COLD, COLD HEART

Previous Books by the Author

Dead Letters (Murder is Academic, US)
Stage Fright
Footfall
Invisible
Deep Water

Christine Poulson was born and brought up in North Yorkshire. She studied English Literature and Art History at the University of Leicester, later earning a PhD. She went on to work as a curator at Birmingham Museum and Art Gallery and at the William Morris Society at Kelmscott House in Hammersmith before becoming a lecturer in Art History at Homerton College, Cambridge. As well as writing fiction she has written widely on nineteenth-century art and literature, and her most recent work of non-fiction was *The Quest for the Grail: Arthurian Legend in British Art, 1840–1920*. Her short stories have been short-listed for several awards, including the 2016 Margery Allingham Prize. She lives in a watermill in Derbyshire with her family.

www.christinepoulson.co.uk
Blog: www.christinepoulson.co.uk/a-reading-life
Twitter: @chrissiepoulson

Christine Poulson

COLD
COLD
HEART

SNOWBOUND WITH A STONE-COLD KILLER

LION FICTION

Published by Lion Fiction
an imprint of
Lion Hudson IP Ltd
Wilkinson House, Jordan Hill Road
Oxford OX2 8DR, England
www.lionhudson.com/fiction

ISBN 978 1 78264 216 9
e-ISBN 978 1 78264 217 6

First edition 2017

Acknowledgments
Cover images: ice © myshkovsky/iStock; scalpel ©
contrail1/iStock; heart © Peter Hatter/Trevillion Images

Scripture quotations taken from The Authorized (King
James) Version. Rights in the Authorized Version are vested
in the Crown. Reproduced by permission of the Crown's
patentee, Cambridge University Press.

A catalogue record for this book is available from the British
Library

Printed and bound in the UK, October 2017, LH26

To the memory of my husband Peter Blundell Jones
(1949–2016)

"We all have our own White South."

Ernest Shackleton

Some say the world will end in fire,
Some say in ice.
From what I've tasted of desire
I hold with those who favor fire.
But if it had to perish twice,
I think I know enough of hate
To say that for destruction ice
Is also great
And would suffice.

Robert Frost, "Fire and Ice."

"Polar exploration is at once the cleanest and most isolated way of having a bad time which has been devised."

Apsley Cherry-Gerard, The Worst Journey in the World

CHAPTER 1

NORTH NORFOLK

As Flora drove up the rutted track to the cottage, she thought for a moment that someone had switched on a light upstairs, but it was only the setting sun striking fire from a bedroom window. She parked the svelte Porsche Panamera that had been Michael's wedding present. It was still a new toy and she'd enjoyed the drive from Cambridge. She got out of the car and shivered, pulled her coat around her. The sun had gone down behind the little grove of pines that served as a windbreak. It was the first time she'd been here alone and it occurred to her that another woman might have felt uneasy. The nearest neighbour was a farmer a mile or two away across the fields. But she wasn't the nervous type, and she was looking forward to having time to herself.

She took the cat carrier from the car. Marmaduke, her long-haired mackerel tabby, liked it here and could be trusted not to run away. "Off you go, little tiger," she said, as she let him out. He snuffed the air, and set off with a purposeful air to patrol the garden.

She had to put her shoulder against the front door to open it. The wood must have swelled in the damp. Cold, clammy air came out to meet her. It was early February and they hadn't been here since the previous autumn. She turned on the water and the heating and decided that she'd have a fire that evening. On the morning of their last visit Michael had swept out the hearth and laid a fire ready for the next time they came. That gave her a cosy feeling, as if he were looking after her at a distance.

She unloaded everything that she would need for her stay, including a stack of ready meals. Michael was the domesticated one and that suited her just fine.

When they had first visited the cottage, she'd been surprised that there wasn't a landline, let alone Wi-Fi, but Michael had explained that that was the point, to get away from everything. And now she appreciated the isolation. Mobile coverage was poor too, but never mind. She thought with pleasure of the three weeks stretching ahead of her. She had her lab books to write up, and a new research proposal to plan. She had no commitments until mid-March when she'd be meeting Lyle and his investors in London. She needed to be fully prepared for that meeting, perhaps the most important of her life.

As she arranged the meals for one in the fridge, she took stock. It had been hard work, but it had all paid off. She was where she wanted to be: married to Michael, her career taking off. The breakthrough in cancer research had been exactly what she needed to establish herself. A shadow fell across her thoughts. Suppose someone were to find out that... But no, she wasn't going to go there. She'd always been lucky and her luck wouldn't fail her now. The patent was in the bag and nothing could stop her. She let herself daydream. Large grants, her own lab, a personal chair, fellowship of the Royal Society, maybe even a Nobel Prize. And then there was the money. Yes, it was all possible. She was only thirty-five. All that was ahead of her.

She ought to ring Michael to let him know that she'd arrived. He was in Melbourne on the first leg of a lecture tour of Australia. She looked at her watch – they were twelve hours ahead so that meant six o'clock in the morning. She put her coat back on and went out into the garden, the only place where she'd be able to get a signal.

The temperature had dropped. There would be a frost tonight. The sun had sunk out of sight and a few stars had appeared in the sky. Far off across the fields a light twinkled from the adjacent farm.

She sent a text to see if Michael was awake yet. Thirty seconds later her phone rang. He *was* awake, suffering from jet lag.

They agreed not to worry about being in touch over the next three weeks. The time difference made things awkward, not to mention the lack of mobile reception, and they were both going to be very busy – Michael moving from city to city and she immersing herself in her work. In any case she wasn't the kind of person to need constant reassurance and neither was he.

As they hung up, and she made her way back into the house, she reflected that theirs wasn't the greatest love story ever told, but she didn't mind that, preferred it really. There was a twenty-year age gap, but that was just fine. What was it they said? Better to be an old man's darling than a young man's fool. Definitely! For one thing he understood that her work came first and he wouldn't be putting pressure on her to have children – he already had a couple of grown-up kids from his first marriage. And there were all sorts of advantages to marrying someone in the same field, especially someone as eminent as Michael. He had already given her more than one leg up in her career. She knew that for his part, he liked playing the mentor and enjoyed showing off his attractive younger wife. It had been almost like an arranged marriage – one that she had arranged herself. She had known what kind of husband she needed and when she'd met Michael she'd known he was it. She smiled to herself. It was a pity that he'd been married to someone else, but really, once she had set her sights on him, he hadn't stood a chance.

She made herself a cup of tea and lit the fire. She spread out her papers on the table in the sitting room. She went into the kitchen and put down food for Marmaduke. She was crouching by the fridge, trying to decide between lasagne and

11

fish pie for supper, when she heard something outside. What was it? A cat maybe? Or some wild animal? A fox? She stood still and listened. There it was again. Something in distress. And yes, that pathetic mewing: it was definitely a cat, close to the house now, and it was in pain. It wasn't Marmaduke, he'd gone upstairs.

She drew back the bolt and opened the back door.

* * *

Upstairs in the bedroom Marmaduke yawned luxuriously. He was tired now after patrolling the boundaries of his territory. There had been no sign of his enemy, the tom belonging to the farm across the fields. Marmaduke was lord of all he surveyed and his kingdom was full of the rustle of small, furry creatures. He had already found and eaten a mouse and he had topped that up with the food Flora had put down in the kitchen. All was well.

He hesitated between the bed and Flora's open case. He was allowed to sleep on the bed when Michael wasn't there, and he would be turfed out of Flora's case when she saw him, but it was too tempting. He climbed in, turned around a few times, and settled himself down on Flora's brushed cotton pyjamas.

There was a crashing and a bumping downstairs. His head shot up. He waited, listening in the dark. The noise stopped as abruptly as it had started. He heaved a sigh and let his head sink down on his paws. He was drifting off to sleep, when he heard a car driving away. Then there was silence.

CHAPTER 2

ELY

Katie paused on the towpath to drink in the familiar scene: the boats in the marina, the picturesque jumble of buildings with the streets leading up to Ely cathedral. It was one of those faded February days when the water was the same colour as the sky. The distant trees were as flat as a frieze and the Octagon Tower of the cathedral was lost in the mist. And yet there was a feeling that spring was just around the corner. The sun was struggling to break through and somewhere a bird was singing.

But Katie wasn't going to see the gradual unfolding of the spring, nor the summer nor the autumn, come to that. I am going to have two winters in a row, she thought, as she walked down the towpath. One less summer in my life.

Rachel waved to her from the deck of the *Matilda Jane*. She looked tired, and the short, dark, curly hair was threaded with grey. Caring for a child with a chronic illness took its toll.

Katie climbed on board the barge and they embraced.

"It's just wonderful, what you've managed to do," Katie said, looking around at the wheelhouse. The boat had been badly damaged by fire the year before last and restoration work had only just finished.

"You're our first guest. Dan's gone to fetch Chloe from her ballet class. Fancy a glass of prosecco while we're waiting?"

"I presume that was a rhetorical question!"

They went down the stairs into the combined sitting room and kitchen. The sun came out, sending ripples of reflection across the wooden floorboards and brightly coloured rugs. The wood-burning stove gave off welcome heat.

Rachel went to the fridge and got out a bottle.

"Here, before I forget," Katie said, delving into her backpack and bringing out a long, narrow box wrapped in red and gold paper. "For your birthday."

Rachel frowned, "But it's not my birthday until – oh."

Katie saw realization dawn.

"You won't be here," Rachel said. "You really are going?"

"Did you think I wouldn't? After all those interviews and these months of training." She brought out another box wrapped in pink paper decorated with fairies. "You'd better hide this before Chloe sees it. I hope she likes the paper. She is still keen on fairies?"

Rachel sighed. "I keep hoping she'll switch to something less girly. Dinosaurs, maybe…"

"Come on, Rachel, she's only five. Give the kid a break. Besides, there's Lego inside. And that's *not* pink."

Rachel drew out the cork with a pop and poured out two glasses. She handed one to Katie and they clinked them.

They sat down opposite each other at the kitchen table.

"I'm going to miss you," Rachel said.

Katie looked with affection at her friend. On the face of it they might not have seemed to have that much in common: Katie, a young scientific researcher in her early thirties, single and childless; Rachel, a wood restorer ten years older, with a husband and child. They had first met when Katie was doing research on Diamond Blackfan Anaemia, the genetic blood disorder that Chloe suffered from. Katie had grown very fond of Rachel and Chloe in the fifteen months or so that she had known them.

"When are you flying out? Saturday?"

Katie nodded.

"So this time next week," Rachel said, "you'll be in Rothera. Here's to new beginnings all round."

Katie hesitated, the glass halfway to her lips. "Well, actually, it's not going to be Rothera."

"It's not? But I thought you said –"

"It was going to be," Katie admitted, "but I had a call from the British Antarctic Survey just now when I was on my way here. I'll be going to the Edward Wilson base instead."

"But can they do that at the last moment?"

"Someone had an accident there and had to be flown out. They need a last-minute replacement. And I did agree to go wherever they sent me." Katie knew exactly what Rachel was thinking. She'd always been doubtful about Katie going to Antarctica. Rothera was bad enough, but the Wilson base! It had only been open for two years and was the smallest and most remote of the three British Antarctic research stations.

"You'll be cut off for even longer there, won't you?" Rachel said, frowning. There was something of the mother hen about her – and it could be irritating.

"Yep. I'll be on the last flight in and then that's it until the beginning of November. It gets so cold that the engine oil gelatinizes. But Rachel, there's always email and satellite phone. It's not like it was in the days of Scott and Shackleton and conditions are pretty good on the base. We even have our own chef."

"What'll you be doing there?" Rachel asked.

"I'll be taking over this guy's research project – I'm well qualified for it. It's about the way human beings adapt to darkness and isolation. Lack of light suppresses the action of the pineal gland with the result that less melatonin is produced. And that's the hormone that sets our body clock. People wintering over tend to get out of kilter, like people suffering from jet lag. They can lose their sense of night and day and become 'free-running', slipping into a cycle that's shorter or longer than twenty-four hours. So I'll be measuring their melatonin levels among other things."

Rachel said, "I wish you didn't have to go. It's so unfair that you couldn't get more funding for your research."

Katie sighed. "I told you, didn't I, what happens to whistle-blowers? Other scientists don't like you breaking ranks and you get a reputation as a troublemaker. But Rachel, no one's forcing me to go to Antarctica – and it's not the scientific equivalent of joining the Foreign Legion! It's the opportunity of a lifetime and I was very lucky to get on the programme."

They had talked it over so many times, returning again and again to Katie's decision to expose a case of scientific malpractice. At the time it had scarcely felt like a conscious choice. Katie had been drawn on from one discovery to the next and had had no way of knowing that it would all end in disaster.

Rachel leaned forward and said, just as she always did, "You did the right thing. Once you suspected, you couldn't let it go. What's that saying: 'Let justice be done though the sky should fall.'"

Sometimes Katie envied Rachel's moral certainty and behind it the religious faith that Katie couldn't quite share.

She said, also not for the first time, "I do regret it sometimes. What good did it do? Careers ruined – mine included maybe – a death –"

"Stop it, Katie. You couldn't have seen any of that."

"Yeah, yeah. The law of unintended consequences..." Time to change the subject. "By the time I get back people might have forgotten about it. Now tell me, how's Chloe? How's the new therapy working out?"

"We go back to the consultant in a couple of weeks." Rachel hesitated. "If it works, it'll make all the difference –"

But before she could say anything further, there was a clattering and a banging overhead. The door to the wheelhouse opened and a small person came skittering down the stairs and headed for Katie like a heat-seeking missile. Katie got to her feet just in time to be clasped around the waist and to feel a head pressed against her side. She couldn't help laughing. Chloe's sheer *joie de vivre* was infectious.

"Katie, my Katie," Chloe said. "Will you bring me back a real live polar bear – a polar bear kitten – to be my pet?"

"Oh, sweetie, there aren't any polar bears at the South Pole."

"And my teacher says are you going to write a blog and can you –"

"Enough with the questions," Daniel said, laughing as he came down the wheelhouse stairs.

He came over and gave Katie a hug. She felt the real affection behind it. What good people Rachel and Dan were: so devoted to Chloe, lovely parents. When she was with them Katie felt part of that magic circle, enveloped in the warmth. She was almost as much of an aunt to Chloe as she was to her brother's little boys. Chloe clasped her small hands around the belt of Katie's jeans and rocked back and forth as she smiled up at Katie.

Katie realized with a pang that she was going to miss her and she thought that Chloe would miss her too. A year is a long, long time in the life of a five-year-old.

She hoped she was doing the right thing. Look on the bright side, she told herself, she'd always wanted to go to Antarctica and it was true, what she had told Rachel, it *was* the opportunity of a lifetime. Very, very few people got to winter over there. She'd be doing useful work there. And she'd already had a lovely email from Sara, the doctor on the base, saying how glad she was that another woman – and a woman with medical training at that – was coming to join her.

But on the other hand, for four months it would be completely dark – night and day – and the temperature could drop to minus seventy or below. And for eight months, she'd be shut in with nine other people – nine *strangers*, all men except for Sara – with no means of escape. At present her family and friends were all in good health but if, for instance, her mother or her brother should become ill, it would make no difference, there'd be no coming back...

"What have I let myself in for?" she asked herself.

CHAPTER 3

NORTH NORFOLK

That first morning at the cottage, Marmaduke saw that Flora's car had gone. There was still food in his bowl and the cat flap was open, so he had a happy day roaming his territory. He expected that Flora would return in the evening. But she didn't come, no one came, and by the next morning he was very hungry. He managed to knock the big box of cat food off the counter and attacked it with his teeth and claws. The kibble lasted for several days and, spread over the kitchen floor, it also attracted mice and even a rat or two, which he quickly despatched and ate. When the food was gone, the mice returned to nibble the cardboard. But when he had caught and eaten them all, life became harder.

He had always been a keen and skilful hunter, but he had hunted simply because it was in his nature. He had never needed to provide for himself before now. He was a big cat and it took a lot of work even to take the edge off his hunger. Water was not a problem. There was a pond at the end of the garden.

Now that Flora wasn't there to keep him in at night, he became nocturnal, hunting at night and sleeping during the day. When, now and then in the grey dawn, prowling through the wet grass, he encountered a fox, they eyed one another with respect and passed on their way.

Flora had sometimes left him alone in the Cambridge flat, but then a neighbour came in to feed him and make a fuss of him. Here there was no one and he was uneasy. He was used to being petted by Flora and he was a cat that needed brushing

18

daily. Although he washed himself assiduously, his fur was growing matted.

Between hunting trips he crept upstairs and curled up on the bed or in Flora's open suitcase. It smelled of her and that comforted him. At home in Cambridge he knew when Flora was due home. No one came up the track, but if they had they would have seen, day after day, a big long-haired tabby cat coming punctually to sit beside the gate every evening at six o'clock.

CHAPTER 4

ANTARCTICA

The flight from Port Stanley on the Falkland Islands to Rothera on the Antarctic Peninsula had taken five hours. At Rothera she had boarded the little Twin Otter aircraft that took her on to Halley Research Station. They had landed only briefly for the pilot to leave supplies, to dump a bag of mail, and to collect one – email hadn't entirely taken the place of real letters. A change in the weather was forecast and they hadn't lingered in case they left it too late and the pilot couldn't get Katie out to the Wilson base – or couldn't get back himself.

Now she was on the last leg of the journey. Thank goodness all the preparation was over: the endless list-making, the challenge of making sure that she had everything, absolutely every single thing, that she would need for eight months from books to Tampax to her favourite chocolate. Anything she didn't have now, she'd have to do without, because where she was going, there were no shops, no mail, no Amazon. Her mother had given her a large jar of Marmite "just in case", though Katie was pretty sure that they'd have that on the base. The place was well-equipped. There was a decent library of books and DVDs (there wasn't enough bandwidth for Netflix) and she also had dozens of books on her Kindle. There was music on her iPhone.

She'd been invited up to the cockpit to sit next to the pilot, an avuncular Edinburgh Scot called Robbie. Looking out of the window, the sheer scale of the landscape staggered her. For the first time she fully grasped how far she was going – truly to the end of the earth. Her eyes began to ache. Not from the glare – she was wearing sunglasses – but from the effort of trying to focus when there was nothing to focus on. There were no landmarks, nothing to break the monotony of ice and snow, just the shadow of the plane moving below them.

She yawned and rubbed her temples. She felt a sense of disorientation, some of it no doubt jet lag. She had been flitting between time zones. At Edward Wilson she would be returning to UK time. Technically Antarctica was in every time zone – or no time zone – because the longitude lines meet at the poles. In practice bases chose the time zones that they wanted to operate in. Imagine! You could choose what time you wanted it to be! It was part of the general weirdness of it all. She looked at her watch. Three o'clock. She'd be in ample time for dinner. Then she remembered. Despite the fact that the sun, though low in the sky, was still shining, it was actually three o'clock in the morning. That would account for how she felt. A couple of lines of verse came into her head: "And this was odd, because it was the middle of the night..." Where did that come from? Oh yes, *Alice in Wonderland*... "The Walrus and the Carpenter"...

The sun was shining on the sea,
Shining with all his might:
He did his very best to make
The billows smooth and bright –
And this was odd, because it was
The middle of the night.

Lulled by the sound of the engine and the monotony of the view she fell asleep and dreamed that she was Alice walking with the Walrus and the Carpenter. But it wasn't a beach, it was an endless ice floe. A crack appeared and she found herself floating away while the Walrus and the Carpenter gazed after her.

Katie woke up with a jerk. There was a crackling in her headphones and, "Nearly there," Robbie said.

At first she couldn't see anything, then she spotted a series of red specks against the white. The plane began to descend and the specks became blocks like pieces of Lego arranged end to end. The wings dipped as Robbie circled the base and Katie saw that it was built to the same kind of design as Halley Research Station: a string of red modules mounted on posts. There was a line of buildings a few hundred metres away: that would be the summer camp. Further off was the telescope, sited in what was called the Dark Sector, well away from the light pollution and radio pollution of the main station, though linked to it by a line of flags on poles. As the plane got closer the modules were less like Lego pieces, more like cartoon characters: like SpongeBob SquarePants, one of Chloe's favourites. Perched on what looked like sturdy trouser-clad legs they looked as if at any moment they might swing their legs in unison and march off across the snow.

The plane was descending. So this was it. This was where she was going to spend the next eight months. She felt a prickle of something that was both anxiety and excitement. At one end of the makeshift runway – no more than a flat piece of ice – stood two figures dressed in red, vivid against the snow, sweeping their arms above their heads in a gesture of welcome.

"Ah, that'll be Sara and the Boss," Robbie said. "Sara's a good lass. She'll see you right."

"The Boss?"

"Graeme. They call him the Boss, because he looks a bit like Kenneth Branagh playing Shackleton in that film, and Shackleton was always called the Boss. And then, Graeme actually *is* the boss. He's the base commander."

"Does everyone gets a nickname?"

"Aye."

"So what's Sara called?"

"Doc."

"That's original."

Robbie laughed. The skis hit the runway and the plane began to slow. Katie unlocked her harness, climbed down the ladder from the deck, and put on her parka and gloves.

When she opened the door, she was dazzled by the brilliant light and the cold made her gasp. It was like being slapped in the face. The mucus in her nostrils froze and the cold, dry air rasped in her throat.

The roar of the engine ceased and a profound silence fell.

The smaller figure came towards her. She was so much muffled up that it was impossible to tell anything about her except that she was tall.

I hope I'm going to like you, Katie thought. *No, that's not right. I* will *like you. I have to like you.*

Sara pushed up her sun goggles and Katie saw brown eyes creased in a smile. "You don't know how glad I am to see you," she said, and Katie knew it was going to be alright.

"The other guys are asleep," Graeme said, "we try to stick to a twenty-four-hour cycle. They did offer to stay up – or some of them did –"

"But we thought you'd be tired," Sara said, "and you'd probably prefer to meet them all in the morning."

Katie was grateful. "You were right."

They helped Robbie and the co-pilot unload the plane and stack the crates and bags onto a trolley. A sack of mail. Katie's bags. A crate of oranges. Meat. Fresh fish. "Chef will be thrilled," Sara said. "The last fresh food until October. Let's get it inside before it freezes."

Katie wheezed, as she carried one of her bags up the steps to the first module. Sara put a hand on her arm. "Take it easy. It'll be a few days before you get used to the altitude. We're about two thousand eight hundred metres above sea level."

Graeme said, "Let these lazy so-and-sos do a bit of work for a change."

Robbie laughed and clapped Katie on the back.

"Sure you don't want to come back with me? Last chance. I'm loath to leave you here with these lunatics."

For a moment Katie was almost tempted. It had all happened so quickly. Too quickly. She laughed and shook her head. She hadn't come all that way to duck out at the last minute: of course she was staying.

The plane had to be refuelled. When it was ready to leave Katie and Sara went back outside to watch as the plane took off and grew smaller in the blue-white sky. It seemed important to go on watching until it dwindled to a dot. When at last it had disappeared neither of them spoke. This was it: it would be eight months before another plane flew in. Katie felt better now that it was too late to change her mind. She'd almost been afraid that she would panic when it came to the last moment. She hadn't and whatever happened now, she would have to deal with it, simple as that. One day at a time, she told herself, and already she was closer to the end of her stay, if only by a few minutes.

As if Sara had read her mind, she put a heavily padded hand on Katie's shoulder and squeezed. "It'll be fine. Not saying it won't be tough at times, but – well, not many people get to do this, we're members of an exclusive club. On the whole continent there are only about seven hundred of us wintering over. That's something special. Make the most of it."

"It's not your first time?"

"Nope. I was here last winter. Come on, let's get back indoors."

CHAPTER 5

"It's not like the old days, when roughing it was a badge of pride," Graeme said. He heaved one of Katie's bags onto the bed. Divested of his outdoor gear, he turned out to be a tall, well-built man of about fifty with close-cut blonde hair and a stubble beard. "For those of us who wintered over in the original Halley station it's sheer bloody luxury. In my view, when you're cut off from the rest of the world for eight months at a time, you need all the comfort you can get. Some of the younger guys think that detracts from the romance of wintering over. Not me."

"We still call bedrooms pit-rooms by the way," Sara said.

There was the sound of a door opening down the corridor and a man in a dressing gown came out, yawning.

"I heard the plane leave," he said, "and I'm thinking that I'll see if you want anything."

Sara said, "This is Chef, aka Ernesto, aka Mother. This is Katie."

He thrust out a hand. He was young, mid to late twenties, Katie guessed, and dark with a five o'clock shadow. "Good to have you on board. Coffee? Scrambled eggs? We've still got real eggs. A nice cup of tea?"

Katie looked at her watch. It was four o'clock. "I think I'll wait and have breakfast at breakfast time."

"Best to get into the station routine," Graeme agreed.

"I'd love a cup of tea, though."

Sara said, "Why don't you two guys get off back to bed? I'll make Katie a cup of tea."

The two women went along to a kitchen, gleaming with stainless steel and spotless. It opened onto an equally pristine

25

dining room. Katie liked the clean lines and pale colours. This was only the second year that the base had been open: nothing had had time to get scuffed or worn.

Sara brewed the tea and set out biscuits. They sat down opposite each other. Now that Sara had taken off her outdoor clothes, Katie saw that she was solidly built. She had shoulder-length brown hair tied back and large, mild brown eyes. She was perhaps late thirties, a bit older than Katie at any rate. She wasn't wearing a ring – probably single then, but she was wearing a small silver cross on a chain around her neck.

"I hoped we'd have another woman on board," Sara said. "It's a bonus that you've got medical training. Nice to know that I won't end up having to take my own appendix out."

It wasn't quite a joke. There had been a famous occasion in the early sixties when a Russian doctor on a Soviet base had carried out his own appendectomy under a local anaesthetic, while a driver and a meteorologist stood by, holding a mirror and handing him instruments.

Katie smiled. "Let's hope it won't come to that."

"Tell me about yourself," Sara said. "Where did you train?"

"I did my medical degree at Imperial College. It was intercalated with a year of microbiology and that was what made me decide to go down the research path. But I thought I'd better leave my options open in case I decided to practise after all, so I did my foundation years before I switched to a PhD. After that I got a couple of research grants. Then I had trouble getting any more funding and I decided to apply to the programme. And here I am."

No need to tell Sara more than that. A lot of people had to move on from doing research in their mid-thirties.

Sara nodded. "I did something similar – went into research, but in the end I missed the contact with other people and went back and did my GP training. Then I came straight out here. I'm not planning to do another year. Two is enough. I'll be going back to join a practice when I go home."

"What happened to the bloke I'm replacing? I didn't hear exactly."

A shutter seemed to fall over Sara's face. Katie wondered if she'd made a faux pas by asking. But it was only for a moment. Then she answered readily enough. "Kevin? That was just unlucky. He'd only gone out to shovel snow into the meltwater tank."

She looked out of the window and Katie followed her gaze. Outside the landscape stretched away like a frozen sea, ice crystals glinting in the blazing sunlight.

"There was a blizzard," Sara said. "Visibility was terrible. We found him lying unconscious some way from the base. He must have got disorientated – that can happen all too easily. We think he slipped and hit his head when he went over. He didn't remember too much about it. We carried out an emergency evacuation and flew him back to England."

"Will he be OK?"

"Yeah, yeah, they think he'll make a full recovery in due course."

This seemed a pretty truncated account of what must have been a dramatic event. And what did "in due course" mean? But Katie got the definite impression that further questions wouldn't be welcome. Perhaps it was regarded as bad form on the base to dwell on things that had gone wrong or might go wrong. Given that from now on, whatever happened, there was no question of flying anyone out, that probably made good sense, psychologically.

Sara went on, "Minor accidents are much more common. That's mostly what the base doctor has to deal with. Everyone is screened before they come out here, after all. And they are mostly young and healthy men in the first place."

She yawned.

"Don't let me keep you from your bed," Katie said.

"You know, I think I *will* get my head down for an hour or two. The blackout blinds are very effective, by the way." She levered herself up from the table. "Breakfast's between seven and eight, lunch at twelve, dinner at seven. Oh, and there's smoko around ten in the morning."

"Smoko?"

"An Antarctic institution. I suppose it actually was for smoking originally. It's just a coffee break now. There's another break at teatime. Ernesto's a red-hot baker and there's usually some kind of cake. Food tends to loom very large here." She smiled at Katie. "Oh, and if you want to explore, go ahead. There are no locks except on the loos."

"What about the surgery?"

"Nope. Though I do have locked cabinets for medical records and for controlled drugs. We may be a long way from home, but the same rules apply."

* * *

Back in her pit-room, Katie unpacked. Deciding what clothes to bring hadn't been much of a problem because everyone was issued with the same utilitarian gear to wear outdoors and T-shirts and jeans were standard wear indoors.

She put up photographs on the pinboard: her parents; her brother and sister-in-law with Harry and Joel, their two little boys; Rachel and Dan with Chloe. She was soon done. It was still only five thirty, but sleep seemed impossible. She had promised to write a weblog for Chloe's school. She was writing from the point of view of a small stuffed penguin. She propped it up against the window, got out her laptop, and began to write. "Penguin has arrived at the South Pole or very nearly. Just now it never gets dark here..."

But she was too restless and too tired to concentrate. She got up and went out into the corridor. She wandered the base, opening doors and peering into rooms. She felt uncomfortable, as though she were prying. But she reminded herself that this was her home now and she could wander at will.

The layout of the main accommodation module was straightforward. A wide central corridor formed the spine of the building and was divided at regular intervals by fire doors. At one end was a combined library and quiet room. She browsed the books: plenty of thrillers and crime novels, but the classics too. She had time now to read things that she wouldn't dream of reading normally. She took a copy of Dante's *Inferno* off the shelf. Well, why not? It was a parallel text. This would be an excellent opportunity to brush up on her Italian. She'd done an evening class a few years ago.

She took it with her as she went on past the pit-rooms on either side of the corridor. Loos and showers next. Then on one side a little gym with a rowing machine and a treadmill and on the other what was clearly the communications room, their link to the outside world. Then a TV room with shelves of DVDs and a music room with a keyboard and a guitar on a stand. Next came an open space the width of the module containing the kitchen and the dining room and bar, where she and Sara had been sitting earlier. This was clearly the heart of the community.

Then she was back in the corridor with rooms on either side. She opened a door onto a gleaming surgery. She went in and had a look around. The base doctor had to be completely self-sufficient. There was a ventilator, an anaesthetic machine, cylinders of oxygen, surgical equipment, and an X-ray machine. There wasn't anything more sophisticated in the way of imaging equipment, no CT, MRI, or ultrasound scanner, and some of the equipment was a bit basic, though still serviceable. The X-ray machine, for example, took X-rays on film, which then had to be developed in the dark room in the old-fashioned way. But basically the surgery contained everything needed for any conceivable medical emergency. And the surgery had its own direct line to the British Antarctic Survey headquarters, so that medical confidentiality could be maintained – because after all the base doctor might have to report on the health of the base commander.

This was Sara's little kingdom and as Katie closed the door she felt thankful that she was only the backup doc.

On the other side of the corridor was a food store; then came a plant generator, the room for monitoring the generators, and the kit room. That was all on this floor. A spiral staircase led to a floor above she knew housed labs and the meteorological room. She decided to leave those for later.

She went back to her pit-room.

There was another hour until breakfast. She was determined to stay awake and opened the copy of Dante's *Inferno*. She was pleased to see that she did recognize some of the Italian. She lay down on the bed and began to read. "*Nel mezzo del cammin di nostra vita mi ritrovai per una selva oscura, ché la diritta via era smarrita.* Halfway through the journey of this life I woke and found myself in a dark forest, lost and with no idea of the way ahead..."

Her eyes were sore. She'd got a little bit sunburned at Rothera, before she'd realized the danger. She closed them, just to rest them. Moments later she was asleep.

CHAPTER 6

ELY

Rachel was woken by the beep of a text coming in on Dan's phone. He hauled himself up in bed beside her. She was aware of him scrolling down the screen and then making a phone call. His side of the conversation was mostly a series of terse monosyllables. "Lyle? Yep... no... mmm..." and then, "Yes, yes. It's fine. Yes, yes... what time? OK."

He hung up and rolled out of bed. A few seconds later, Rachel heard the swoosh of the shower. She drifted off again and woke to the smell of coffee. Dan was standing by the bed, wrapped in a towel, smelling fresh and soapy. He put a mug on her bedside table. She looked at the clock. Oh goodness, it was seven forty-five already. They must have forgotten to put the alarm on. It had been another bad night with Chloe.

"That was Lyle," he said.

"So I gathered."

She pulled herself up on the pillows and watched him assembling his lawyer's uniform, laying out a pinstriped suit on the bed, putting on a cotton shirt with a fine pink stripe.

He was in underpants, socks, and shirt when the phone rang again. It was Alison, his secretary. He jammed the phone between his ear and his shoulder, while he struggled to thread a cufflink into a sleeve. Rachel beckoned him over. He sat down on the bed and offered her first one cuff and then the other, swapping the phone over to continue the discussion with Alison. "I'll be in the office in ten minutes or so," he said, and ended the call.

"Thanks, love." He leaned over absent-mindedly and brushed her cheek with his lips. "About Chloe..."

31

"Do you think you won't make it?" She couldn't keep the anxiety out of her voice.

"No, I'll be there, I promise. But I might have to meet you at the hospital," he said, as he reached for his tie.

He pulled on his trousers and shrugged on his jacket.

"Don't forget to have some breakfast," Rachel said.

"I'll ask Alison to go out for some croissants. See you later." He bent to kiss her.

To all intents and purposes she saw that he'd already gone. In his head he was at work, organizing his day, planning what could be passed on to his assistant, what could be shifted to make room for a meeting with Lyle. Rachel listened to his footsteps going down the stairs and then the sound of the door closing behind him.

She got up and put on her dressing gown. She went into Chloe's room. Chloe had half thrown off the covers. She tucked her back in. She went over to sit on the window seat and cradled her mug of coffee in her hands. There was ten minutes or so before she needed to wake Chloe for school.

Their little house on Quayside looked over the marina, but the *Matilda Jane* wasn't visible from here. She was moored around a bend in the towpath. They only lived on the boat in the summer.

It was March now and just yesterday she had heard a thrush singing its heart out. There was a mist of green on the weeping willows that overhung the towpath. She thought of what Katie was missing and wished she wasn't so far away. They were in regular email contact, but it wasn't the same as sitting down together with a glass of wine.

Of all her friends, Katie was the one who most understood what Chloe's Diamond Blackfan Anaemia meant. Ever since she was a baby she had had to have a blood transfusion once a month. And with the transfusion went a risk that dangerously high levels of iron would accumulate in her heart and liver. Five times a week she had had subcutaneous infusions to shift the iron deposits. So five nights a week, Rachel or Daniel had had to put a needle into her leg or waist and tape an infusion pump to her body to deliver the therapy overnight. It was a tough regime for anyone, let alone a little girl.

And then a few months ago, their consultant had suggested a new therapy that could instead be delivered orally.

And this afternoon, they would learn whether or not it was working. She hadn't said anything to Dan, but she didn't have a good feeling about it.

* * *

Daniel made his way up Fore Hill to the Market Place. People were sometimes surprised to hear that a firm of lawyers in a sleepy little place like Ely, known mostly for its cathedral, could have a global reach. But Daniel's firm, specializing in patent law, was ideally placed close to Silicon Fen or the Cambridge Cluster, one of the most important technology centres in Europe. A thousand high-tech businesses focusing on software, electronics, and biotechnology were based there, many of them with connections to the University of Cambridge. That meant that the area also attracted venture capitalists, big consultancy firms, bankers – and lawyers.

Lyle Linstrum was one of those venture capitalists and Daniel was curious to find out what brought him to Ely. About eighteen months ago Linstrum had been head of a biotech company and had employed Daniel in a case where there had been a dispute over which research team had made the first discovery of a therapy to combat obesity. The case had almost been concluded when Linstrum was sacked from the board of his own company.

You can't keep a good man down. Daniel had been sure that Lyle would soon bounce back. He had followed his progress in the financial pages of the newspapers and it was as he had foreseen: raising money, funding new ventures, was what Lyle did – and he'd gone on doing it. He had set up his own firm of venture capitalists. There were even rumours that he might be back on the board of his old company soon. He was like one of those toys with a ball for a base: when you pushed him over, he popped back up.

Daniel reached the office before Lyle arrived. He just had time for a cup of coffee before there was a knock on his door and his secretary put her head around the door. She looked dazed. Lyle had that effect on people and Daniel braced himself.

Lyle appeared in the doorway. He had a lean, leathery face, and was well over six foot, made even taller by the cowboy boots he was wearing. The boots, the bolo tie, the photos in the press of him riding Western style, wearing chaps, reins held loosely in his hand on his ranch in Texas: they all contributed to a public image of him as a buccaneering, larger-than-life character. The truth was more complicated. He was also a former academic, a scientist who had grown more interested in the development of discoveries than in doing the discovering himself.

"Hey, Daniel." He offered his hand. "Great to see you!"

Daniel put out his own hand, resigning himself to having it gripped to the point of discomfort – if not beyond. He gestured to two chairs on either side of a coffee table and Lyle folded himself into one of them.

"What can I do for you, Lyle?"

"Well, it's pretty urgent –"

It would be. It always was with Lyle. In spite of that Southern drawl of his, he didn't do patient or measured. He was tapping one foot as he spoke. He never sat still. He must be getting on for sixty, but you'd never have guessed it. A lot of people thought Lyle could be brash, abrasive, even downright rude. That was true enough, but Daniel liked him: what you saw was what you got. And there was something about his overflowing energy that was invigorating.

"And you want me to drop everything else and concentrate on it," Daniel said.

"Well, yeah. There's a small biotech company called Theseus that we're planning to invest in."

"I've heard of them. A couple of years ago? They made a breakthrough in cancer research. Concerning apoptosis, wasn't it?"

Apoptosis was the mechanism by which a cell was programmed to destroy itself; the possibility of finding a way to trigger that selectively in cancer cells was a recent and very promising area of research. Daniel was not surprised that Lyle was keen on investing in it.

"That's right. A research team came up with it – a woman called Flora Mitchell was running the show and she had a postdoc working with her. Just a couple of young researchers – came across it almost by accident – that's the way these things happen sometimes – and the university established Theseus to develop it. My, but these guys like their classical references."

"In this case, it's apt. Exploring a labyrinth in order to discover and then slay the monster."

"Sure, sure. Exactly what those guys are aiming to do. You know the basic idea?"

"They used an artificial virus to deliver a biochemically benign electron carrier –"

"Yeah. Cytochrome *c*. It's been shown to trigger apoptosis in lung cancer cells. Think of it, Daniel. A treatment for cancer that has none of the brutal side effects of chemotherapy or radiotherapy. Of course it's only *in vitro* at the moment."

It's a big jump from something working *in vitro*, in a petri dish in a lab, to working in an actual living being. And that would be where Lyle and his investors came in.

Lyle went on. "Flora Mitchell got more research funding on the back of her earlier work, and it's all looking great. They're reaching the point where they need big bucks to take it further and develop a therapy. That's where I come in. So far I've been relying on the advice given by their own retained patent attorneys. Now that I'm planning to bring in other potential investors, I need to be sure that that advice is sound and there are no potential holes in the intellectual property protection."

Daniel nodded. It would take a huge amount of work to develop an actual pharmaceutical product from research like this and would cost hundreds of millions of pounds, far beyond the scope of a university budget. "So now you need a second opinion. And that's where I come in."

"That's where you come in."

"Any problems that you're aware of?" Daniel asked.

Lyle raised a hand in denial. "This isn't like the last time I employed you. It all looks hunky-dory – and I'm not anticipating any irregularities. Of course they put in a patent application as soon as they realized what they'd got, but there could be additional patents or protections that we might want to seek. Flora's done some further work in the meantime on how the therapy could be delivered."

This all seemed straightforward enough. Once outside parties were considering investment there would inevitably be some fairly heavy due diligence on the patent front because no one would want to invest if there were any doubts about who owned the rights. It would be Daniel's job to make sure that all that was in order: as well as looking at the patent application, that meant going through the lab books that had recorded the experiments.

Lyle looked at his watch. "Got to get back to London." He got to his feet. "So are we on?"

"We're on."

"Great. My PA will be in touch."

Another bone-cracking handshake followed.

"Heard anything from Katie?" Lyle asked as he released Daniel.

Katie had been best friends at university with Juliet, Lyle's daughter.

"Rachel's in touch by email and she rings up now and then and speaks to Chloe. She seems fine."

"Great, great. Glad to hear it."

He made for the door and had his hand on the knob when he paused.

Dan waited. He thought of this as the Columbo moment. It was surprising how often clients did this. What was presented as an afterthought was often a worry that they hadn't quite been able to put into words or to acknowledge until the very last moment. Sometimes it was the most important part of the interview.

Lyle turned and leaned against the door.

"There is one thing. Flora Mitchell, the principal investigator. Very smart, very determined, very personable. A high-flyer if ever I saw one. She'll be heading up the project and she's part of the reason we're prepared to dig deep for this one." He paused.

"And?"

"Probably nothing. It's just that she's a bit elusive at the moment. Not an immediate problem, I've got all the documentation that we need for now. But my secretary tried to get hold of her to remind her about the meeting with investors that's scheduled for next week. Couldn't be done."

"Well, is she away?"

"According to the department's administrator Flora's holed somewhere, getting a run at some work she needs to complete. Well, OK, but she's not even replying to emails or texts!"

"I wouldn't read too much into it, Lyle. Not everyone's umbilically attached to their smartphone."

"I guess you're right. Let's not get ahead of ourselves."

And then he did go. Daniel walked him out and watched him climb into the red Audi that he had left right outside the office, parked on a double yellow line. Being Lyle, of course, he hadn't got a ticket. He went roaring off down the street.

A shadow fell across Daniel's thoughts. What was it?

Oh, yes, Chloe. That worry was never far away. He hadn't said anything to Rachel, but he had a bad feeling about this afternoon's meeting with the consultant.

CHAPTER 7

NORTH NORFOLK

Two weeks had passed since Flora had gone. The days were growing longer. There had been rain and high winds. The garden was full of noise and movement and fascinating rustlings in the undergrowth.

Marmaduke had made many nocturnal excursions and his bed in Flora's suitcase was now felted with fur and lined with little twigs and dead leaves. It was beginning to resemble a bird's nest. Marmaduke had grown leaner and fitter. With practice his hunting skills had improved. He had added rabbits and the occasional bird to his repertoire, but he was still hungry a lot of the time. And he was becoming increasingly bedraggled, his fur in clumps and tangled with burrs. He worried them with his teeth, but he couldn't get them all out. They worked their way in close to his skin and irritated him.

He still waited for Flora every evening. During the day between naps he lay on the bedroom windowsill and watched for a car to drive up. He began to make occasional trips to the edge of his territory to look for someone to care of him. And that was when he ran into trouble in the form of the big tom from the farm across the fields. He had to defend his territory at all costs and a fight ensued, fur flying and fearsome yowls. He saw off his enemy, but not before the tom had managed to inflict a long, deep scratch down the side of his face. Marmaduke had cleaned himself up as best he could, but the wound ached and was beginning to throb.

CHAPTER 8

ANTARCTICA

Katie was disappointed in herself. She had thought she'd cope better than this. It was galling. Of everyone on the base, she was the one who was having the most trouble with her sleep patterns – along with Adam, the heating and plumbing engineer who was the youngest on base. He was really suffering, too. She hadn't imagined she'd find it so difficult to adjust to twenty-four hours of daylight. Ironic really, when it was what she had come here to study.

She looked at the digital clock on the shelf beside the bed. It was four forty-five and she had been tossing and turning all night – if you could call it night, when it never got dark. She knew that by mid-afternoon she would be fighting to stay awake. Better get up. She reached and pulled on the blind without getting out of bed. Brilliant sunlight streamed in. It would be a good idea to go outside too, while that lasted. It wasn't always sunny and the frequent blizzards could reduce visibility to virtually nothing. She tried to get out every day if the weather permitted. Claustrophobia and cabin fever were real threats to mental and physical health.

She got up and put on her thermal T-shirt and long johns. She pulled on a pair of trousers over her long johns. She walked through the silent building to the boot room at the far end and put on her outdoor gear: first her thermally insulated overalls, then a thick fleece jacket. On top of the jacket went her green polar parka. She pulled a balaclava over her head and a woolly hat on top of that. Finally she pulled on her mukluks, bulky boots with thick soles and cotton uppers that allowed your feet to breathe.

Out in the corridor the thermometer by the exit read twenty-five degrees below. She hesitated. Should she sign out? She thought back to her training and decided that as long as she wasn't going off the base and visibility was good then she didn't need to. But she would take her radio – just in case.

She pulled up the hood of her parka, took a breath to ready herself, and opened the door. Stepping outside was like being plunged into icy water. She climbed slowly down the stairs and looked around, blinking in the intense light. The undulating landscape stretched away like a frozen white sea. Ice crystals danced in the air and formed twinkling haloes around the sun.

She decided to give herself a goal for her walk by going out to the caboose. It was a small caravan-like structure that could be moved around on skis and at present it was out on the perimeter of the base, a walk of about a kilometre.

The silence and the stillness were absolute. All she could hear was the rhythm of her pulse in her ears and the crunch of her feet. And yet silence didn't seem quite the right word for this – dullness, this blankness. When she stood still it was as if she had suddenly gone deaf. She thought of home, of the English landscape with its layers of human history, its richness, its domestic scale. She hadn't known what an important part of her life that was until now. The vast emptiness of this continent was scary, but exhilarating too. It seemed somehow to wipe the slate clean.

She glanced back at the platform to judge the distance she had come. At one of the windows, she glimpsed a pale disc. Only when it moved back and out of sight did she realize that it was someone's face. That hasty and surreptitious movement made her uncomfortable and so did the thought that someone had been watching her when she had thought she was alone.

She reached the caboose. The door was iced up and she kicked it open. Her breath hung in the air as she lit the stove and made some tea. The place was soon so hot – at least above waist level – that she was able to strip off her parka and fleece jacket, while freezing drafts wafted around her ankles.

How distant her old life was beginning to seem: that world of long days in the lab and uncertain results, of tedious and time-consuming grant applications, of anxiety about achieving the publications that were so essential for success. When she thought of her stalled career, the whistle-blowing and what had come in its wake, it somehow didn't seem so important any more.

The tea drunk, she washed up and got dressed again for the outdoors. As soon as she opened the door she realized that something had happened.

The brilliant sunshine of earlier had gone.

In fact everything had gone. Katie's first thought was that there was something wrong with her eyes. She couldn't see anything. She was suspended in a void. Then she realized what must have occurred. Clouds were blocking out the sun – at least that was what she assumed, because she couldn't actually see any clouds. This was a whiteout, not the kind created by a blizzard, but the kind caused when sunlight is blocked and scattered by ice crystals in low-lying clouds. Land and sky merged in a flat, featureless vista of white. She had never experienced anything remotely like it. Her eyes were struggling to focus, but there was nothing to focus on.

She glanced back into the caboose to reassure herself and to rest her eyes. She could, if she wanted, stay out here at the caboose where there was a cache of food and plenty of fuel. She had her radio and could contact the base.

It wasn't like being lost in fog. She knew she was seeing for hundreds of metres, but overlapping shadows cancelled each other out so all definition and sense of depth were lost. She took a few steps and her feet crunched in the snow, but when she looked back she had left no footprints. She squatted down and touched the snow. She could feel the indentations, but she couldn't see them. Her sense of disorientation was so strong that she felt a wave of giddiness. She turned back to the caboose and went inside to watch and wait it out.

It didn't take long. The first thing to become visible was one of the black oil drums that marked the perimeter of the base. The cloud cover was lifting and gradually the world acquired definition. She set off for the platform.

* * *

She hadn't been in any real danger, she told herself as she stripped off her outdoor clothes in the kit room. And yet the whiteout had shaken her. It was partly the strangeness of it and partly the suddenness. She had been told how rapidly conditions could change out here and now she knew the truth of that. She was glad she had taken her radio even though she hadn't needed it.

She made herself coffee and toast in the kitchen and took it back to her pit-room.

There was someone awake somewhere. As she went down the corridor she caught a distant strain of music, very faint. She couldn't tell where it was coming from or make out the words, but from what she caught of the twanging melody, it seemed to be country and western. It was probably Craig who was a country and western fanatic. Nick on the other hand had a tendency to play Shostakovich at full volume and sometimes walking down the corridor was like listening to a piece of music by that American composer who had two tunes blasting out from different directions.

There was still an hour before the day properly began and Ernesto would be making porridge and frying bacon.

She decided to use the time to catch up on her correspondence. She owed Rachel an email. She propped herself up on her pillow, opened her laptop, and began:

"Hi Rachel,

"You asked me what I'm missing most? Well friends and family obviously. But also trees. Grass. Flowers. (I didn't realize I'd miss colour so much.) And fresh milk. We are also getting low on fresh veg and fruit – though we are still OK for potatoes and carrots and onions and apples. And we have eggs. Apparently they keep for quite a while if you store them properly and remember to keep turning them. It's strange being in a world where there are no children and no old people. And no money (nothing to buy). On the other hand there are no viruses now that we're cut off from the rest of the world. No one's going to get flu or even have the common cold until late October when outsiders – as I already think of them – arrive.

"Of course there are things that we've got plenty of: silence when the wind dies down. Ice. And space – once you get off the base. And the weather's been good, it's only got down to minus twenty-five (!) and there's been plenty of sunshine. So for those who want it, there've been trips out on the Skidoos accompanied by Alex. Alex has got two roles on the base. He's our mechanic, but he's also our mountaineer and all-round outdoor man. He's climbed Everest and has worked in Mountain Rescue back in the UK. He's responsible for supervising any trips off base. We call him Mr Fix-it. He can turn his hand to anything. He's Scottish – there seem to be a lot of Scots out here – with a rather attractive west coast accent. A lean, lanky guy with hair that flops over his forehead.

"Time, above all, I've got plenty of time. Yes, I've got my work to do and my share of the chores. The chef has one day off in seven and then the rest of us take it in turns to cook. There are cleaning duties too – that's called being on gash – and meltwater duties. But basically it's office hours with nowhere to go after work or on weekends. It's years since I've had so much free time. I'm racing ahead with the *Inferno*. And

I'm using some of that time to think about what I'm going to do when I get back home.

"You'll want to know about the other guys here. Well, Sara's great. We have a giggle about things.

"Graeme – the Boss – is the electrical engineering technician and the base commander, not that he needs to do much bossing. Everyone is responsible for their own work and they just get on with it. But the base commander is sworn in as a magistrate before the season starts so the buck does stop with him (wonder if he's allowed to marry people, like captains at sea – not that I have any plans...). He never loses his cool. If something does go wrong he just starts to sing in a low voice, 'When this lousy war is over, no more soldiering for me. When I get my civvy clothes on, oh, how happy I shall be.' Sara says that when he moves on to 'There's a long, long trail awinding' you know he's really fed up. He's something of a father figure – no surprise, given that he's got four grown-up children and three grandchildren that he's very proud of.

"And then there's Ernesto, the chef. He's only half-Italian. His mother was from Naples, but his father was from Peckham. It's a combustible mix and his accent is unlike anything I've ever heard. His cooking is terrific. We do eat a lot of pasta, but everyone is fine with that. You need plenty of carbs when you're out in the cold. And meals are important to punctuate the day.

"There are lots of little rituals. For instance it's traditional after the last summer visitors have left for the winter crew to have a back-to-back screening of three horror films, *The Thing from Another World* and two versions of *The Thing*. They're about aliens from outer space taking over remote snowbound research stations! The guys waited for me to arrive. We had popcorn and ice-cream (no problem keeping things cold, it's more a matter of not letting them get *too* cold).

"It took me a little while to get some of the guys straight in my head. There are four or five blokes who seemed more or less the same person at first glance – doesn't help that everyone wears the same clothes, and they've all got beards, but of course once you start to get to know them, they're quite different.

"What's great is that we all muck in together, even though on the face of it, you might not think some of us have got much in common. On one hand there's Adam (the Kid), the youngest on the base, who's from Sheffield and calls everyone 'duck' – male and female."

Katie paused to reflect. She was pretty sure that Adam – only twenty-five – had a bit of a crush on her. He was a pale-skinned redhead and blushed when she took his pulse. She decided to make a point of treating him like a younger brother and to play up the age difference.

She went on:

"On the other hand there's Nick the astronomer (the Posh One), who went to Eton. I know that because Justin teases him about it – he's the other astronomer. Justin I think of as the Surfer Dude, because he's got longish blonde hair and has the build for it. They're the telescope nannies. Twice a day you see them trudging off to the Dark Sector to take readings and one or other of them has to be on duty all the time in case something breaks down – and it quite often does.

"And then there's Rhys, the meteorologist, Mr Mastermind. He could answer questions on Antarctica and its history – and virtually anything else. He knows a hell of a lot, and he lets everyone know it. (But as Sara remarked to me the other day, he doesn't know as much as he thinks he does. No one could.) At the same time, he's always making cups of tea for people, would do anything for anyone – so it's swings and roundabouts, as it always is. We all have our annoying little ways – except me, of course!

"That's everyone."

But was it? Katie stopped typing and thought about it. Her and Sara, the Boss, Chef, Adam, Justin and Nick, Rhys. What about Alex? Yes, she'd mentioned him earlier. But still that was only nine.

She stared at the screen, baffled. For a few moments she just couldn't think and then – Craig! She'd forgotten Craig! That was awful!

She deleted "that's everyone" and typed:

"Lastly there's Craig, our Comms person. We rely on him for our satellite contact with the outside world and that's ironic, because he's about the least communicative person I've ever met. He isn't unfriendly or difficult or anything like that. He just hardly ever speaks. Talk about the strong, silent type! Craig is big – and I mean BIG. He's well over six foot and broad with it. He's one of those guys who makes you want to step back, he takes up so much room. Always wears those knee-length shorts indoors – looks a bit like an overgrown boy scout."

Before Katie left home, there had been plenty of jokes about being alone in the base with eight men and no way in or out. However, Katie was there in a medical capacity and everyone on the base was her research subject, so it would be best to avoid getting into a sexual relationship with anyone. If there was anyone Katie did fancy, it was Nick. With his sooty dark hair and his tattoos there was something of the louche bad boy about him. But she wouldn't do anything about it. In a small, isolated community that could lead to jealousy and bad feeling. It was important to be friendly, but not too friendly. And that cut both ways. She ought to know something about everyone on base. Had she even tried to have a proper conversation with Craig or sat next to him at a meal? She decided to get to know him a bit better.

Katie became aware of a commotion outside in the corridor, and the thud of running feet. She turned to look at the door, just as it burst open. Adam was standing there, eyes wide. "Doc! Doc!"

Katie got to her feet, her heart thumping. "What's the matter? What is it?"

"Big Doc wants you in the surgery! It's Justin. He's hurt! He's hurt bad!"

CHAPTER 9

Katie forced herself not to run. Panic never helps. She walked briskly down the corridor with Adam at her side, trying to make sense of what he was babbling – "we were helping Alex in the garage – a burst of steam – his hand – and his arm – it were awful – his leg" – and knowing that whatever had happened, there was now no way at all of getting help or of having Justin flown out. They'd just have to deal with it. Fragments of her training came back to her – how to deal with burns – what to do if someone died on base – no, don't go there...

They reached the surgery door, Adam hovering anxiously behind her. She braced herself as she opened it; Justin was lying on the examination trolley. He looked round as she came in. He was pale, his hair plastered to his forehead with sweat. He was clearly shocked, but he was at least conscious and alert. Perhaps it wasn't as bad as all that.

Alex was waiting near the door. He looked concerned, but not desperately worried, Katie was relieved to see.

Sara was leaning over Justin, and was trying to remove a dressing from his right hand. He took a sharp intake of breath and gritted his teeth. "Sorry," Sara said, "the painkillers should kick in any minute. I'll wait."

"OK, Adam," Alex said. "Everything's under control now. Let's get off to the kitchen and get Ernesto to make us a nice strong cup of tea."

"Is he going to be OK?" Adam was on the verge of tears.

Alex clapped him on the shoulder. "Hey, of course he is. He's got these two lovely doctors all to himself. Lucky guy!"

The little joke reassured Adam. But still he looked to Sara for confirmation.

"He's going to be fine," Sara said firmly.

Alex and Adam departed and Katie closed the door behind them.

"Are you feeling any better?" Sara asked Justin.

He nodded. "Go ahead."

With infinite gentleness she eased the dressing off. Katie looked over Sara's shoulder and winced in sympathy, but at the same time she was relieved. The palm of the hand was as red as a lobster, swollen and blistered, but the skin wasn't charred or leathery. It was bad, but it didn't look as if it had gone through the dermis. It was probably just a second-degree burn – though that was bad enough. That hand was going to be out of action for quite a while.

"It still hurts like hell," Justin complained.

Sara said, "Believe it or not, that's a good sign. With third-degree burns there can be numbness. This isn't quite that serious."

"I've got to be able to go out to the telescope!"

"Are you right-handed?"

He nodded.

Sara was sympathetic, but firm. "It's going to be out of the question, Justin, for the time being. Even if you're up to trekking over there – and we haven't looked at your ankle yet – you won't be able to use this hand for weeks."

Justin cursed. "I don't believe it!"

Katie understood how he felt. The telescope was the whole reason for his presence at the base. Every day, twice a day – at least – he and Nick did what she had done this morning and went through the laborious process of donning thermal underwear, fleece, double-thickness gloves, triple-thickness socks, padded overall, and parkas. Whatever the weather, they slogged across the snow and ice to the telescope to do, well, whatever it was they did do. And that wasn't all. Things could – and did – go wrong. At any time of day or night the alarm might sound on their laptops to warn that the telescope had stopped working, interrupting the flow of data from the stars that was sent on to researchers in faraway labs. They would have to dress up again, go out to the telescope, and try to figure out what had gone wrong: maybe a bearing that needed lubricating or a broken fan.

There was no way Justin could do all this with one hand.

Sara gathered what she needed to dress the hand.

Justin lay back on the couch with his face set. Katie took his other hand and he gripped hers as Sara dabbed on the antibiotic cream and applied the dressing. She arranged a high arm sling so that his hand could be elevated to reduce the swelling.

"All done," she said. "We'd better get this ankle X-rayed – just in case."

"What happened there?" Katie asked.

"When the steam hit my hand, I stumbled back and twisted my ankle. What an idiot!"

Katie and Sara helped Justin across to the X-ray machine. With Justin's arm around her shoulder, Katie was conscious that it was a while since she'd been this close to a man. There was a smell of soap and fresh sweat, not unpleasant, and she couldn't help noticing how muscular his shoulders were. He was a good-looking guy if you went for the type, which Katie didn't. But she couldn't help feeling a frisson of interest all the same. *If it's like this now, what's it going to be like by October?* she wondered.

It took a while to take the X-rays and develop them in the dark room. Justin rested while it was done.

When the X-rays were up on the light box, Sara said, "You're fine. No signs of a fracture. You'll need to keep your weight off that ankle, Justin, for a week or two. That's all. We'll get it strapped up."

While she was doing that, he apologized for his earlier bad temper. Katie found herself liking him better than she had before.

Sara showed Justin how to manage his crutches. She and Katie watched as he hobbled off disconsolately down the corridor.

As they turned back to the surgery, Sara said, "It's going to be tough on him psychologically. He's used to being a fit young man – did you know he's a keen cyclist and was almost selected to train for the Tour de France? He takes every opportunity to get outdoors and he's in the gym for at least a couple of hours every day."

"And now he's going to have to sit by while other people do his work. He's going to get bored and frustrated," Katie agreed. "It's not going to be easy on everyone else either. His work'll have to be covered somehow."

They looked at each other with a tacit understanding of what this might mean for the atmosphere on base. Everyone would have to pull together, work harder, take on tasks that weren't part of their job description. This was when any problems of attitude or weaknesses of personality would become apparent. In a team of ten it made a big difference to be one man down.

Sara frowned. "The second accident on base in a matter of a few weeks. You know, some winters the doctor has hardly anything to do."

"I'd been meaning to ask you," Katie said, "have you had any news of Kevin?"

Sara brightened. "Just this morning. He's going to be fine. Still doesn't remember anything at all about the accident – or about the entire day. That's not uncommon with head injuries. I'm so relieved. I'd been feeling bad about it."

"But it wasn't your fault."

"Well, that's the thing. It kind of was. You see, I was supposed to be on meltwater duty that day, but I had a migraine and Kevin offered to do it for me – that's the kind of guy he was. He shouldn't have been out there at all. It should have been me."

In spite of the good news about Kevin, she still looked worried.

"Is there something bothering you?" Katie asked.

"Well, there is, a bit. Probably nothing. But you know that business with the corkscrews?"

There had been a spate of practical jokes on the base. Katie had taken a joke carton of milk out of the fridge: it mooed when she tried to pour some into her tea. Ernesto had found a plastic spider in the flour. Mysteriously, Penguin had gone missing and around the same time both the corkscrews had disappeared. With so many practically minded people to hand, getting corks out of bottles wasn't a problem, but it was annoying all the same. A few days later, Katie had noticed them in the surgery, camouflaged in a tray of medical instruments.

"What about the corkscrews?" Katie asked.

"It made me feel a bit uneasy. Not sure why, but I decided to do an inventory to see if anything was missing."

"And was it?"

"Yes. We're short a scalpel."

53

CHAPTER 10

"There's a long, long trail a-winding..." Graeme sang in a low voice.

He saved the document he was working on – a revised timetable taking Justin's injury into account – and sat back.

His eyes strayed to the framed photos on his desk. He missed Helen and the kids and the grandkids. Wintering over on the ice was a single man's game, but he had had to come here just one last time. The place had called to him. At unexpected moments – in a traffic jam, putting out the dustbins, even at a football match – he had felt that craving, that yearning to be on the ice. The cleanness, the emptiness, the space – it was like a drug. He'd promised Helen that it *would* be the last time. Of course she hadn't liked it but, bless her, she knew what Antarctica meant to him and she hadn't objected. He felt a surge of love for her: what a great girl she was.

It got under your skin, this place. There was literally nowhere on earth like it and he loved the camaraderie on base. But this year... there was a bad vibe. Of course, Justin's accident was just one of those things – no one was to blame – but so too had Kevin's accident been just one of those things. He didn't like it. When you had a run of bad luck like this, you never knew how it might end.

And there were other things he didn't like. These practical jokes for instance. Of course there was always a certain amount of joshing on base, some of it pretty puerile. The departing summer crew and scientists always left various little surprises behind – that was a tradition. The mooing milk carton was probably one of them, and the spider in the flour. That kind of thing was nothing to worry about. But the other things...

The first thing to go missing had been Penguin. He had disappeared – from Katie's room, she thought – and that was very unfortunate, because she was doing that blog about him for schoolkids. She'd had to make up a story about him being a naughty penguin and running off to ski to the South Pole. Everyone on the base had looked for him, but to no avail. Then, when he had been gone a couple of days, Graeme had spotted him through the open door of Sara's pit-room. He was sitting on her pillow. The episode had left a bad taste in the mouth. Perhaps whoever had done it hadn't realized about the blog before they took Penguin. He hoped not, because if they had, there was something mean about it.

And then there'd been the missing corkscrews. That was just silly – or was it? Maybe it was a little bit sinister, too?

Then there had been this morning. He'd gone into the kitchen to find Ernesto in a mood.

"I dunno what's happened. I got the fish out of the freezer last night," Ernesto told him, frowning. "I put it to defrost in the fridge."

It was 21 March, the autumn equinox. The day before had been Nowruz, the Persian New Year. Ernesto was planning a special Nowruz meal of fish and rice with green herbs. There was no one Persian on the base, but having lots of little celebrations was part of keeping up morale. Ernesto's excellent cooking gave them something to look forward to every day and a reason for spending time together. And the routine of mealtimes kept them anchored in time.

"Shall I have a look?" Graeme asked.

Ernesto nodded and stood glowering as Graeme opened the fridge and scanned the shelves. "Not there," he agreed. "Is there time to defrost some more?"

Ernesto looked at the kitchen clock. "Just about, but..." He shook his head. "Don't like people mucking about in my kitchen."

Graeme wondered if Ernesto had only thought he'd got the fish out, but it didn't seem a good idea to suggest it.

However, Ernesto got there himself. "Maybe I just thought I had," he conceded. "Hope I'm not going toast already."

Graeme hoped not, too. "Going toast", or "winter-over syndrome" as psychologists called it, was a recognized condition. There was evidence that the prolonged isolation and perhaps the lack of light actually altered brainwaves. "Going toast" was characterized by the "Antarctic stare", the tendency to gaze into the middle distance for minutes at a time. People could become vague and forgetful, their eyes unfocused, voices trailing off in the middle of a sentence.

"Bloody sure I'm not though," Ernesto muttered.

"Nah, course you're not, mate." Graeme clapped him on the back.

No, what had worried Graeme as he made his way down the corridor to his office was not "winter-over syndrome". It was too early for that – they were only a month into their isolation – and the weather had been good. It was only twenty-five below zero with plenty of sunshine and for those who wanted it, there had been trips out. The dark and difficult days still lay ahead. No, at this point everyone should be fine.

He looked thoughtfully at the wall where photos of all the crew were posted. Someone was playing games. Who was it? He thought he could rule out Ernesto. He had seemed genuinely puzzled and annoyed. And he took food far too seriously to joke about it.

His eye travelled along the line of photos. What about Alex? Graeme liked Alex. He was proving to be an asset to the station as an all-round handyman. He seemed too grown-up for these silly stunts. But then were any of the others more likely? Justin? If it was Justin, he wouldn't be in any mood for joking now. Rhys? Nick? Craig? Maybe Craig? Sometimes these quiet types... Ah now, what about Adam? He was always telling bad jokes. Though some of the things that were happening weren't really that funny – they almost didn't seem like jokes. But it might be worth keeping an eye on Adam. After all, he was the youngest and a bit immature.

Continuing along the line of photos, his gaze lingered on Sara. The toy on her pillow and the corkscrew in the surgery: were these jokes deliberately aimed at her? A thought struck him: could she even be responsible? Surely not...

He suddenly realized what the time was. Hell, he was supposed to be in the dining room, addressing a meeting that he himself had called!

* * *

Everyone was sprawled on dining chairs – Justin with his leg up – except for Ernesto who was standing with his back to the kitchen door, a clean tea towel over his shoulder.

Graeme cleared his throat and said, "You all know by now that Justin's going to be out of action for a while. I've called this meeting, because I was going to ask for volunteers to cover Justin's trips to the telescope and to share emergency duties with Nick until Justin's back on his feet. And we'll have to cover Justin's meltwater duty. But it's not necessary for me to ask for volunteers."

He paused for effect and there were sideways glances as people wondered what was coming next.

"That won't be necessary," Graeme went on, "because all of you have already been to my office over the course of the day, volunteering your services. It's only what I would have expected, but all the same... good going, guys. So I've drawn up a rota accordingly. Have a look at it and let me know if there are any problems."

There were nods all round.

"That's all," Graeme said. "As you were."

"Just a moment." Justin raised an awkward hand. "I just want to say thanks, guys. I'll be working at my one-handed typing, so if anyone wants data inputting, anything like that – just let me know. And as soon as my ankle's better – which the Doc says shouldn't take long – I can take a bigger share of the night watch."

There was a buzz of conversation. Ernesto brought in two trays of lasagne. Graeme began opening bottles of red wine. Some bases discouraged alcohol, but social drinking was fine on the UK bases and he felt this was a day when a drink or two was just what was needed.

It looked as if the situation was bringing everyone together, even having an energizing effect. Even Craig looked mildly animated and was actually having a conversation with Justin. Wonders would never cease.

* * *

The killer watched the two women over the rim of his glass as they chatted and laughed together. Big Doc and Little Doc.

He was still kicking himself over Kevin. Of course he wasn't to know that Kevin had swapped meltwater duties with Sara at the last moment. Everyone looked the same in their outdoor gear and Sara was a big woman, so his mistake was understandable. But just at the last moment, he'd had an inkling that something was wrong and had pulled back, hadn't hit Kevin with the full force of the blow. Under the circumstances it was lucky that Kevin wasn't dead – also lucky that he didn't remember what had happened. There would have had to be a full-scale enquiry and that would have attracted way too much attention. As it was, the accident had put everyone on edge and now this with Justin, too.

But maybe the situation could work in his favour. Everyone would be that much more distracted and busy.

He looked again at the women, sneaking a glance. They were leaning in towards each other, looking serious now, Katie frowning and nodding. He liked Katie and in other circumstances he would have liked Sara, too, perhaps even fancied her. Sara was a good doctor, too, no doubt about it, and it was a pity in a way that she wasn't going to see the winter out. But that was the way it had to be.

He was in no hurry. After all, no one was going anywhere!

The days of twenty-four-hour daylight had ended and the sun rose and set now. The days were growing shorter and shorter. The huge blood-red ball seemed scarcely able to hoist itself above the horizon. It rolled along for a few hours and sank out of sight as if exhausted. The day had come when it was dissected by the horizon, and now only a third remained. Soon the sun would be going down for the last time and the long Antarctic night would begin.

Darkness was his friend. He could afford to wait for the perfect opportunity and this time there must be no mistake.

CHAPTER 11

Katie said, "I don't care which token I have as long as it's not the iron or the thimble."

Alex said, "There's no gender stereotyping here, I'll have you know. Anyway, the thimble's missing. How about the racing car – or would you prefer the Scottie dog? Me and my brother used to fight over that when we were kids."

So had Katie and her brother. Children always went for the Scottie dog.

"What's this?" she said, picking up a small black and white object. "Is it... yes, it's a penguin!"

"I made that," Rhys said, "to replace the thimble."

"Cool! I'll have the penguin."

Rhys looked gratified. "It's actually made of pewter."

Knowing Rhys, it would be.

"The Scottie dog for me," Alex said.

"I'll have the boot," Justin said.

Craig took the battleship and Nick took the iron.

Rhys said, "Did you know you can date a set by the tokens? This has to be from before 2013, because that's when the iron was replaced by a cat. Other retired tokens include a rocking horse, a sack of money, a man on horseback, a lantern, and a purse. The game was invented in 1913 and it was originally intended to promote the economic theories of Henry George –"

Everyone groaned and Alex said, "Enough! Rhys, you're like a walking Wikipedia entry."

Rhys grinned. He never took offence. Yes, definitely a touch of Asperger's, Katie thought.

"I'll have the top hat to go with the rest of my elegant attire," he said.

Katie wondered how she could ever have thought that these guys were alike. By now their personalities were so distinct and were expressed even in the way they wore their clothes. They were all wearing T-shirts and jeans – except Craig who was wearing the inevitable shorts and Justin who was wearing a shirt because it was easier to get on over his bandaged hand. Yet even so there were differences. Rhys's T-shirt proclaimed "There are ten types of people in the world: those who understand binary and those who don't" and he had actually ironed it, while Craig's looked as if it had been crunched up while still wet and chucked in a corner. All the men had beards. It was a tradition, but it was practical too, warmer when outdoors. Nick wore an earring. Craig wore a gold neck chain. And indoors everyone wore different shoes.

"Who's going to be the banker?" Katie asked.

"I don't mind doing that," Nick said. He reached for the money and started to distribute it. Katie was fascinated by his tattoos. Black and red roses entwined his right arm from the wrist upwards and disappeared into the sleeve of his T-shirt. She couldn't help wondering where the tattoo ended.

Justin was having trouble fanning out his money. Katie resisted the urge to help him. He wouldn't appreciate being treated like a child. He was learning how to do things with his left hand and was determined to be as independent as possible, though he'd had to accept that he needed help cutting up his meat.

Nick had all his money squared up. So did Rhys. But Nick had also divided his money into two piles. She wondered why. Alex hadn't sorted his at all. Justin's was ordered, but not excessively so. Katie's was the same. Craig's was all in one pile – his properties too, so that you couldn't see what he'd got.

The Mystery Man even in that, Katie thought. She had tried to get in conversation with him, but she had learned nothing except that he liked country and western music – which she already knew – and oh yes, he had once had a holiday in Nashville and gone to the Grand Ole Opry. When she had decided on the direct approach and asked him outright why he had come to Antarctica, he had just shrugged and said, "Oh, you know..."

They began to play. There was something strangely reassuring about it. It was such a family game, associated for Katie with Christmas. Here they were playing it in the middle of the Antarctic, hundreds of miles from any other person, while outside it was perpetual twilight and forty degrees below zero. They were following in the footsteps of generations of earlier winterers. The cards for Chance and Community Chest were soft and grubby from long use. The thimble wasn't the only token missing; the wheelbarrow had gone, too.

Alex opened a can of beer and shook the dice. "Great. A double six. That takes me to Marylebone Station. I'll buy it to go with the station I've already got."

Rhys said, "Remember the last time we played this? Kevin got all the stations and cleaned up."

It was Katie's turn. She landed on Park Lane. She'd already got Mayfair. "Hey, I can start building houses."

"Jammy beggar," Justin grumbled.

"Funny," Rhys said. "Some winters nothing happens – other winters... well, Kevin and Justin, that's two accidents, one really bad, the other pretty bad and both in a matter of weeks."

"It's a hostile environment," Alex said. "You could say it's surprising that things don't go wrong more often, when you think how dangerous it is out here. Some countries don't even allow their guys to go off base."

"Remember when they managed to fly that guy out of the South Pole?" Nick said as he shook the dice. "It was the beginning of April. The doctor got ill – gallstones, wasn't it? Whitechapel. Not worth buying."

"Pancreatitis. 2001. Ron Shemenski. They said he wouldn't last the winter," Rhys said. "Graeme happened to be wintering over that year. He was telling me about it. They flew Twin Otters down from Canada and landed them at Rothera. At the Pole they worked thirty hours straight to make a runway. They were only just in time and it was touch and go whether they'd get the sick guy out."

"You really don't want your doctor to be taken ill," Craig said. Miracle of miracles, he had actually spoken. "Or your heating and plumbing engineer. Whose turn is it?"

"Mine," Justin said. "That's right. Without them we'd be in deep do-do. And personally I wouldn't want to get through the winter without Ernesto. Whereas we mere scientists are expendable." He moved his piece and landed on Chance. He picked up a card. "Advance to Pall Mall," he read. "If you pass 'Go' collect £200. Great, and I'll buy Pall Mall, too."

"Lucky we've got Katie here as a backup," Alex said.

"I only finished my medical degree. I didn't do GP training or anything like that," Katie reminded him.

"Sure, but on the other hand how hard can it be, removing someone's appendix?" Nick said.

"Yeah, you're right. Piece of cake. There's bound to be a demonstration on YouTube. Just as long as I don't have to remove my own," Katie said, remembering what Sara had said.

Or treat my own breast cancer, she thought, as had happened to an American doctor wintering at the South Pole. They'd had to airdrop chemotherapy supplies to her. Perhaps it wasn't a good idea, from the psychological viewpoint, to dwell on possible disasters. Or was it better to get them in the open and defuse anxiety with black humour?

"I'm sure Ernesto would be happy to remove your appendix if you asked him nicely," Justin said. "Apparently he's done a course on butchering. He was telling me all about it the other day."

"Oh, thank you," Katie said. "That makes me feel so much

better. Luckily Sara and I are in excellent health, so hopefully we won't need to take him up on that."

"My pleasure," Justin said. "Oh and by the way, you've landed on Regent Street. You owe me twenty-six quid."

Craig rolled the dice and moved his token to Community Chest. He picked up his card, read it, and laid it on the table without speaking.

Alex leaned over and read it: "Go to Jail. Move directly to jail. Do not pass 'Go'. Do not collect £200. Oh dear, what *have* you been up to, Craig?"

Katie happened to be looking at Craig and saw his eyes shift.

There was a moment's silence, enough to tell Katie that she wasn't the only one to speculate about what had brought Craig to the Antarctic.

* * *

Two hours later and Katie had got to grips with the playing style of her companions. Nick was extremely cautious. She knew now that one pile of money was for buying properties and the other for paying and receiving rent. Rhys had noticed Nick's strategy and had quietly rearranged his money to copy it. Alex was the most reckless and the most competitive. He had already nearly gone bankrupt, before coming back from the brink. She hadn't really noticed what Craig was up to until everyone suddenly saw that he had completed the second most expensive set of properties – Regent Street, Oxford Street, and Bond Street – and was starting to build houses. Justin was somewhere in the middle: methodically collecting what he could, and not taking too many risks. He'd managed to get two stations as well as the Water Works and the Electric Company and they were nice little earners.

And what about her? She had Mayfair and Park Lane as well as Trafalgar Square, Fleet Street, and the Strand and she might very well win. She wasn't taking it as seriously as the others. As she watched Alex's furrowed brow as he threw the dice and heard him groan when the wrong number came up, she couldn't help feeling that some of them were taking it *too* seriously. He handed over a wodge of money to Craig – and not with good grace. She could tell he hated to lose, though he was trying not to show it. For goodness sake, it was only a game. Luck played a big part in it – as in life generally. She found herself yawning and glanced at the clock. It was eleven o'clock.

"Shall we call it a day?" she asked.

Reproachful eyes were turned on her.

Rhys said, "We used to pull all-nighters last year. All the time. Running on from one game to the next."

"Sorry, guys, I won't be spending the next six months playing non-stop Monopoly."

"Just this once," Rhys pleaded.

"Well…"

She was still hesitating, when the fire alarm went off.

Instantly Craig and Rhys were on their feet. Almost before Katie had registered the alarm they were out of the door and heading for the Comms room where the firefighting equipment was kept. Everyone had received basic safety training, but these two had enhanced training in dealing with fire. It was probably just Graeme putting them through their fire drill, but it had to be taken seriously.

Nothing was feared more than fire on the base, especially during the winter. If the base were destroyed, there was nowhere else to go. True, there were emergency rations and fuel dumps located out on the perimeter and on the other platforms. There were tents too, buried out there in the ice. The odds were that they would survive the winter one way or another, but it would be desperately hard. Katie had no desire whatsoever to relive the experiences of Scott and Shackleton.

Justin grabbed his crutches and the four of them made their way to the mustering station in the corridor outside the kit room and next to the exit. Graeme and Ernesto were already there, waiting for them. Sara appeared in her dressing gown, yawning and pushing her hair back. She'd obviously been asleep.

The alarm stopped, leaving a silence that tingled in their ears. Just a drill then, thank goodness.

"Where's Adam?" Graeme said, frowning.

They all looked around, as if they might somehow have overlooked him.

"I thought I saw him going to his pit-room earlier," Sara said.

Justin said, "He was hitting the sauce at supper time."

"I'll go and look for him," Katie said.

Surely, she thought, as she headed off down the corridor, no one could sleep through this, however drunk they were.

But somehow Adam had. He was sprawled out on his bunk, face down, still fully clothed, snoring, and he stank of beer.

She shook him awake. He moaned and muttered and opened his eyes.

"The fire alarm!" she said. "Didn't you hear it? Everyone else is at the mustering station."

"What?" He stared blearily at her, struggling to focus his eyes and work out what she was saying. "Wha's that you say?"

"The fire alarm! Come on!" She pulled on his arm.

He half-rose and fell back on the bed with a groan. "Not well."

Finally she got him on his feet and out into the corridor. He made his unsteady way towards the mustering station with Katie following behind to make sure he didn't veer off somewhere en route.

Graeme would be annoyed. It was one of the few things he was really strict about. He didn't mind people having a drink or two, but it was vital that they were "fit to muster". Otherwise, they imperilled not only themselves, but everyone on the base.

* * *

They went back to the game of Monopoly but it had gone off the boil, and they agreed to finish it the next day.

But Katie was never to know whether she would have scooped the pool. When Graeme, who was on night duty, went into the dining room around two o'clock, he found the board overturned and the money, the tokens, and everything else scattered all over the floor.

When he'd tidied it all up, he found that the little penguin was missing.

CHAPTER 12

NORTH NORFOLK

The journey from Cambridge railway station to the flat Michael Cameron shared with Flora was scarcely half a mile, but twice in the taxi he fell briefly asleep and woke with a start. *I'm getting too old for this*, he thought. Three weeks of back-to-back lectures, receptions, dinners, followed by the long, long flight from Sydney. It would have been sensible to have stayed a few days longer, relax, have a holiday, but he had been desperate to get back to Flora. He had no illusions. It was like that French saying: there is always one who kisses and one who offers the cheek. Flora was the one who offered the cheek. Yes, Flora did love him – and was appreciative of everything he had to offer her – but there was an element of the pragmatic in it, he knew that. He, on the other hand, adored her. He was afraid to let her know how much and was careful not to crowd her. He hadn't been able to believe his luck when she'd agreed to marry him. He would do anything for her. Sometimes he lay awake at night, thinking about what he *had* done for her. But there was no danger really: only the two of them knew...

The taxi pulled up outside the flat. The driver helped him to heave the suitcases into the hall and Michael gave him a generous tip.

He was surprised to find the flat empty. He'd expected Flora to be here. She'd planned to return from the cottage the previous day as she'd had a meeting with important investors in London that morning. He looked for a note, and checked his phone to see if she had texted him, but there was nothing.

Probably she had just popped out to the shops. Or maybe the meeting had run over and she was on a later train. He sent her an affectionate text.

He decided to lie down – just for half an hour while he waited for her. He woke up three hours later. He had been sleeping open-mouthed and had drooled on the pillow. He wiped his mouth with the back of his hand. He hoped Flora hadn't seen that, but no, he could tell from the stillness that she hadn't returned. The bedside clock said five o'clock and he wondered for a moment if it was morning or evening. He felt a twinge of anxiety. She surely should be here and something else was nudging his thoughts, warning him that something wasn't right. What was it?

The phone rang. Ah, that would be her. He reached out for it and, as he did so, realized what was bothering him. If Flora had arrived back yesterday, then where was Marmaduke?

It wasn't Flora on the phone. It was Lyle. Flora had not turned up for her meeting. He wanted to know what on earth was going on? Was she there or did Michael know where she was?

It took Michael a while to get to grips with what he was saying. Jet lag had slowed down his thought processes and he was having difficulty putting things in order.

"Flora's not here," he told Lyle. A thought struck him. *Had she ever been here?* "Just hang on a moment," he said.

He put down the phone and went into the bathroom. None of Flora's paraphernalia was there. So she had not been there the previous night. His heart lurched. She had left him and had taken Marmaduke with her. The next moment he realized that even if this were true, this wouldn't explain why she hadn't shown up at such a crucial meeting. He felt the first cold trickle of apprehension.

He went back to the phone.

"When did you last hear from her, Lyle?"

"Not for – what? – three weeks, maybe, something like that – not since she went off to the cottage anyway. And neither has the departmental secretary. I rang her after Flora didn't show. And she's not answering calls or text messages."

"Just let me check my phone." Michael thumbed through the messages. Nothing from Flora. And no reply to his earlier text.

"No, and I haven't spoken to her since she arrived at the cottage," he told Lyle. "There's no landline or Wi-Fi there. No signal either."

"Well, is she still there, do you think? Did she get confused about the date?"

"Not Flora," Michael spoke with conviction.

His thoughts went into overdrive. Something must have happened to her: he saw her car in a ditch, her body slumped over the steering wheel. Get a grip, he told himself. Someone would have informed him if she'd had a road accident. Instantly the picture was replaced by one of Flora lying at the bottom of the stairs at the cottage.

"Something's wrong," he said. "There's a local farmer who keeps an eye on the cottage. I'll give him a ring."

* * *

While Michael waited for Mr McGuire to ring back, he made himself a pot of strong coffee. He didn't feel hungry, but made himself some toast from a loaf of sliced bread that he found in the freezer.

The farmer rang on his mobile. He had checked the cottage. The front door was locked but the back door wasn't. He had gone in and had a quick look around. There was no sign of Flora and her car had gone. Michael considered this. To go anywhere at all – even to buy a newspaper – she would have had to get in the car, so there wasn't much in that. As for the back door, they often didn't bother to lock it during the day. But still... his gut was telling him that this wasn't right. It was unthinkable that Flora had forgotten that meeting: he knew how much the project meant to her.

He couldn't just sit and wait for her to contact him. He rang Lyle and told him that he was going to drive to the cottage.

* * *

Everything looked normal as he bumped down the track and parked in front of the house. He didn't bother with the front door, but went straight round to the back. He opened the door and called Flora's name, knowing as he did so that if her car wasn't there, neither was she. Yet the house was warm, the heating was on, and that gave him hope.

But that hope dwindled as he went around the house and pieced together what he saw. The teapot had not been emptied and was full of mould. The fridge was packed with food past its sell-by date. He went upstairs to the bedroom. Flora's case lay open on the floor. She hadn't even unpacked. Inside there was a circular depression in the clothes, lined with fur and dead leaves and bits of twig. The bed didn't look as if it had been slept in.

In the sitting room he saw that there had been a fire in the grate and it had burned itself out.

Full of foreboding, he went back outside. It was getting dark now. He called her name. The sound of his voice drifted forlornly away. There was a rustling in the hedge and a creature emerged. At first in the dusk he didn't recognize it. Then it ran towards him and he saw that it was Marmaduke, carrying a mouse in his mouth. When Michael bent down to stroke him, he released the mouse and it darted away. Marmaduke was beside himself with excitement, rubbing round Michael's legs, talking to him in urgent chirrups and meows. Michael picked him up. He was so thin that Michael could feel his ribs. His fur was matted and there was a sticky, weeping wound on his cheek. He rubbed the other side of his face against Michael's shoulder and began to purr.

Michael carried him into the kitchen and put him down. He searched the cupboards, Marmaduke winding himself around Michael's feet all the while, pleading for food. Michael found a tin of tuna, opened it, and tipped the lot into a bowl. He put it down and watched for a few moments as the cat ate voraciously. The poor old boy was starving. He must have been alone here for weeks. Flora would never have left her beloved cat to fend for himself. Something had happened to her, probably soon after she had arrived here and soon after he had last spoken to her. Three weeks and no one had known that she was missing.

Full of dread, he got out his phone and rang the police.

CHAPTER 13

ELY

Lyle came into Daniel's office with a face like thunder, just behind Alison, who was bringing in a tray of coffee and biscuits. He took the tray from her with the usual courtesy that he showed towards women, but one look at his face and she made herself scarce without even thanking him.

"How far have you got with the lab books?" Lyle demanded.

"Almost there. Just a few very small queries."

The lab books were at the heart of due diligence. They recorded everything that took place in the lab: every detail, every step, every formula, every calculation, and, of course, every result. This was essential if an experiment were to be replicated and it meant too that if someone got knocked down by a bus, their work wouldn't be lost. It was also possible to establish the date of a discovery from them, and that was vital in taking out a patent.

Daniel was working his way through two sets of lab books, one belonging to Flora Mitchell and the other to Sara McKee. The two scientists had very different styles and there were one or two points where their lab books didn't quite dovetail. Not significant, but he would need to cross the "t"s and dot the "i"s when he saw Flora and that would need to be soon. He also had to talk to her about the new work, before he could settle down to drafting patent specifications.

Daniel continued: "Nothing I can't iron out, when I see Flora Mitchell."

"You won't do that."

"I beg your pardon?" Daniel stared at him, wondering if he were being sacked. "Is there a problem?"

"I'll say there's a problem. Flora Mitchell has disappeared."

"What? Lyle, stop looming over me." Daniel got up from his desk. "Sit down. Have a cup of coffee and tell me what's happened."

"I blame myself," Lyle grumbled, as he did what Daniel had suggested. "My instinct told me something was wrong and I took my eye off the ball. I've been in the States talking to investors and only got back to the UK yesterday; I was in London this morning. Flora didn't show. I rang the lab. Emily, she's the administrator, hadn't seen or heard from her either. At first she didn't think anything of it, because she knew Flora had a lot of paperwork to catch up with – a big grant application for one thing – you know how time-consuming they are. So she wasn't surprised at Flora wanting to hole up for a while and get her head down – and she's done that before. But Flora should have surfaced by now and she was worried."

"Maybe Flora lost track of time?" It was a feeble suggestion and Daniel knew it. An ambitious young scientist miss a meeting that was vital to her career? Hardly!

"Emily doesn't think so and neither do I. Not now. I've been sending messages to say that she must contact me with the utmost urgency – and nothing: nada, zilch." Lyle flung himself back in his chair. "No answer at her Cambridge flat, until I got her husband who's just got back from a lecture tour of Australia. He drove out to their house in Norfolk. She's not there either and he says that she must have been gone for weeks. Her bed's not been slept in and the cat was starving. He's called the police. Her car's not there. And he says he hasn't been able to find her laptop either."

"Maybe she's had some kind of breakdown?"

"Nah, not Flora."

"We don't know for sure that something serious has happened to her," Daniel pointed out.

"I do," Lyle said. "Someone as ambitious and driven as she is doesn't just drop out of sight for weeks on end."

Lyle threw himself back in his chair.

"Maybe that's why," Daniel said. "Sometimes these high-powered types just … burn out." He spread his hands.

"Not Flora. I tell you – she's the last person to have a breakdown. She wasn't stressed, far from it, she was thrilled at the prospect of more investment, more research. That's why the alarm bells started ringing when she didn't show at that meeting and didn't call in."

"Maybe she's run off with another man – or woman."

"I just can't see it. Flora's too level-headed. That marriage was all part of it for Flora. I'm not saying that there wasn't love, but you know, that sort of marriage – it's kind of like a strategy. All part of the game plan, marrying a successful older man, who can help her in her field."

"That's a bit cynical," Daniel protested.

"No, no, it's not – well, maybe just a little – I guess he started off as her mentor and it grew from there. It was the perfect set-up for both of them. And then – he won't want children, he's already got them from a previous marriage, so that won't get in the way of her career. I've seen it time and again. She gets support and the connections she needs, he gets an attractive younger wife. Everyone's a winner."

Daniel was surprised. He hadn't had Lyle pegged as being so alive to the nuances of relationships.

"Except for the first wife," he pointed out.

Lyle grinned. "There is that."

"So what's the next move?"

He sat up in his chair. "Well…"

Daniel didn't like the speculative way that Lyle was looking at him. It suggested that what Lyle was going to ask was a bit of a stretch by anyone's standards.

"I've told her husband that I urgently need to get hold of any papers Flora was working on – her current lab book in particular – and he said to send someone to Norfolk to pick them up."

"Fine. Good. Who are you sending?"

"Well, I thought… you."

"Me?"

"I can't go myself – got to meet a big investor in London – and it can't just be anybody. I need someone who, well, someone who'll find out what's going on."

"I'm a patent lawyer, Lyle, not a private detective!"

Lyle leaned forward, clasped hands dangling between his long legs. "It's a matter of making sure you've got the right documentation as well."

Daniel looked at him quizzically. "So you're expecting me to make a round trip of several hours?"

"That's about the size of it," Lyle admitted.

Daniel thought about it. A cross-country drive on a fine spring day would be no hardship.

"If you want to use a highly qualified patent lawyer as a courier, and are willing to pay, who am I to complain?"

"Good man."

"And after that I'll have to get hold of Flora's assistant on the earlier research. What's her name? Yes, Sara McKee. I'll need to set up a meeting with her."

Lyle grimaced. "Didn't I tell you?"

Daniel stared at him. "There isn't another problem, is there? Don't tell me she's missing too?"

"Well, no. Not that, exactly. But she's not doing research any more. She's working as a medic on an Antarctic research base. It's satellite phone or email contact only, I'm afraid."

"Which one? Which base?"

"Wilson."

"But that's where Katie is! What a coincidence!"

Lyle looked shifty. "Weeell." He drew the word out.

So it wasn't a coincidence.

Lyle continued: "It was Sara going out there that put the

idea in my head and I suggested it to Katie. The atmosphere in the UK's been pretty toxic for her since she blew the whistle about what had been going on in Honor's lab – and I felt some responsibility for that. It was thanks to me that she got involved. I thought it might do her good to get away. And then when she did decide to apply to BAS, I gave her a storming reference – she deserved it."

CHAPTER 14

ANTARCTICA

"Katie? Katie?"

"Yes, yes, I'm here!"

"Oh, wow, you could be in the next room!" Rachel said.

"Reception varies quite a lot. How are you?" Katie asked. "How did you get on with the consultant?"

The tiny pause told Katie all she needed to know.

Rachel said, "It's bad news, I'm afraid. They've had to stop the new therapy. The blood test showed that it's affecting her liver."

Katie had been afraid of this. Some patients did develop problems with liver toxicity. No one knew why exactly. It might be some kind of allergic reaction.

"So you're back on the old regime of infusions five nights a week?" Katie said.

"It was so wonderful not to have to do that. And now of course it's all the harder, going back to it. Before, we just accepted it and Chloe'd never known anything else. It wasn't easy, but it was as much part of her everyday life as brushing her teeth."

"How has she taken it?"

"Badly. Just how badly I only realized today, when Miss Marley, Chloe's class teacher, asked to see me. Actually I'd been planning to see her anyway. Chloe had burst into tears a couple of times and when I tried to find out what had upset her, she said that one of her friends had been mean to her. Something about being called 'a big fat bum' and a drawing being torn up."

"Oh, poor Chloe!"

"No, wait. So I went in at lunchtime today. I like Miss Marley. She's tiny – it's as if she's the right size for teaching little ones. But she's got an air of authority about her. I had to squeeze myself into one of those little chairs. I do wonder how larger parents manage when they come to talk about their children."

Katie could tell that she was reluctant to come to the point. "So what did she say?"

"She said that Chloe's a lovely little girl, bright as a button, but she was well aware that she had a lot to cope with... I could see that she was choosing her words carefully. And then she said there'd been one or two incidents... I asked if this was to do with what Chloe had told me about her friend being mean to her. Miss Marley looked thoughtful and she said, 'Is that what Chloe told you? I'm afraid it was the other way round. It was Chloe that called a Harriet "a big fat bum" and she tore up her drawing, too.' I couldn't believe it. My Chloe!"

"Oh Rachel!"

"I know," Rachel wailed. "I was mortified, Katie, just mortified. My child, a bully!"

"Oh, hardly that. It was probably just a one-off thing."

"Miss Marley said that it wasn't an isolated incident. There was a pattern emerging of Chloe getting frustrated and upset and taking it out on Harriet. And that's even though she likes Harriet, Harriet's her best friend. She's moved Chloe so that they're not sitting together. And the lunchtime supervisors are keeping an eye on the pair of them in the playground."

Katie sighed. "Poor little soul. It must be hard. What a pity the new drug didn't work. One day there'll be a cure for DBA."

"Yes, but when?"

That was the question. Would it come before Chloe was a teenager and the day came when she would have to manage those overnight infusions herself? It was a tough regime for a young person. Those who couldn't cope risked dying of cardiac failure.

Katie knew better than to hold out false hope. Her own research had only shown that a potential therapy might work *in vitro*, outside a human body. What worked in a Petri dish might not work in a human being. There'd have to be more experiments using mice and then primates and then human trials. A cure was still a long way off.

The best chance remained a bone marrow transplant from a suitable donor and the best way of producing a suitable donor was for Rachel and Dan to have another baby. Rachel had once mentioned that she had been very ill after Chloe's birth and another baby wasn't on the cards, but she hadn't gone into details and Katie hadn't asked. But now, somehow the distance seemed to help and the intimacy of talking on the phone, and Katie heard herself say, "What a pity you couldn't have another baby."

She heard Rachel sigh. "It was a fluke that I even had Chloe. I had endometriosis and I didn't think I could get pregnant."

"You have still got your ovaries – and your uterus?"

"Oh yes."

"Well, have you thought of IVF?"

"Even if I did get pregnant – well, it wouldn't be straightforward. After Chloe was born I had a post-partum haemorrhage and nearly died. They say it could happen again."

"Wow, that must have been scary!" Katie thought back to her medical training and her time on the obstetrics unit. Yes, the chances of post-partum haemorrhage recurring in a subsequent pregnancy *were* high, but forewarned was forearmed and the risks could be managed.

She said, "It wouldn't be nearly as dangerous the next time round. There's so much they can do."

There was a silence. "That's enough about me," Rachel said, closing down the discussion. "We'll get back into the old routine and hopefully things will settle down with Chloe. How are things going with you?"

Now it was Katie's turn to hesitate. "Do you know, I'm not entirely sure."

She told Rachel about the wrecked game of Monopoly. "We haven't played it since."

"Perhaps it was an accident?"

"Maybe, but no one's owned up. And it doesn't explain why the token, the little penguin, went missing. We really looked hard for it. Swept the floor and everything. And then there was the fish."

"The fish?"

"Ernesto missed some from the fridge. Then a couple of days ago, Sara noticed a bad smell in the surgery. It got worse and worse and finally we did a thorough search and we found the fish hidden in a filing cabinet. It's not very nice, knowing that someone's sneaking around the base doing things like that and not knowing who it is."

They chatted for a while, then Rachel had to go and collect Chloe from after-school club.

Katie pondered what Rachel had said. There was something she didn't quite understand here. The haemorrhage must have been a terrifying experience, but was it one that would put Rachel off permanently, when the stakes – the chance of a cure for Chloe – were so very high? This didn't fit with what she knew of Rachel. Surely she was the kind of woman who could get over something like this for the sake of her child. She was sure there was something Rachel wasn't telling her.

CHAPTER 15

NORTH NORFOLK

The drive to Norfolk gave Daniel a chance to think about what Rachel had told him about the incident at school. They had decided to talk to Chloe about it that evening. The pain of knowing that there is nothing you can do to heal your sick child… If only they could have had another baby. He reminded himself that even then there would have been only a one in four chance of a match. Unless they had IVF and embryo selection. And he knew that Rachel had a problem with the idea of discarding healthy embryos because they weren't a match. That was all academic anyway, because no way could they risk another pregnancy. But there was another possibility, something he had kept at a distance and not allowed himself to think too much about. Now it came sidling into view. Surrogacy. It was much more common now than when Chloe had been born. In fact you read about it in the papers all the time. Perhaps now was the time to consider it. At any rate there could be no harm in doing some research into the possibilities. He silenced the little voice that said, "Just because something is being done all the time doesn't mean it's right."

The satnav told him he had arrived at his destination. As he turned into the drive he saw a little Georgian cottage – a gem of a place – with a sweep of lawn leading down to a stream under a brilliant blue sky. Gold and white and purple crocuses were scattered under the trees that lined the bank. A plum tree bore stars of white blossom.

They certainly weren't short of money. But of course Michael

Cameron must be in his late fifties at least, at the height of a distinguished career, and besides he'd probably bought this before the property boom.

He parked by the front door with its original cobweb fanlight, got out, and rang the doorbell.

It was some moments before the door was opened by a craggy-faced man wearing a tracksuit. He had a couple of days' worth of stubble and the hair that ringed the dome of his bald head was tousled. The man looked haggard, there was no other word for it.

He said, "You'll be... Sorry... Lyle did say..." He had a deep, rather actorly voice.

Daniel put out his hand. "Daniel Marchmont."

The man took the proffered hand, but hesitantly, as if he wasn't quite sure what he was supposed to do with it. "Michael Cameron. Come in, do."

His hand was clammy and Daniel resisted an urge to get out a handkerchief and wipe his own hand. Daniel caught a whiff of something – whisky? – on his breath.

"Let's have some coffee, shall we?" Cameron said. "I need something."

Daniel followed Cameron through a hall that led to the back of the house and into a cast-iron conservatory that looked out over the garden. Cameron left him there and went off to make the coffee. Daniel sat down in one of the Lloyd Loom chairs and looked around. There were terracotta pots – empty at the moment, because this was the summer house. A vine had been trained up the outside and sunlight filtered through to make shifting patterns on the flagstoned floor.

Cameron came back with a tray bearing mugs and a cafetière. There was even a jug of milk and a sugar bowl. He put the tray down on a glass-topped table and sat down opposite Daniel. He pressed the plunger and poured out the coffee.

Perhaps the act of making it had steadied him, allowed him to get a grip on himself. His manner had changed. The hesitancy had gone. "I rang the police before you came. They didn't have any news."

"I'm sorry," Daniel said.

"I'm worried sick," Cameron admitted.

"When was the last time you saw Flora?"

"It was the day I flew to Melbourne. She planned to come out here the next day and I know she did because she rang me when she got here."

"And then you didn't hear from her for..."

"I didn't hear from her at all after that. But I didn't expect to. We don't have a landline here or Wi-Fi and mobile coverage is terrible." He rubbed his hand over his chin. "And then there was the time difference. We agreed to meet up back in Cambridge."

Daniel tried to imagine having the sort of arrangement with Rachel where they'd be out of touch for several weeks. He always rang home once if not twice a day, when he was away. Of course, Flora and Cameron didn't have children and that made a difference, but still...

Cameron guessed what he was thinking. "Look, no point in beating about the bush. Flora's twenty years younger than me. Didn't want to be breathing down her neck all the time. But now – God, I wish I'd got her to check in with me –"

Daniel didn't know what to say. He realized that Cameron was probably a bit drunk.

There was a chirruping sound and a cat emerged from the house. Cameron patted his knee and it jumped up. It was a strange-looking beast. Great hunks of hair seemed to be missing, as if someone had attacked it with a pair of shears.

Cameron saw Daniel looking and explained. "Had to get the vet to cut out burrs and knotted fur. He was in a terrible state. He must have been here on his own for weeks, poor old boy." He stroked the cat's head. "That's how I know something must have happened to Flora. She'd never have left him to fend for himself."

Daniel realized that Cameron believed that Flora was dead – or perhaps to hope was too painful.

Cameron straightened his shoulders. "Anyway... About these papers..."

"It would be helpful to see what Flora was working on... any notes, for example."

"Of course." He lifted the purring cat off his lap and placed him gently on the floor. "There's a little room off the hall that we use as a study. They'll be in there."

They went into the house, the cat close on their heels. It was as if he couldn't get enough of human company.

It was cold in the study and the air was musty. Surely no one had used this room in a while. Cameron looked around, frowning. There was a desk, but no papers.

Cameron said, "She might have decided to work in the sitting room. I saw she'd made a fire in there."

They went across the hall. The sitting room had a shabby, comfortable feel. It had been furnished in a country cottage style with sagging chintz chairs and a row of earthenware jugs on the broad white-painted windowsill. A big mahogany table was positioned for a view of the garden. A chair had been pushed back from it. A pen, pencil, and eraser lay scattered on the table – but no papers and no lab books.

"I'll check upstairs," Cameron said. "Maybe she hadn't unpacked them."

He went out. Daniel wandered around the room, inspecting the framed prints and watercolours, a pleasantly random collection, probably picked up in local antique shops. On the mantelpiece was a line of pink lustre plates on stands. The house told the story of a long marriage and a holiday home lovingly furnished and decorated over many years. He felt sure this was the work of the first wife. Probably she had kept the family home and Cameron had kept this.

The cat jumped on the windowsill and began to watch a bird.

On the hearth were the remains of a fire that had died down leaving half-consumed logs and scraps of paper. If Flora had laid the fire, that meant that she had at least had time to begin settling in before – well, before whatever it was that had happened. He looked again. Scraps of papers... He took a pen out of his pocket and gently stirred the charred fragments. Underneath there were parts of pages that had escaped the flames. He saw part of a formula written in a large, looping hand.

He had solved the mystery of the missing lab book.

CHAPTER 16

ELY

"It's not fair. Harriet doesn't have to go to the hospital! She doesn't have to have a needle stuck in her every night. I hate you! I hate you! I hate you!"

Chloe ran upstairs and they heard the door of her bedroom slam.

Daniel put his head in his hands and groaned.

"That went well," Rachel remarked.

"We had to talk to her. We don't want her growing up thinking that she's a special case – that it's OK to be mean to other people when you're miserable."

"Of course. But maybe we didn't have to go in mob-handed? Just one of us would have been enough."

"Yeah, maybe," he conceded.

There was the ping of an incoming text on Dan's phone; he looked at the screen. "It's Lyle. I'd better ring him. Do you mind, love?"

"I'll go and check on Chloe."

Chloe had calmed down and was chatting to Quack-Quack, a small stuffed duck. That was one thing about her: she wasn't a sulker, thank goodness. She was already in her pyjamas and had brushed her teeth earlier and – thank God – tonight was one of the two nights a week when she didn't have an infusion. Rachel eased Chloe under the covers and tucked her in. She switched on the pink-shaded bedside light, switched off the overhead light, and sat down in the little chair by the side of the bed.

Chloe's favourite story was currently Cinderella. Rachel

had only got as far as the coach arriving at the ball when she saw Chloe's eyelids drooping.

She went on sitting by Chloe's bedside, glad of a quiet space and time to think.

She wished now that she had told Katie the truth, when they had talked about why Rachel hadn't tried to have another baby. She had sensed that Katie was puzzled. All their friends and family had accepted long ago that there wouldn't be another child. The fact that Rachel had almost died giving birth to Chloe and that there was a significant risk of another post-partum haemorrhage had been accepted as sufficient reason. But it wasn't, not really. Katie from her medical knowledge and what she knew of Rachel had guessed that.

Then, as she gazed at the face of her sleeping child, it happened: without warning the warm bedroom dropped away, she was back in the maternity unit. It had been a routine C-section. Daniel was holding her hand. The midwife lifted up her baby for her to see and someone said, "A perfect little girl." And then everything had changed. She'd had an epidural, so she felt no pain – and she couldn't see what was happening. The first thing that registered was the shock on Dan's face, then the pressure of the surgeon's fist as he jammed his fist into her uterus in an attempt to stem the bleeding. Then a bitter, coppery smell. Dan went as white as a sheet. The next moment they had put the baby in his arms, and he was being hurried out of the room.

Someone said, "We've got to get more blood into her" and someone else was searching her arm for a vein. There were urgent voices, telling her to stay awake. They were trying to keep her with them, and she wanted to stay, but it was no good... She was drifting away. She knew that she was dying and a strange peace settled on her. There was no regret or sadness. She had given birth. Their baby was fine. Dan would take care of her. She was so tired, so tired, fading... fading...

Chloe murmured something in her sleep – and Rachel was back in the present, her heart beating fast.

"Rachel... Rachel," Dan was calling softly up the stairs.

"Coming!"

She gave herself a few moments. In the first year after Chloe's birth she had often had these flashbacks, then they had been fewer and fewer and eventually they had stopped altogether. Perhaps this one had been triggered by the worry over Chloe.

When she went down the TV was on for the news, and a full-face photograph of a fair-haired woman filled half the screen.

"Is that –?" Rachel began.

Dan held up a hand.

The newsreader was saying "went missing from her home near Walsingham on or around the nineteenth of February". There was a picture of a pretty Georgian house. He continued, "Doctor Flora Mitchell is a leading cancer researcher. Police are asking anyone who has seen her to contact their local police station or ring this number..."

When the newsreader had moved on to the next item, Dan clicked the TV off.

"That's the house that you went to today?" Rachel said.

He nodded. "Her husband's beside himself with worry."

"What do you think's happened?" She sat down next to him.

Dan shook his head. "Doesn't look good. It's a long time to go missing. Lyle fears the worst – that someone took her. Either that or that she's had a catastrophic breakdown of some kind."

He told her about finding the lab book burned in the grate. Luckily there was a PDF, but still, a scientist's lab book was precious. If Flora had destroyed that, then she was in a bad way. But if it was someone else who had done it, well, that was worse, because that meant it was a deliberate and malicious act.

"She looked young in that photo," Rachel said.

"She was – is – young. Only mid-thirties. Oh well, let's hope for the best. Perhaps the publicity will flush her out. Maybe she's taken off with some other man – or woman – and once she's got over the embarrassment of being splashed all over the headlines, she'll be back."

"Do they have children?"

"Children? No, no, they don't."

"What's this going to mean for you – and for what she was working on? How important was it?"

"Very important. It could usher in a whole new generation of cancer treatment. Flora was the lead researcher. On the other hand very few people are indispensable. I guess the actual work will go on one way or another. For Lyle it's a matter of whether or not the investors are going to get the jitters. As for me, I'm just the hired hand. I work with what I'm given. I'm going to talk to Sara, the woman who worked with her on the earlier research. In fact," he glanced at his watch, "I'm supposed to be putting through a call around now."

"Funny her being in Antarctica and Katie being out there as well!"

He laughed. "Only if you don't know Lyle. Typical of him to have a finger in every pie. Nothing he likes better than pulling strings!"

* * *

The line wasn't great and at first Sara McKee didn't seem to grasp what he was saying.

"But where did you say Flora had gone?" she kept saying.

"That's just it. No one has seen or heard from her for three weeks."

Finally the penny seemed to drop. "You mean she's gone missing? But what can have happened?"

"We don't know." Daniel was afraid that the connection was going to be broken at any moment and was anxious for Sara to get the point. "That's why I need to talk to you about the apoptosis research. I'm reviewing the patent application and there are a few details I'm not absolutely clear on. Can you think back to the summer when you and Flora made the apoptosis discovery? I've got your lab book here."

There was silence and he guessed that she was trying to call up her memories.

At last she said, "What you've got to remember is that I was the junior partner. Flora was the senior researcher. I was decent enough at what I did, but I didn't have her flair. That was what made me realize that I was never going to be more than mediocre at best. And besides, I missed working with people. That's why I decided to go back to medicine."

"So, the apoptosis research?" he prompted.

"That's an example of what I mean. I'd never have come up with that on my own. It was a stroke of genius on Flora's part. She came in one morning and said why don't we try delivering excess cytochrome c directly into the cytoplasm and triggering apoptosis. Well, it was a bit more involved than that of course with self-assembled viruses and monoclonal antibodies and a whole load of weird chemistry I'd never heard of, but she had worked out a protocol and had a guy over in chemistry help us out and it worked. Complete cell death in two lung cancer cell lines *in vitro*! It was a game-changer. We had both our names on the research paper that we submitted to *Oncogene*, but it came from her really."

"Do you mean it didn't come directly from what you were already doing?"

The line crackled and he missed what she said next.

"What was that?" He found himself raising his voice – as if that could make a difference. Then suddenly he heard her loud and clear.

"I said, yes and no! Using monoclonals was one of the options, and we'd probably have got a result, but this came out of left field. No one was expecting something so radical."

"You rate her highly."

Sara said, "I think some people have an instinct for what will work. They make a leap of the imagination. It's like…" she paused as she sought for the word, "an intuition, yes, a kind of intuition. Flora has it. That's what makes her such an exceptional scientist. I just did the donkey work. Is that what you need to know?"

"I've got a clearer picture now, thanks." A sudden thought occurred to him. "I suppose you haven't heard from her yourself recently. You can't shed any light?"

Sara hesitated. "We didn't keep in touch. We, well, we weren't friends, not really. I mean, I respected her and admired her as a scientist, but she wasn't –"

And then, quite suddenly, the connection was severed and the line went dead.

CHAPTER 17

ANTARCTICA

There was something wrong with Sara. They were in the surgery and Katie had been telling her about the latest set of data, but she just wasn't listening. Ever since the phone call with Dan last week, she'd been distant and distracted. She hadn't even noticed that Katie had stopped talking. Katie waited.

Then Sara did notice and said, "What was that?"

"You haven't been listening to a word I've said, have you?"

She looked embarrassed. "I'm sorry, Katie."

"What's the matter?"

"I keep thinking about Flora. I emailed that lawyer, that friend of yours, Daniel, again this morning, but there's still no news. I can't stop wondering what's happened to her."

"Perhaps it all got too much for her..."

"But it seems so unlike her. She wasn't the type to buckle under stress."

"Is there a type? Can't it happen to anyone under the right circumstances?"

"Maybe. But what circumstances? Her career was going from strength to strength and she'd recently got married. And then I keep thinking about the questions Daniel asked me, about our research and how we came up with the idea. At the time I didn't think there was anything wrong and I still don't see how there could be. But he got me thinking..." Her voice trailed off. "Oh, it can't be anything," she concluded.

"Tell me," Katie said.

"Well, something happened very soon after our research was published. Someone showed up at the lab – a man, he managed to blag his way in and claimed that we'd stolen his work. He was clearly unbalanced, well, raving really. We had to get security to remove him from the building." She frowned, trying to remember. "I can't think what his name was. Did it begin with a K? One of those Irish names. Kieran something, maybe? It turned out he *was* a scientist, but he'd had a psychotic episode and had managed to walk out of the hospital where he'd been sectioned. We'd never heard of him or his research project, so there was no possibility that we could have been influenced by what he'd been doing. But he just didn't believe us."

Katie nodded. It happened often enough that people were working on parallel lines. And though it was unusual for people to be unaware of similar research projects, it did happen.

Sara said, "Oh, there can't be anything in it." She broke off. "What was that? I thought I heard..."

Katie thought she'd heard something too – a sound out in the corridor. "Someone waiting to see you?" she suggested.

Sara shook her head. "I'm not expecting anyone."

Katie got up and opened the door. She looked up and down the corridor and shrugged. "No one there. What were you about to say?"

"Oh, it was obvious that he was suffering from paranoid delusions, poor guy. It's just that – Flora going missing. It's spooked me. I mean what if he still thinks that and, well, somehow got to her..." Sara looked at Katie. "I'm talking rubbish, aren't I?"

Katie wasn't so sure. "I think you should tell Daniel. He can hand it on to the police. It's like you say, probably nothing in it, but if someone threatened her, I'm sure they'll want to know. What's she like, this Flora?"

Sara considered. "She wasn't an easy person to know. She was so focused on her work. And she wasn't really interested in socializing outside the lab. On the other hand I did work at the bench next to hers for two years so I did get to know her to some extent."

"Was she in a relationship?"

"I think there *was* someone. Sometimes she'd let drop that she'd been somewhere that you'd usually only go as a couple. A weekend away – that kind of thing – but she never went into detail and I can't remember hearing a name. Actually, I wondered if he was married."

There was a thump on the door. They heard Graeme's voice. "Sara. Katie. Come on. It's nearly time. Get yourselves kitted up."

"We'd better go," Katie said. "But look, why don't you get on the phone to Daniel this evening? Probably it is nothing, but once you've told him about it, you can stop worrying."

* * *

They dressed in their outdoor gear and went out to join the others gathered on the ice. They waited in silence, their eyes fixed on the horizon. Luckily it was a clear day. Then it came, a flash of red as the edge of the sun appeared. Moments later it was swallowed up again. It was as if a day had passed in a flash, sunrise followed immediately by sunset. Over four months of night had begun. It wouldn't always be total darkness. Sometimes there would be moonlight or starlight or the aurora australis, but they wouldn't see the sun, their source of heat and light and energy, until August.

Sara, standing next to Katie, said something that Katie didn't catch.

"What was that?" she asked.

"'The bright day is done, and we are for the dark.' Shakespeare. From *Antony and Cleopatra*."

Katie couldn't see Sara's expression under her ski goggles, but her tone was sombre and Katie felt a chill that wasn't just from the cold. Yes, they *were* for the dark. And that was scary. No wonder people used to feel a superstitious dread of solar eclipses and feared that the sun had been swallowed up. They were right to fear that. One day – millennia ahead – the sun would grow old and die, turning their Earth to a dead, dark, cold sphere spinning lifeless through space.

Graeme as the eldest on the base climbed onto the roof to lower the British flag. It had been there only since sun-up the previous year, but was already bleached and tattered from its exposure to a summer of intense twenty-four-hour daylight and the blizzards of early winter. A fresh flag would be hoisted by Adam, the youngest, when the sun returned in the spring.

Graeme clambered back down. "Have a good winter," he said. He went round the group, slapping the men on the shoulder. "Have a good winter," they all chorused.

When he reached Katie, their eyes met and on an impulse she opened her arms and went in for a hug. They were both so heavily padded that Katie was reminded of two sumo wrestlers grappling and said so as he released her.

He laughed. He went on to hug Sara too. Nothing went unnoticed on the base and he was careful to treat both women the same.

Ernesto raised his voice to get everyone's attention. "Special 'sundown' meal coming up! There's lamb, I'm roasting the last of the potatoes, and I'll be cracking open some bottles of Chianti."

As they climbed back up to the base, Katie heard Sara telling Graeme that she wanted to make a satellite call later that day.

* * *

He was sticking close to Sara these days. Following her up the gangway to the station he heard her requesting a satellite call.

Earlier he had managed to overhear some of Katie and Sara's conversation. Better if that call didn't happen.

He had thought to wait a few days until the sunset glow had faded from the sky and it was completely dark, but maybe after all, this was the time? The weather forecast was predicting a blizzard later today. Visibility would be virtually nil and a blizzard would fit in with his plans in other ways.

And also today was a holiday, a break from routine. There would be a heavy meal and more to drink than usual. Everyone would be sleepy and sluggish, less inclined to keep track of the others. Yes, if he chose the right moment, it could work.

Katie was saying something to him. He smiled at her and gave her his full attention. It was more important than ever to seem his usual self and give no grounds for suspicion.

CHAPTER 18

Graeme was dreaming that he was in the Botanical Gardens in Christchurch. It was summer and the light was dazzling. He could feel the sun on his skin, smell the flowers.

Someone was shaking his shoulder.

"Graeme, Graeme, wake up! She's gone!"

For a moment or two he didn't know where he was, or what was happening, even if it was night or day. He squinted at the window. It was dark outside, so that – ah, no, it was dark outside all the time now. The bedside clock said 18.47.

The lamb, cooked with rosemary, garlic, and anchovies, had been delicious. He had eaten far too many roast potatoes and had had two helpings of tiramisu as well as a couple of glasses of wine. The rules about alcohol at lunchtime were relaxed for special days like this. He'd lain down on his bunk to read and must have fallen asleep. He shouldn't have done that: sleeping during the day – or what passed for day – could send your body clock seriously out of whack now that there was no sunshine to help reset it.

Adam was standing by his bed. "Big Doc has gone!" he said.

Graeme pushed himself up the pillows. His mouth was dry and he felt groggy. What Adam had said didn't make sense. She couldn't be gone. There was nowhere to go to.

Adam said, "We were meeting for a game of ping-pong at six thirty. When she didn't turn up, I went looking for her. Graeme, she's not here! I've looked everywhere – the loos – everywhere!"

"OK. Have you said anything to the others?"

Adam shook his head. "Only that I was looking for her. No one had seen her."

"That's good. Before we do that, we'll have another look together."

"Yes... perhaps... I suppose... I *must* have missed her somehow."

He saw the relief in Adam's face. Graeme had taken charge. Graeme would put things right. That was part of his job as Station Leader, to shoulder the responsibility.

"Of course you've checked her pit-room?"

Adam nodded.

For the sake of thoroughness, Graeme knocked on her door. When there was no answer he pushed the door open. The bed was made and the room was tidy – nothing out of place. There was a faint scent in the air – face cream? Shampoo?

They walked past the other pit-rooms to the end of the module that was closest, where the combined library and quiet room was located. Baby Doc, aka Katie, was there, lounging in one armchair with her feet in fluffy slippers resting on another, deep in what Graeme guessed was Dante's *Inferno*. She looked up briefly as they glanced through the glass door, and raised a languid hand in greeting. Justin, seated with his back to the door, was so engrossed in what he was reading that he didn't even notice them.

They went back up the corridor past the pit-rooms. Next were the male and female toilets and shower rooms, ranged on either side of the corridor. They pushed open the doors. There was no one in any of them.

Next, the communications room, which was empty. In the small gym opposite Rhys was on the rowing machine and Alex on the treadmill.

No one in the TV room or the music room, which also doubled as a games room. On the table tennis table the ping-pong ball and the bats lay ready.

Graeme began counting heads. Katie, Justin, Adam, Rhys, Alex, and Graeme himself so far, that made six. In the dining room Craig and Nick were playing Scrabble. That was eight. In the kitchen Ernesto was kneading dough. Nine. Everyone was accounted for. Except Sara.

The warmth and the good smells made the kitchen a favourite spot to hang out. They declined Ernesto's offer of an espresso "that'll take the top of your head off".

"Seen Big Doc?" Graeme asked, keeping his tone casual.

"Not since lunch, I don't think," Ernesto said.

They went on through the fire door to the last section of the module. Graeme knocked on the surgery door. No answer. He pushed open the door and surveyed the silent, gleaming room.

The remaining rooms were storage rooms, kit rooms, and the room that housed the generator. Graeme and Adam searched them all in silence. The last room was the boot room for outdoor clothing and footwear.

She wasn't there.

They went up the spiral staircase to the next floor which contained offices and labs.

Overhead they could hear the thrumming of the halyard on the flagpole and the wind howling through the rigging of the antennae on the roof. From time to time the whole building quivered and strained like a ship at sea.

They walked through, flicking on lights as they went, until they reached the meteorological room at the end.

They looked at each other without speaking for a few moments. Graeme could tell Adam was scared.

"We've looked everywhere now," Adam said.

"Not quite," Graeme said. "We'd better go back and check the other pit-rooms."

But they were all empty, too. For the sake of thoroughness, Graeme opened all the wardrobe doors, disturbing a tottering pile of soft porn magazines in Rhys's: it was a well-known collection dating back to the 1980s that had been donated from the Halley station. Rhys just happened to be storing it.

Now there could be no doubt. Everyone on the platform was accounted for – except Big Doc.

"Could she have gone out to the telescope or the summer quarters?" Adam asked.

"On her own?" Graeme said. It was strictly forbidden to leave the base alone in conditions like this. "Is her outdoor gear here?"

They looked along the pegs, which were labelled with their owners' names, like the ones at nursery schools.

"Her parka's gone," Adam said.

Graeme studied the signing-out sheet. Nick and Craig had been out to the telescope earlier that day before the sundown ceremony and had signed back in. No one had been out since.

"And there's a radio missing too," Adam said. "But why? Why would she have gone out on her own? Without telling anyone and without signing out?"

Why indeed? Graeme thought, when there was – quite simply – nowhere to go. When it was seventy degrees below zero and there were no other human beings closer than the Russians over at the Vostok station hundreds of miles away. This was a place more isolated, more remote than the International Space Station.

He looked out of the window at a scene that was illuminated only by the lights of the station. It wasn't actually snowing – it rarely snowed in the Antarctic – but the gale-force wind was blowing the ice crystals up from the ground into furious, swirling clouds. The scene reminded him of that famous picture of Captain Oates staggering away from the tent to die.

There had been some strange undercurrents recently and he'd been half expecting something to happen. But this! Sara had seemed the sanest of them all. He would have put money on her surviving the winter in good shape.

"We've got to get out there and look for her!" Adam said. There was a note of panic in his voice.

Graeme put up a restraining hand. He would not be rushed into making a hasty and perhaps ill-advised decision. "First we'll find out when she was last seen and if she said anything to anyone."

* * *

It was an anxious group that assembled in the dining room. Graeme quickly established that Big Doc had said nothing to anyone about going outside.

"Who was the last to see her?" he asked.

It turned out to be Rhys, who had gone to see her in her capacity of base doctor earlier that afternoon.

Looking round at their faces, Graeme saw surprise, even bewilderment, but also a calmness and a readiness to deal with whatever came – for which he was thankful. They looked like a pretty tough crew – and they were. These guys had been picked for their personal qualities as well as their expertise. The loss of one of their companions would be profoundly upsetting, but they probably wouldn't show it and they wouldn't panic. The only one he was worried about was Adam, young and inexperienced as he was, compared to the others.

Katie was the backup medic and the assistant on Big Doc's research programme. A lot would fall on her shoulders if – well, if they couldn't find Sara. Katie was frowning and biting her lip, but Graeme saw that she had herself well under control.

None of them said anything, but glances were exchanged and Graeme knew what they were thinking. There was a whole mythology surrounding wintering over and the toll it takes on the mental health of the winterers: stories of stations where no one talked to anyone else for months on end; of people who went berserk and had to be restrained and locked up for their own sake. And then there were people who were overcome by such claustrophobia that they simply walked out into the snow and had to be chased and dragged back.

"We'll have to look outside," Graeme said. Immediately hands were raised. "Thanks, guys, but it has to be Alex. A no-brainer." No one protested. Alex was officially in charge of expeditions off base and was experienced in Mountain Rescue. It had to be him.

A thought occurred to Katie. "Have her skis gone? Has she taken a radio?"

"There's a radio missing. We'll check the skis. Katie, come with me and Alex. And, everyone, no point in contacting Rothera – or anyone else – until we've got a clearer idea of what's happened."

He didn't add that there was absolutely nothing Rothera could do about it anyway. Everyone knew that whatever had happened, they were on their own.

"I will make coffee," said Ernesto.

"Good idea." Even in the grim circumstances, Graeme had to suppress a smile. It was a station joke that Ernesto regarded coffee as the cure for all evils.

Katie and Alex went with Graeme back to the kit room. Graeme let Alex go in ahead, and put up an arm to hold Katie back.

In a low voice he said, "You know Sara better than anyone. Has she been – I mean, has she been OK lately?"

"She'd been a bit worried by some news from home – someone she knows has gone missing – but nothing that'd explain this."

Inside the kit room, Alex was examining the ski rack. "Sara's skis are still here," he said. "So she can't have gone far."

"We'll have to check the vehicle bay," Graeme said, "and we'll go over to the summer research module. She'd have no reason to go over there, but who knows?"

Katie watched them as they began to dress to go out.

"Take me, too," she said. "You might need medical assistance."

Graeme hesitated. She had a point. Even if they found Sara alive out there, the fact that she had gone out alone without signing out and in this weather might indicate some kind of mental disturbance, a breakdown even.

"OK, get your things on."

Craig put his head around the door. "There's no response from Sara's radio. I've got yours here."

The three of them signed themselves out and checked that their radios were working.

Chunky as astronauts in their gear, they made their way to the door to the outside world.

It was like dropping into a cold, fast-moving river. Graeme gasped and heard the others gasp in unison. Ice granules scraped his face. His head was filled with the rushing noise of the wind. Conversation was impossible. He signed to the others to follow him down the stairs.

At the bottom he seized a hand-line decorated by triangular red flags that whipped in the wind. This would take them to the vehicle depot and from there to the summer station. He turned, awkward in his thick clothes, to check that the others were also grasping the line. He noted that Alex had automatically taken the rear so as to protect Katie a little from the wind. It wasn't just chivalry. She was the least experienced.

They both nodded to him and he set off.

He hoped to God that Big Doc had taken shelter in the depot or the summer station. She could not have survived long out here. He didn't hold out much hope of the search being successful. It had to be done though. They had to know that they had done everything possible. After a few minutes of struggling against the wind, his beard and eyebrows and eyelashes were already frozen. He looked back.

The others were still with him.

The station itself had completely disappeared into the murky gloom of the Antarctic night.

CHAPTER 19

It wasn't possible to worry about Sara, or even to think. Though Katie was sheltered to some extent by Graeme in front and Alex behind, the sheer effort of moving and bracing herself against the wind required total concentration. It drove the whirling snow before it and Katie's head was full of its constant howl.

They toiled up the steps to the summer station. Snow was backed up against the door and Alex dug it out with the shovel that was kept on the outside of the door for just that purpose. At last Graeme pushed it open. They staggered in and Alex slammed the door behind them. The relief was instant. Now they could actually hear themselves speak.

Graeme shone his torch around and found the light switch.

"Sara! Sara!" His voice echoed down the corridor.

They had already checked the depot. Nothing was missing and there was no evidence that Sara had been there, though the blizzard would have covered up any footprints almost instantly.

In the summer station the heating was kept on low to prevent the whole place from freezing solid. In comparison with the temperature outside, it seemed balmy. Already Katie was sweating under her layer of clothes.

"We'll search the place together," Graeme said.

They opened door after door on empty labs and pit-rooms. The dryness of the air meant that it didn't smell musty. There was something eerie about the place. It was as if some catastrophe had descended and its inhabitants had been forced to abandon it. There were reminders of its absent occupants – a pair of windproof trousers hanging on a peg, a sci-fi novel, a toothbrush left in a bathroom, a discarded dog-eared copy of *National Geographic*.

Outside the wind was still howling. Graeme was methodical, opening cupboard doors, looking under bunks. It seemed clear that no one had been there since the place had been shut up for the winter. But it had to be done. They had to know that they had checked everywhere. A horrible thought struck Katie: if Sara really had – gone, there would be an enquiry and they would have to be able to say that they had done everything they could to find her.

At last they were back at the entrance.

"That's it, then," Graeme said. "We've searched everywhere on base."

Katie said, "But we can't just leave it at that. We must –"

She was interrupted by Alex. "No, we haven't! We haven't searched everywhere. I can't believe we didn't think of this before. We haven't searched the caboose!"

Katie felt a rush of hope. Perhaps Sara had simply wanted to be alone. But even so, it was about a kilometre from the base and there wasn't a flag-line...

"Surely no one would go out to it in weather like this," Graeme said, taking the words out of her mouth.

Alex said, "Perhaps she went out there and the weather turned and she decided it was too dangerous to make her way back."

"What about her radio?" Graeme said.

"Lost? Damaged? I don't know –"

Looking at Graeme's face, Katie saw that he thought it was a possibility. It was at least a reprieve. As long as there was somewhere that Sara might be, they didn't have to believe the worst.

"Katie, I want you to stay here," Graeme said. "We can collect you on our way back to the base. If we need you before then, I'll send Alex back for you."

Katie opened her mouth to protest, then closed it again.

Graeme was the boss, and anyway it made sense. They were both far more experienced than she was. It would be tough enough without them having to worry about her. She would only hold them back.

"There'll be tea and powdered milk in the kitchen," Graeme said. "Make yourself a brew."

He pulled his visor back down and adjusted his head torch. Alex did the same. Thus attired, they looked like a pair of monstrous insects.

Graeme pulled the door open. The wind slammed it back against the wall, a river of freezing air rushed in. It took Graeme and Alex heaving from the outside and Katie pulling from the inside to close it. Eventually it latched shut. Katie moved to the window and was just in time to see Graeme and Alex vanish into the blizzard.

* * *

Behind her stretched the empty corridors and deserted labs. She imagined it as it was in the summer, bustling with life. She had never felt so lonely in her life. She radioed to the base to tell the others what was happening, and it was a comfort to hear even Craig's voice.

Better to be active. She went into the kitchen. There was hot chocolate, even a packet of biscuits, tins of soup. She remembered that there was a whole cache of tinned and dried food, plus a freezer containing frozen food. Similar supplies were stashed around the rest of the base, in case of emergencies.

Abruptly the wind dropped. For a few seconds there was absolute silence, then the wind roared as loudly as ever, but perhaps that meant that the blizzard was abating. She went to the window that looked out in the direction of the caboose. It was too soon to expect them back, but still her eyes strained against the swirling drift. She went on gazing into the night, mesmerized by the constant movement. It seemed to her though that the drift was thinner, that she could see a little farther.

Sara would be in the caboose, she had to be. They would get her back to the warmth and safety of the base and everything would be alright. In her mind's eye she followed the progress of Graeme and Alex to the caboose. The path to it was marked by a line of empty forty-five-gallon drums as was the perimeter of the base, so there should be no chance of them wandering away into the night. But still, it was dangerous. Visibility was almost non-existent and the temperature was so low. It was easy to get confused.

She decided that she would heat up some soup. The men would need it when they got back. She opened two tins of Heinz Tomato – the comfort food of her childhood – and put it on a low heat. Her stomach rumbled. It wasn't that long since she had eaten an enormous sundown meal, but she was famished. She began opening cupboards to find bowls and spoons. As she set things out on the table she realized that something had changed – she wasn't sure what. She stood still and listened. The wind had stopped roaring. She went to the window. Yes, the blizzard was dying down. In the distance she could see the light of the main platform. And now she could see two little lights bobbing towards her: head torches. Only two. Her heart skipped a beat. They hadn't found Sara.

Katie rushed to open the door and they staggered in.

Graeme pulled up his visor. He had beads of ice on his eyelashes. She looked at him without speaking, not daring to ask. He shook his head. "She's not there."

Alex said, "But we think someone's been there recently."

Graeme said, "What could have happened – she went out there to be on her own for a bit and didn't realize that the weather was getting worse. She left it too late and got caught on the way back."

Alex said, "It would be all too easy to wander off base."

Katie had a sudden wild hope. "Perhaps she's managed to get back to the platform while we've been away."

The two men said nothing, but Graeme shook his head and Katie remembered that of course Craig would have radioed them with the news.

Graeme said, "Now that the wind's dropped, we can organize proper search parties, including one to go out to the telescope. We'd better get back to the platform."

Katie looked more closely at his face properly, noticing now patches of white: frost nip, the precursor of frostbite. She looked at Alex. His eyes were red-rimmed. They were both on the verge of exhaustion.

She thought, *I'm the doctor on base now. I've got to look after these guys*.

She said, "I don't think that's necessary, Graeme, you can mobilize the others on the radio. It's important that you both get warmed up before you go out again. There's hot soup waiting for you in the kitchen."

CHAPTER 20

ELY

Lyle came in with a sheaf of newspapers and spread them across Daniel's desk. Daniel took in the headlines:

Tragic accident
Polar Doc missing feared dead
Tragedy at Pole

The same photo of a woman in her thirties smiled out from all of them. It looked like the kind of formal picture that they have on university websites.

Lyle flung himself down in a chair. "What's going on, Daniel? Now both Flora and her researcher are missing. This can't just be a coincidence."

"Can't it?" Daniel had already read the online accounts and had had time to think about that. "Of course it can. What else can it be? Sara McKee was just one of the researchers who's worked with Flora over the years and it was a while ago at that. She doesn't have anything to do with the current research – but even if she did, the cases are quite different. Sara has to be dead."

"They haven't found a body. And if she had survival gear with her..."

"Wishful thinking, Lyle. Why would she leave the base? There's nowhere to go and if there was, there's no way to get there. It's hundreds of miles to the nearest human settlement. No. This time the headlines have got it right. A tragic accident." He tapped the copy of the *Guardian* that lay uppermost on his desk. "It's like it says here. The Antarctic is the most hostile environment on earth. She got lost and confused, wandered off base, and maybe fell down a crevasse or simply froze to death. The authorities must be pretty sure she's not going to be found or at least not found alive or they wouldn't have made it public."

Lyle thought about it. He heaved a sigh, "OK, yeah, she's dead. Has to be... I guess they'll find her body when the sun comes up."

"Whereas we still have no idea what happened to Flora."

"I spoke to Michael this morning. The police say that she hasn't used her credit cards or taken money out of any of her accounts since the day she arrived at the cottage. And they still haven't found her car."

"It's not looking good," Daniel admitted. "And the longer she's gone, the worse it looks. But still, we don't know. Anything could have happened. She could be wandering around somewhere in a fugue state. Or she could have run off with someone who's paying the bills. For all we know, Flora's sipping rum punch on a beach in the Caribbean."

"Do you believe that?"

"Well... not really."

"Neither do I. I think she's dead. One of these days they're going to find a body – and I hope they do. Because I can't imagine anything worse for Michael and for Flora's family than never knowing what's happened to her."

* * *

In Brancaster on the north Norfolk coast, a man was getting up before it was light. Marcus had stayed so many times at the same B & B that he was almost one of the family and he was allowed to get his own breakfast. He made bacon and eggs and washed up after himself. He got the packed lunch his landlady had left for him in the fridge and stowed it in his khaki canvas bag along with his binoculars, his camera, and his battered copy of *Collins Bird Guide*.

The dawn-streaked mudflats, the cry of wild birds, the sheer romance of the north Norfolk coast: these were the days that he lived for. Only a few years now and he'd be able to retire from his civil service job in Birmingham. Then he planned to sell up and move here permanently. For diversity of habitat it was one of the best year-round birding areas that he knew. Cley, Blakeney Point, and Titchwell were excellent for spotting rare birds.

It had been a stellar holiday. So far he had spotted Slavonian grebe, water pipits, shore larks, tundra bean goose, short-eared owls, and green-winged teal as well as lots of the commoner birds. The previous day on the salt marsh he had heard the distinctive booming cry of the Eurasian bittern. The bird was notoriously shy and their plumage allowed them to hide, camouflaged, among the reeds. He hadn't actually managed to see it, so he was going back today. If he did manage to spot one, his holiday would be complete.

There had been a frost and it was a clear, chilly morning in late March, perfect for birding. He was pleased to see that his was the first car in the car park. He opened the boot and sat on the edge while he pulled on his waders.

He began to make his way across the marshes, moving inland along a path from the beach. This was a magical place between land and sky. The civilized world seemed to drop away. The marshes belonged to the birds and he was an intruder or, no perhaps not that, more like a guest, full of respect for the creatures that lived here.

A light breeze rustled the reeds. He caught a glimpse of pale plumage and dark streaks. His heart leaped. This could be it. It was splashing, moving further away. He took a step towards the edge, trying for a better view. His foot slipped and the next moment he was sliding down into the water. Luckily he managed to stay upright and though the water was above his knees the waders protected him. But the noise had frightened the bittern – if that was what it was – and it knew he was there now. There was no more splashing. It was lying low, trying not to be noticed. He put his binoculars to his eyes, hoping to spot it among the reeds. What was that? Something in the water, out of sight from the path, but from here, the tip of a black plastic bag was visible. The end had come open and he could see something moving gently in the current. Fronds of waterweed? It had to be, because it wasn't, it couldn't be – but he knew that it was. What he was seeing was human hair.

CHAPTER 21

ANTARCTICA

Katie unwrapped the dressing on Justin's hand and examined the burn. "It's doing fine – not infected, that's the main thing. Another week or two and you should be able to use it, though you'll have to be careful for a while."

Justin sighed. "I hate being out of action when there's so much to do. Couldn't I just –"

"Do as you're told, Justin. If you're in too much of a hurry, you'll open the wound and you'll be out of action even longer. Let me dress it again."

But she could well understand Justin fretting. It was six days since Sara had disappeared. Every day that the weather permitted a team went out to look for her. Though no one had said so, they all understood that they were looking for a body now. At the same time, they had to keep the work of the base going and that wasn't easy when they were a person down and Justin could only use his left hand. At the end of each day Katie was so tired that she fell into bed and dropped instantly into a pit of sleep.

"What are you going to do when all this is over, Katie?" he asked her.

"You mean when we get out of here? Not sure. I'm wondering about doing GP training."

"You won't be coming back next year?"

She shook her head. "Nope."

She didn't need to say why. Their eyes met in silent understanding.

Justin said, "Anyway. You'll make a great GP. There's

something about you that inspires confidence. You've got a gentle touch..."

"That's not what you said last time I changed your dressing!" Was he flirting with her? No, she could see he was serious.

"No, really, gentle but firm."

"Makes me sound like a brand of loo paper!" She tied off the ends of the bandage. "That's you done. So how about you? What are your plans?"

He sang a couple of bars in imitation of Graeme: "'When this lousy war is over, no more soldiering for me...' I'll be going back to my job in Cambridge. I've done three years on the ice and that's when I promised myself I'd stop. It's not good to be here too long. It's too easy."

"Too easy!"

"It's very rare for something like this to happen – what happened with Sara, I mean."

"Yes, but what did happen? Honestly she's the last person... I just can't understand it. It just seems so unlike her to have gone out in the first place. I keep going over and over that last day wondering if there was something I should have spotted. But she was just as normal." Katie hesitated. "Though..."

"You've thought of something?" Justin said.

"Just something she said that day when we were outside at sundown. 'The bright day is done and we are for the dark.' It's from *Antony and Cleopatra*. That wasn't really like her and I wonder now if she was depressed and I just didn't pick up on it. I knew she was upset about her colleague disappearing, but I didn't think she was *that* upset. It wasn't as if Flora was a close friend."

Justin said, "Accidents... errors of judgment. They happen everywhere, but out here you can't take your eye off the ball for a moment. One slip... It nearly happened to me, the last time I wintered over. I went out to the telescope. It was pitch dark and I somehow lost the flag-line and got turned round. I thought I was still heading for the Dark Sector, but I found myself back at the station. Man, that was scary. I might have missed my way completely and just wandered around there in the dark until I was exhausted."

Katie nodded. She remembered the whiteout on the way back from the caboose, the utter sense of disorientation. That had to be what had happened, that or something like it.

Justin went on.

"I meant what I said though. In some ways it *is* too easy; everything's here for you. You don't have to decide what to wear or what to eat or where to go of an evening. There *is* nowhere to go. Even your friends are provided: a ready-made social life. It's a special experience, and it's a kind of specialness that you can get too used to. It's as if you've stepped off the real world for a while. If you stay here too long you might find you can't get back on. Yes, three years is ample..."

"I'm guessing there's no one waiting for you back home?"

"Only Maudie."

"Maudie?"

"My dog. Standard poodle. My mum's looking after her. What about you, Katie?"

"Nope. Just family and friends."

There was a silence. Then they both started to speak at the same time, and both broke off to let the other speak. Uncertain who should speak first, neither did. They burst out laughing.

Katie broke the impasse. "Nearly time for smoko. Shall we go along to the dining room?"

"Sure."

Today there were hot sausages, crispy bacon, porridge, and home-made croissants. Smoko was a sociable occasion. Every day Rhys put together a short quiz or a crossword, and there was fierce competition to see who could finish it first. Craig in his role as Comms officer monitored incoming news bulletins so that he could put together a daily news-sheet. It always contained football results when Adam's team, Sheffield Wednesday, were playing.

As Katie sat down at the dining table, she reached for today's news-sheet. Her eye was caught by an item halfway down.

"A woman's body has been found in Norfolk," she read, "and is thought to be that of missing scientist, Flora Mitchell."

* * *

"Yes, it *was* Flora," Dan said. "It was a bloke out birdwatching who found her."

Katie had managed to put a call through to Rachel. Dan was at home, as she had hoped, and answered the phone.

"But what do they think happened?"

"It was definitely murder, I'm afraid. She'd been stabbed. They think from the state of the body that she died shortly after she arrived at their holiday cottage. It's out in the wilds of Norfolk. Then the killer probably used her car to transport the body to the coast."

Katie said, "There's something I think I should tell you. Sara was going to ring you just before she, well, before she went missing. She'd remembered that a man came to their lab – this was just after she and Flora had published their work on apoptosis – ranting and raving about them having stolen his research. They had to get security to throw him out."

"Did she have a name for this guy?"

The line began to break up and she could hardly hear him over the hiss and crackle of interference.

"Kieran, she thought. She couldn't remember his surname."

"What was that? Kevin?"

"Kieran!" she shouted.

"Oh, Kieran? Yes?"

"Yes!"

Then the noise on the line died down and his voice was as clear as if he was standing next to her.

"Were the police called?"

"I think so. Yeah, must have been, because he'd been in a

secure unit and they took him back there. Turned out he was a scientist, and he *had* been working on something similar, but he was mentally ill – psychotic breakdown, paranoid delusions – and he'd managed to walk out of the hospital where he was sectioned. Of course they hadn't really stolen his research. But Sara wondered – maybe if he believed that they had, he might have come after Flora and done her some harm."

"Most schizophrenics are more of a danger to themselves than to anyone else," Daniel pointed out. "Worth following up, though. I'll tell the police and I know Lyle will be interested, too. I'll ring him this evening. Thanks, Katie."

"Perhaps I should have told you this before..."

"Don't worry about that. You've got enough on your plate. It must be pretty grim where you are? No news about Sara, I guess."

"No, nothing."

"And what about you? Are you OK?"

She'd thought she was, but the sympathy in his voice got through her defences. Tears welled up.

He must have realized that, because he said, "I'll get Rachel now and I know Chloe will be desperate to say hello."

Chloe came on first. They chatted about school for a few minutes, and Katie promised to update the blog. Oh, the blessed normality of it all. Chloe was bright and cheery and confiding. Katie wondered if the problem at school had subsided.

She heard Rachel in the background. "That's enough; now, chickadee, run along off to bed and I'll come to tuck you in a bit later."

As soon as Chloe was out of the room, Rachel said, "How are you, really, Katie? I've been worrying about you."

"Mostly I don't have time to think about it. There's so much to do that I've had to put grieving on hold for now. The worst thing is not being able to get away from it all. That's why it's so great to talk to you. Tell me what you've been doing, tell me something ordinary."

"Well, Lyle came for a meal. First time I've met him. What a charmer! He showed up with a huge bunch of flowers and he'd brought a book for Chloe that was exactly right. He treated her as if she were as important as anyone else in the room and told her about the horses on his ranch. He didn't talk shop over the meal. He asked me about my work and asked intelligent questions. *And* he helped to clear the table."

Katie couldn't help smiling. "Oh yes, that's Lyle all over. He didn't get to where he is without plenty of charm. But tell me, how are things going with Chloe?"

There was no answer.

"Rachel? Rachel?"

Just the whine of static. The contact had been broken.

Katie couldn't help herself. Tears rolled down her cheeks. She was groping in her pocket for a tissue when Craig came in.

He went back out and she thought she'd embarrassed him, but he came back a minute or two later with some kitchen roll and thrust it into her hand. He squeezed her shoulder briefly and sat down beside her. Tears continued to fall and she mopped them up.

After a while he said, "It's a crying shame alright, but we'll get through it." And that was all.

But after all, what else was there to say?

CHAPTER 22

"Katie, can I have a word?"

It was the following day and Graeme had poked his head out of his office as she was passing.

"Sure. What's up?"

He gestured her to a seat. "Just wanted a catch-up. How are you doing?"

She sat down and considered the question. Not very well, was the truth. She was sleeping badly, having dreams that jerked her gasping awake. Mostly she didn't remember them, but in the ones she did, she would be searching for Sara in a blizzard. She would suddenly realize that she was out of sight of the base and that she herself was lost. She'd wake up, sweating.

"I've been better," she admitted.

"And the others?" he asked. "How do you think they're bearing up?"

She considered. "I think they're coping by being very much focused on the job in hand. A tendency to drink a bit more, maybe. Nothing much more than that." Though it was true that meals were more sombre occasions than they used to be.

"I've been wondering about Adam."

"He's lost his sparkle," she agreed. There had been no more practical jokes lately. Maybe that had all been down to Adam. "It's natural that he'd be upset. He's young..."

"Of course," Graeme said. "It's bound to be hard on him. But I'm wondering if it's more than that. I was watching him today at lunchtime. Nothing I can put my finger on, but he doesn't seem quite right to me. I'd like you to find a reason to give him a once-over, just check there's nothing wrong physically."

Ought Katie to have realized that Adam was off colour? She glanced at the photos of Graeme's family. Perhaps having four children had honed his diagnostic skills! She felt, well, what? Not rebuked, no, she felt sure there was no criticism implied, but it occurred to her that in spite of her best intentions, she hadn't fully adopted the role of base doctor. She was still behaving like a second in command, waiting to be told what to do. Well, she'd better get a grip.

"I'll keep an eye on him," she promised, "and I'll make a few tactful enquiries when I take his next blood sample tomorrow morning." Was there anything else that Sara had done that she wasn't doing? Yes, there was! "Maybe it's time for another Doc School?" she suggested. "Everyone enjoys them – they're as much of a bonding opportunity as anything."

Graeme beamed. "Excellent idea. This afternoon maybe? I'll announce it at lunchtime."

* * *

Warmed by Graeme's approval, she went on down the corridor to the surgery. Doc School would also give her a chance to spend time with some of the guys and have a good look at everyone, assess their condition, do a kind of medical inventory.

Doc School was the name given to the regular sessions run by the base doctor over winter. It was all part of the ethos of the base which involved training up the others in one's own skills. Katie had already helped Adam to service the generator – something that had to be done every four weeks – and Alex had taught her how to use the digger and how to navigate by the stars. As a sole medical practitioner, it was important to have another pair of hands to assist in an emergency. And then of course the base doctor herself might need treatment and you can't put your own arm in plaster. Before she had disappeared, Sara had run a couple of sessions on intravenous cannulation and suturing. Katie considered what remained and settled on plastering as being the most fun – and most useful too as a fall on the ice and a resulting fracture was one of the things they were most likely to have to deal with on base.

At lunch the announcement of a session of Doc School was greeted with mildly ironic cheers.

Katie made a point of taking a seat next to Adam. Was he paler than usual? Maybe, but the lack of daylight was having its effect on everyone. It could just be that. But certainly he was subdued. It was Ernesto's day off and Graeme had cooked bangers and mash. Adam usually had a hearty appetite, but today he was only picking at his food. Yes, she'd make a point of giving him a proper check-up when she got him into the surgery. Meanwhile she got him talking about his favourite football team, Sheffield Wednesday, and his family back home. He soon cheered up, discussing transfer deals and prospects for the next season.

And when Alex said, "Anyone fancy a quick game of Cluedo over coffee?" he brightened up even further.

"Count me in," Justin said.

Graeme nodded, "Me too."

"And me," Rhys said.

Katie met Alex's eyes over Adam's head and he winked at her. She knew perfectly well that he didn't care for Cluedo. Actually none of them did really. But it was Adam's favourite game and Alex had clearly noticed that Adam was a bit down. They had truly become a family, pulling together to support the youngest.

"Ernesto had better be Mrs White the cook," Adam said.

Ernesto raised his eyebrows wearily, but he didn't object and he sat down at the table willingly enough.

"And Graeme should be Colonel Mustard," Adam went on. "I'll be Professor Plum."

"Bless you, my children," Justin said. "I'll be the Reverend Green."

"And Katie, can you be Miss Scarlett?"

"Sorry," she said, "I need to set everything out for Doc School."

"Which leaves me and Rhys to be Miss Scarlett and Mrs Peacock," Alex said. "OK. Don't mind a bit of cross-dressing. Who do you want to be, Rhys?"

Rhys picked Mrs Peacock and as Katie left to get everything ready, Rhys was explaining – to the accompaniment of theatrical groans from the others – that the game had been launched in 1949 and originally the lead piping token had actually been made of lead before they realized that it posed a risk of lead poisoning. The original revolver had been a Dreyse M1907 semi-automatic pistol, which was of German manufacture and...

As Katie went down the corridor his voice faded away. She shook her head and smiled to herself. What Rhys had to say was often pretty interesting – at first – but he never knew when to stop.

* * *

The killer had enjoyed his lunch. He had felt so much better since he had acted. A balance had been restored. A world out of kilter had been put straight. It had all been over very quickly. He wasn't a cruel person and he hadn't wanted Sara to suffer. It was just that she had to pay when her actions had done such grievous harm to someone he loved. Some things are worse than death.

Luckily she had been a little bit drunk. She hadn't suspected a thing until the very last moment. And even then – had she really grasped what had happened? He had held her for the few seconds that it took for the light to leave her eyes.

There was one thing left to do, and that would have to wait until the Skidoos were usable again and he could get off base. Some of those crevasses were very deep and once he had tipped Sara's body down one of them, he was confident that it would never be found.

Meantime all he had to do was sit tight. He had been careful to feign being as upset by Sara's disappearance as anyone else. As far as the others were concerned, it was a tragic accident. Or, should that be *most* of the others? He wondered about Katie: she didn't seem convinced that Sara would have gone out alone and got lost. But she would accept it in the end. The Antarctic was a treacherous place after all. Accidents did happen.

But what if she didn't accept it? What if she started poking around? He'd already overheard her asking one or two awkward questions. But no, he was quite safe. He had covered his tracks with his usual efficiency and no one would ever find out. And anyway he liked Katie and it wouldn't be right to hurt her. After all, she hadn't done him any harm. Not like Sara.

CHAPTER 23

"So to recap," Katie said. "Position the limb with the ankle at ninety degrees. Apply the stockinette – it's important that it's smooth and wrinkle-free – and then the under-cast padding. You start at the knee end and work down to the ankle working from the outside in and as you wind it round the leg you take care to cover fifty per cent of the previous turn. OK, guys?"

She looked around the room. They were all there except for Graeme who had a lot of paperwork to catch up on and anyway felt he had been to enough Doc Schools to see out his time in Antarctica. Justin wasn't able to take part, but had come to watch, and she had used him to demonstrate how to put a leg in plaster.

When they had nodded in agreement, she went on. "So then you're ready to apply the actual cast. You take the plaster of Paris bandage and dip it in a bowl of warm water. You squeeze out excess water. Then, as with the under-cast padding, you wind it round the leg, again taking care to cover fifty per cent of the previous turn. Then you take the second roll and repeat. Get to it, guys, and there'll be a prize for the best cast."

They got into pairs: Ernesto and Nick, Rhys and Craig, Adam and Alex.

"Fancy a bet?" Justin murmured in her ear.

"I'll have to make the final decision," she reminded him.

"I trust you."

"Alright then. You're on. Who are you fancying?"

"I'm going for Alex. I saw him stripping down an engine the other day. Excellent manual dexterity."

Katie considered. "My money's on Ernesto." What were needed here were excellent fine motor skills and she thought he would be the deftest of the lot – and most efficient too. He'd already got hold of everything he needed and had set it out just as he was used to setting out what he called his *mise en scène* in the kitchen. Besides, he'd been on an enhanced first aid training course before coming out to the ice. There were always a couple of people on base who had done that and Craig was the other one: so he was one to watch, too.

"What are we wagering here?" she asked.

Justin said, "I'll make you one of my killer cocktails."

She groaned.

He looked hurt. "I could have had an alternative career behind the bar at the Ritz, I'll have you know. And if I win, you'll make your special lamb stew next time it's your turn to cook."

"Fair enough." She drifted around the surgery, watching and offering a word of advice here and there. Rhys was struggling to wrap Craig's leg in the under-cast padding. He kept getting it twisted and it didn't help that Craig was lying back with his arms folded and a sceptical look on his face.

Ernesto, as she had expected, was ahead of everyone and was about to soak the plaster of Paris bandage.

"Do we have a choice of colours for the plaster?" Nick asked. "I'd like black."

"Sorry," Katie said. "We only have bog standard white here."

Alex was also doing well on Adam's leg. But she didn't think he was going to be as fast as Ernesto.

The first two stages, the stockinette and the under-cast padding, were fairly straightforward. The fun started with the wet plaster of Paris bandage. Once again Ernesto was ahead of the field. Katie stood and watched him as he manipulated the bandage with the same dexterity that he used for his pasta dough. All the same he was finding it hard to apply the bandage evenly.

There was a protesting yelp and Katie turned to see that Rhys had somehow managed to wind the bandage around his own arm. He hadn't squeezed enough water out of it. The sodden bandage clung to him, dripping chalky water. "Oh hell," he said.

He put his hand up to his head and it left a white streak in his hair.

Everyone laughed.

Katie went to untangle him. She started him again with a new bandage. As she showed him how to get the right amount of water out of it, she was conscious of a happy buzz of conversation around them. Graeme had been absolutely right. The messy physical activity had released the tension they had all been feeling. The mood had lightened.

Even Adam was smiling, looking more animated.

She went over to see how he and Alex were doing. Alex had started the second layer and it was going to be a close thing between him and Ernesto as regards who would finish first. He had forgotten to put on surgical gloves – a point against him – and she watched the blunt fingers with their oil stains under the fingernails as they carefully aligned each new turn of the bandage to cover precisely half of the one before. He was doing a much better job in that respect than Ernesto. She couldn't believe that this was his first attempt.

"Have you done this before, Alex?" she asked.

He looked up startled and for a few moments seemed lost for words. She got the feeling that she had somehow caught him out. Then he shook his head. "No, never."

"I thought maybe your Mountain Rescue training..."

"Just basic first aid stuff."

She wasn't sure that she believed him – and yet what possible reason could he have to lie?

She didn't have time to reflect further. There was a loud groan and Katie turned in time to see a spasm of pain cross Adam's face. His hand went to his lower abdomen.

"What's the matter?" she asked.

"I had a bit of a tummy upset earlier. Something hadn't

127

agreed with me. Then it went off and I thought I was alright. But it's come back and I feel proper poorly. Much worse than –" He broke off and closed his eyes and groaned again.

Around them everyone had stopped what they were doing and had fallen silent.

"OK. Everyone out, please. I need to have a look at Adam." She had a horrible feeling that she already knew what was wrong. But surely they couldn't be that unlucky?

When the others had left the room, she lifted Adam's T-shirt to expose his abdomen.

"Where does it hurt?" she asked.

He indicated a place on his lower right side. She applied gentle pressure, and he didn't respond, but when she released the pressure he winced and gasped. That was known as rebound tenderness and it was indicative of peritonitis.

"I feel sick. Have I got food poisoning?" he asked.

"Let me just take your temperature," she said. She found the digital thermometer and put it in his mouth.

As she stood and waited, Adam's hand sought hers and gripped it. She squeezed back.

When she took out the thermometer, it read just over thirty-eight degrees Celsius. She thought for a few moments. Adam was still lying back with his head on the pillow. He opened his eyes and looked at her.

Katie answered his unspoken question. "I'm not sure what's wrong yet."

"You can make me better, can't you?" She could tell he was frightened. She stroked back the ginger hair from his damp forehead.

"Yes," she said with a confidence that she didn't feel. It was part of her job to reassure him.

But who was going to reassure her?

* * *

128

"What's the situation?" Graeme asked.

"It could be appendicitis. I've started him on a course of powerful antibiotics."

"Will that be enough?"

"Hope so. When I was on the training course they said that ninety-nine times out of a hundred it wouldn't be necessary for the base doctor to operate."

There was a silence. Then she said, "But what if this is the one time in a hundred? Could we get him out? It's been done before, hasn't it?"

Graeme made a face. "Very rarely."

"Rhys was talking about someone they got out – from the South Pole. Pancreatitis, I think he said?"

"Yeah. That was Ron Shemenski in 2001. That was around this time of year," Graeme admitted. "It wouldn't be my call. And the time factor would be crucial. It'd take days to get the Twin Otters down from Canada and there's no other aircraft that could land in these conditions. And even then the weather might prevent them from doing the last leg of the journey. I'll ring HQ now."

Katie listened with half an ear as Graeme outlined the situation. She really, really wanted to avoid giving a general anaesthetic to Adam unless she absolutely had to. For a major abdominal operation like this, he would have to be given paralysing drugs to relax the muscles so that she could cut through to the appendix. That would mean that he wouldn't be able to breathe, so she would have to get a tube into his airway to enable a ventilator to breathe for him. And that was a very risky procedure for someone with hardly any anaesthetic experience and no backup.

She hoped, oh, how she hoped, that she wouldn't have to do it.

Graeme hung up and turned to Katie. "HQ have told us to prepare a runway. They'll try to get a flight in at the full moon – if the weather holds. I'm afraid there's a lot of ifs. Scientific work will have to be suspended."

The lights flickered and went out. Katie barely had time to register it before they came back on. She looked at Graeme in alarm. What if this happened when she was operating?

Graeme read her thoughts. "Don't worry. There's a backup generator, remember. I'll get the guys cracking on a runway."

"I'll have to see who I can train up to help me if I do end up having to operate, God forbid."

"That's right. Hope for the best, prepare for the worst."

But he made no move to bring the conversation to a close and she sensed there was more to come. When he didn't speak, she said, "Was there something else, Graeme?"

"What? Oh, yes..." He hesitated, then seemed to make up his mind.

"What I'm about to tell you mustn't go any further. It's not been made public. There's news about Kevin. I heard from HQ earlier this afternoon."

"Kevin?" She couldn't think whom he meant.

"The guy who was injured and flown back to the UK. He's come round and there's every chance that he'll make a good recovery."

"That's great," Katie said. But why was Graeme looking so worried?

"His memory's coming back. And here's the thing. He's remembered the accident, only he's not sure it *was* an accident. He says he heard someone behind him. He was turning to see who it was and then there was a blow and that's the last he knew."

"He thinks someone hit him on the head deliberately?"

"Yep – though I don't think he's a hundred per cent sure. So what I want to ask you is – how much do you think his memory can be relied on? I mean, the guy does have a head injury..."

Katie considered this. "Well, often people don't have any memories of the time immediately before an accident, that's more usual, but I believe confabulation *can* occur afterwards. Head injuries are tricky things."

"Confabulation?"

"It's a memory disorder," Katie explained, "where people have false or distorted memories and experience them as if they are true. But what do his doctors think?"

"They're inclined to believe him – something to do with the nature of the injury. More consistent with a blow on the head than with a fall. But it's not conclusive. Oh, hell." He threw up his hands. "I don't want it to be true. I'm just grasping at straws. Like I said, can you keep it to yourself? Best not to let everyone on base know about it."

She wondered why he had told her, but before she could formulate a question, he said, "I'm telling you because you are the one person on base that I can be absolutely sure didn't do this. It happened after the summer workers left and before you arrived. So you're in the clear."

She felt a chill. "So you think..."

He gave a bark of unhappy laughter. "What is it that they say in those corny old movies? 'It could be any one of us.' Even me, Katie!"

"I don't think you'd be telling me about it, if it was you."

"Well, no, fair enough."

"Why would anyone have wanted to hurt him? Had he fallen out with anyone?"

"Not as far as I know. He hadn't been here long enough for that. It was his first season on the ice. But, look, I've decided not to make it common knowledge. It's tough enough as it is. It's hardly going to improve matters, to have everyone looking at everyone else, wondering if they're liable to be struck over the head any minute. I thought long and hard about telling you, but two heads are better than one and on balance I felt it was better for at least one other person on base to know. And perhaps you have a right to know."

"So what are we going to do?"

"There's nothing much we *can* do. I doubt if there can be any evidence left out there – the snow's drifted over the place where it happened. Any footprints will be long gone."

"What about the – well, the weapon, whatever he was hit over the head with? If he was hit over the head."

"I don't think we can go round the base confiscating all the blunt objects, do you? No, we'll keep it under wraps for now. HQ have agreed to that, though there'll have to be some kind of investigation when the winter's over, if only for Health and Safety purposes."

CHAPTER 24

ELY

Daniel had wondered if Lyle would be wearing Western riding gear, chaps maybe and a cowboy hat. But it must be a case of "when in Rome" because Lyle was sporting a tweed jacket, jodhpurs, and a hard hat. He was cantering around the exercise yard, on a brown horse – chestnut did they call it? It looked enormous to Daniel, who was waiting at the rail. Lyle's secretary had told him that Lyle was at a local riding school, getting in an hour's exercise with his mobile phone switched off. It was only a ten-minute drive from the office, so Daniel had gone straight over.

Now Lyle had spotted him. He slowed the horse down to a trot and came over. The horse stuck its head over the rail and snorted and rolled its eyes. It towered over Daniel, who stepped back hastily.

"Oh, don't mind Samson," Lyle said. "He's an old softie. He's just hoping that you've got a treat for him."

Samson shook his head and nickered. Daniel eyed him warily.

Lyle swung his leg over the horse's back and lowered himself to the ground. Samson turned his head and gently butted him.

"Alright, alright." Lyle took a carrot from his pocket.

Samson's enormous teeth made short work of it. Lyle beckoned to a young woman, who came over and led the horse away.

Lyle said, "I rang Michael yesterday evening. The poor guy's devastated – as you might imagine. He didn't know anything about this Kieran fellow – and Flora had never mentioned

133

having trouble at the lab. He didn't think there was anything in it."

"I've had better luck. I put an assistant onto it and she's come up with a name. Kieran Langstaffe."

Lyle considered it. "Kieran Langstaffe. No, don't know the guy."

"It's true that he was working on something related to what Flora and Sara were doing, but only tangentially and nothing was published. He hasn't worked since. He had a catastrophic breakdown and spent a couple of years on a locked ward. He's apparently better now. I think I'd better speak to him."

"Surely you don't think there's anything in it? That Flora and Sara pinched his research?"

"No, of course not. I don't see how that could have happened. But it's best to cover all the bases."

"Yeah, you're right. Don't want this coming back to bite us at some later date. Is the guy still in hospital?"

"Nope. They moved him out of the secure unit and now he's out and living with his parents in south-west London."

Lyle took off his hard hat. He rubbed his hair where it was plastered to his forehead.

"Wait a minute. Did he get out before or after Flora disappeared?"

"I thought of that. He's only been out a fortnight. He was still in a secure unit when Flora went missing."

* * *

The streets of between-the-wars houses seemed to stretch on forever through the outskirts of south-west London, but eventually Daniel found the house and pulled up outside. It was just like all the other houses around it, with Crittall windows and a front garden where paving stones alternated with overgrown rose bushes to create a chequered effect.

Daniel had spoken to Kieran's mother that morning and

134

she had told him that Kieran was having a good day. "But I don't know how long it'll last," she'd said. "I should come soon if you want to talk to him." They had agreed that he should go down that afternoon.

Daniel rang the doorbell and heard it echo through the house. No one came, but then through the wavy glass of the front door he saw movement. The woman who answered the door was short and dumpy with curly grey hair, in her sixties, Daniel judged. There were deep lines on her forehead.

"You must be Mr Marchmont?" she said. The slight lilt hinted at Irish origins. "Come in. We'll just go through to the kitchen first."

As he followed her through the hall he was aware of distant music, something familiar that tugged at a memory just out of reach.

In the kitchen Mrs Langstaffe turned to face him. "It's just – I'd better tell you what to expect. But – you'll have some tea, won't you? We'll take it in and have it with Kieran. It's his teatime and it's important to stick to a routine. I'm afraid I do have to be there, otherwise he might get upset. Though he might get upset anyway. But I'm hoping it'll do him good to talk about his work. That is what you're here for, isn't it?"

He explained about the patent and she busied herself as she listened, filling the kettle, setting out a tray with china cups and a plate of biscuits. When he mentioned Kieran showing up at the lab, she paused. "Yes, I remember that. He's much better now, but he's not exactly normal. He has some obsessions and he's a bit unpredictable. No, don't worry," she said, answering the alarm on his face, "he's not violent, but he might take against you and refuse to speak or he might like you and be happy to chat. There's no way of knowing and even if he does want to talk he might not want to answer your questions – or even be able to. I'll have to draw things to a close if he starts to get upset."

The kettle switched itself off.

"I understand," Daniel said, wondering if he did. "I'll be guided by you. Just let me know if you think it's getting too much."

She made the tea. Everything was assembled now on the tray.

Daniel said, "Let me carry that."

"No, no, thank you, that might disturb him. I'll lead the way, and you can open the door." She hesitated. "Kieran's a very clever man, you won't forget that, will you?"

"I won't, I promise."

He sensed that there was something she was holding back, and wondered again what he was going to find. As he followed her to a room at the back of the house the music increased in volume. He recognized it now: country and western – it was Hank Williams singing, "Cold, Cold Heart". An ex-girlfriend from years and years ago had played in a country and western band and had been keen on that song.

He pushed open the door for Mrs Langstaffe to go in first and followed her in.

It was a big room that looked out onto a dank sunless little garden surrounded by tall hedges. He glimpsed that through a kind of tunnel: each side of the room had a series of tables lining the wall and the tables were crowded with complex, colourful structures. They looked like something out of the lair of the mad scientist in a fifties B-movie. Or would have done if they had not been made out of Lego. There had to be tens of thousands of pieces there. He gazed at them in fascination. It was hard to say what they represented – a futuristic city maybe, all walkways and stairs and tunnels? He thought of those drawings by Escher where the perspective leads around to where you came in: they were something like that.

By the window a man sat at a desk strewn with A4 paper and coloured pencils. He turned to look as they came in.

"We've got a visitor, Kieran," Mrs Langstaffe said brightly. She put the tray down on his desk. "Mr Marchmont has come all the way from Cambridge to see you."

"Oh, call me Daniel, please."

"And you can call me Deirdre."

Kieran had a round, puffy face – maybe the result of his medication? – and guileless blue eyes. He stared at Daniel, as unselfconscious as a child. He did in fact look extraordinarily young for someone who had to be at least thirty. Perhaps that was the drugs, too.

"Have you come from the government?" he asked.

"No," Daniel and Deirdre said in unison.

Kieran looked downcast. "I would have thought they'd send someone," he said. "In the circumstances. With its being so important."

"Perhaps they will," Deirdre said. Her voice was soothing. "Let's have a nice cup of tea, shall we?"

He nodded. "Are there chocolate Hobnobs?"

"Of course." She began pouring out cups of tea.

In the background Hank Williams had moved on to "Your Cheating Heart".

"Would you like to see my diagrams?" Kieran asked. He didn't seem to be interested in who Daniel really was and why he was there. "Are you sure you're not from the government?" he added hopefully.

"'Fraid not," Daniel said, wishing he'd dressed more casually. Perhaps it was the suit that was misleading him.

"Oh well. Here are my diagrams." He gestured to the sheets of paper that littered the table. They were covered with interconnected shapes and what were definitely chemical symbols. There was something organic in the way they flowed across the page. Some of the shapes looked like planets, some like cross-sections of plants, some like sexual organs. They were beautifully coloured in.

"Of course it's three-dimensional really. That's why I have to make models."

He waved a hand at the Lego constructions.

"Is this something to do with your cancer research?"

Kieran considered. "Not really. Well, in a way it is, because it's about everything, so naturally it's about that, too. But I don't want to talk about that now." He sipped his tea. "I did think the government would send someone. Are you sure that you're not..."

"Sorry. But this is all very impressive," Daniel got up to look at the models. "I've never seen anything like it." That was true enough.

Kieran started to explain. At first it seemed to make sense, drawing on the laws of physics, but as the explanation grew convoluted, Kieran started to use terms that Daniel didn't understand and he lost the thread of the argument. He tried again more than once to ask Kieran about the cancer research, but the first time Kieran ignored him. The second time his eyelids began to flicker and he started to look around in an uneasy way. Deirdre, who had faded into the background, stepped forward then and caught Daniel's eye. She asked him if he'd like to see the garden. He took the hint and they went out through the French windows.

When they reached the end of the small garden and were out of earshot, she said, "I'm sorry. It looks like you've had a wasted journey."

"I don't quite understand. What is it that he's doing?"

"He thinks he's found the secret of life, the secret of the universe. That's what the model and the diagrams are about. On a good day – like today – he thinks he's going to win a Nobel Prize and be more famous than Einstein."

They looked back at the room where Kieran was tinkering with some pieces of Lego. The plaintive strains of Hank singing "I'm so Lonesome I Could Cry" floated out into the garden.

"And you know, sometimes I almost believe it myself!" Deirdre added.

"What's a bad day like?" Daniel asked.

"He's paranoid. Thinks that people are out to steal his work. He can flip quite easily and I saw that he was beginning to get upset when you asked him about the cancer research."

"It must be very hard. Are you on your own looking after him?"

"There's my husband, too, but he's out at work during the day. I'm a teaching assistant, but I'm not doing that now. Someone needs to be here with Kieran."

Daniel wondered how it had happened, how a bright postdoc had ended up like this. "When did it...? How long...?"

"He's always been sensitive and highly strung," she said. "But so clever with it. The first person in our family to go to university and he got a PhD! When he started to get ill, it began with little things. He thought that things were missing from the lab, that people were taking things, and then that they were moving things around deliberately to confuse him. There was a conspiracy against him, that was what he said. At first I believed him, and then I started to realize..."

"I'm very sorry," Daniel said.

"They've been very good at the university. His head of department still rings up to ask how he is. But he doesn't get many visitors now. People don't know what to say to him. We'd better go in. He gets very absorbed in what he's doing, but he might start wondering what we're talking about. That's one of the problems with being paranoid. People really do talk about you behind your back!"

They went back inside. Kieran looked up and smiled.

"Here. I've made this for you." There was a little figure made of Lego on the desk.

Daniel was aware of an anxious sideways glance from Deirdre. She visibly relaxed when he said, "Thank you, Kieran" and slipped the Lego man – woman? hard to tell – into his pocket.

"It's time for me to go now," Daniel said.

Kieran nodded, but his attention was back on his diagram. He chose a violet crayon and began to colour in what looked like a leaf.

Hank Williams must be on a loop. They were back to "Cold, Cold Heart". Daniel and Deirdre went out into the hall, followed by its plangent strains.

"Might it be worth my coming back and trying again?" he asked.

"Well, it might be. He did like you. That's why he wanted to give you a present."

Daniel gave her his card so that she could contact him if she thought Kieran might be willing to talk about the cancer research.

"Does he do that all day?" Daniel asked. "Drawing, I mean, and the Lego?"

"Pretty much. I do usually manage to get him out of the house most days for a walk. We go to the park and feed the ducks. And sometime he'll watch TV in the evening – he likes the nature programmes."

"And the music? Is it always..."

"Yes, always country and western and most of the time it's Hank Williams."

"Doesn't it drive you –" Just in time he stopped himself from completing the sentence.

She did it for him. "Bonkers? Well, yes." The smile she gave was a blend of weariness, wry humour, and resignation. "On a good day I can get him to switch to Patsy Cline – or even Willie Nelson."

There was something heroic about this dumpy middle-aged woman. Daniel liked her very much.

He said, "It must be hard work."

"It is. But he's my son and I love him."

* * *

The rush hour was beginning and it was a slow drive home. Daniel couldn't get "Cold, Cold Heart" out of his head. It seemed so dreadfully apposite, so mournful and despairing, with its reference to doubtful minds and being shackled to a memory. In a way it described Kieran and he knew that he would always associate it with that room and the poor young man and his ruined mind. "Mad" wasn't a word used much these days, but it somehow seemed the right one. What a tragic waste: all that intellect and energy directed into something so futile. Was there a chance of Kieran recovering sufficiently to go back to scientific work? It didn't seem likely, but even if he did, the scientific world is highly competitive and moves on very quickly. It was probably already too late for Kieran to get back on board.

Crawling along the M11 he thought of what Deirdre had said. "He's my son and I love him." Is there any greater love than that of a parent for a child? No wonder the idea of the father and the mother was so important to Christian faith. His thoughts turned to Chloe whom he loved more than anything in the world. One thing about having a sick child: it sorts out your priorities. He and Rachel knew now what really mattered. They didn't care about her being academic or anything like that. All they wanted was that she should be a happy person, a decent person – and healthy. He thought again about how they could make that happen. He was right about surrogacy being much more common these days. A browse on the internet had confirmed that. There were sites advertising surrogates in the Ukraine. He didn't like the sound of that and he knew Rachel wouldn't either. It smacked of exploitation, of poor women renting out their uteruses. But there were also UK sites which specialized in introducing prospective parents to women who were prepared to act as surrogates for largely altruistic motives. His thoughts wandered to a possible future. He saw Rachel's face as she received a newborn baby into her arms... then later a laughing toddler with arms outstretched... and Chloe, cured, radiant with health...

He found himself pulling up outside his office with no memory of driving the last few miles.

His secretary was putting on her coat as he went in. She said, "Lyle rang. He's booked a table for two at the Old Fire

Engine House for seven. And there's a message on your desk from a Mrs Langstaffe. She wants you to ring her."

Had Kieran already said something about the research? He rang her straightaway.

She said, "I don't know why I didn't think to ask you while you were here. Have you spoken to Alistair?"

"Alistair? No. Who –"

"Alistair Johnson-Marsh. He used to work with Kieran. He'll know about the research. He's been ever so loyal, such a good friend, coming to see him all the time when he was in hospital. He's Kieran's best friend, really. Kieran being so ill, it's been very hard on him."

"Have you got a number for him or an email address?"

"Just a mobile number." She gave it to him.

In the background he could hear Hank Williams singing "Hey Good Lookin'".

He couldn't believe he hadn't asked about that. But as he tapped in the number he thought he knew why. The meeting with Kieran had thrown him off balance. There was something profoundly disturbing about someone who was so removed from reality. It was almost as if it would be possible to be sucked into this parallel world, as if Kieran's craziness might be catching. He admitted to himself that he had been glad to get away.

The mobile number wasn't active, it seemed. He Googled the name instead. He soon found what he had been looking for. Yes, Alistair Johnson-Marsh had worked on the cancer research, but Daniel couldn't find anything more recent that he had worked on. His scientific career seemed to have ended at the same time as Kieran's. Of course the shelf-life of a postdoc researcher is a short one. By their mid-thirties they are getting too expensive and need to move on to a new stage in their career. But it was strange all the same that he seemed to have completely vanished from view.

* * *

Daniel scanned the menu. Trust Lyle to have homed in on the best restaurant in town. He used to bring Rachel here when they were courting and it was still where they came for special occasions. "Celery and stilton soup and then roast guinea fowl for me."

"I'll have smoked eel," Lyle decided, "and – what's this? – roast leg of English Nedging lamb? What's Nedging?"

"It's a village in Suffolk," the waitress explained. "Local lamb."

"That'll do for me. And I think, let's see, a bottle of Château Patache. That OK with you, Daniel?"

"Fine." He wouldn't be driving and it was easy to walk home from here.

Lyle picked up the conversation where he'd left off when the waitress arrived. "It's not that odd, is it, that this Johnson-Marsh character isn't on the scene any longer? A lot of people in their early thirties get out of the scientific life and train to do something quite different."

"Agreed. But what is unusual for someone of his age is that he doesn't seem to have any kind of profile on social media. No Facebook account, nothing on Twitter."

Lyle considered. "Yeah, that is strange."

"I'll get my secretary to dig around a bit more, see what she can come up with."

The wine arrived. Lyle tasted it and nodded. The waitress filled their glasses.

Daniel took a grateful swallow and sighed.

"Tough day," Lyle stated. Daniel had already given him an account of his visit to Kieran. "You look tired."

Daniel hesitated, wondering how open to be. But, after all, Lyle had already met Rachel and Chloe. As they ate their first course, he told Lyle about Chloe's blood disease and the punishing regime that they had just been forced to resume.

Lyle was a good listener. He quickly grasped the essentials.

"So your best hope is a donor sibling?" he said. "So the obvious question is..."

"Yes, why didn't we have another baby. The chances of Rachel conceiving are pretty small. It was a fluke that she had Chloe."

"But you've tried, right? And you've considered IVF?"

Daniel was silent.

"You *haven't* tried?" Lyle asked.

"The thing is, Rachel nearly died giving birth. Postpartum haemorrhage. She lost so much blood that the hospital ran out of her blood type. It really was touch and go."

Lyle said, "Even a normal birth is pretty awesome. What you guys went through must have been scary stuff."

Dan nodded. "They don't tell you this could happen. There was no warning. Her pregnancy was fine, everything seemed set for a normal birth. But then she was in labour for a long time, the baby was getting distressed, and they decided to do a C-section. It all still seemed pretty routine. Everyone was relaxed about it. I was holding her hand. They lifted the baby out of her and then it all happened so fast... blood everywhere. I actually saw the surgeon jam his hand into her to try and stop the bleeding. A nurse handed me the baby and then they were rushing me out of the room."

"Oh, man," Lyle said.

Dan stared into space, remembering. "Suddenly it was just me – with my daughter in my arms. I remember walking down the corridor and looking out of the window. It was beginning to get light. I've never felt so alone. Just me and the baby, and there was this one star left low in the sky. I tell you, Lyle, I thought I'd be bringing our baby home alone."

"A hell of a thing. No wonder that's put her off having another baby. But it's not likely to happen again. Or is it?"

The waitress came to clear their plates away. For a few moments neither of them spoke. Lyle began to tap something into his phone.

"Also best to know what you're dealing with," he said. "Let's have a look at the statistics. Here we are. The UK: 8.5 deaths for every 100,000 pregnancies. The risk is vanishingly small, and you need to bear in mind that post-partum haemorrhage will be only one cause of those deaths."

"Yes, yes – but having had one, Rachel's more likely to have another one –"

"But now that you know, the risk can be managed, surely? Still, I can see that it must have been a traumatic experience for her, but given what's at stake –"

Daniel raised a hand. "No, no you don't understand, it's not Rachel, *she* wants to try again. Rachel's got over it. I haven't."

"Ah." Lyle looked at Dan and sighed. He put his phone away. "It's no use telling you that this isn't a rational response, is it? Any more than it's any good telling people who are afraid of flying that it's the safest method of transport."

"Those hours when I thought that Chloe might be without a mother – and that I might lose Rachel.... . No, Lyle, I can't go through that again."

CHAPTER 25

ANTARCTICA

Katie couldn't stop herself constantly checking the weather. Outside a full moon shone on a landscape bleached of colour. It was ten o'clock at night. Would the weather hold until the next day and the day after? The forecast was uncertain. The Twin Otters were being flown down from Canada, but it would still be days before they arrived in Rothera. The guys were taking it in shifts, working round the clock to smooth out a runway.

Graeme would not allow her to help. She was needed indoors to look after Adam and he didn't want her exhausted and liable to make mistakes. He had also insisted that she get a good night's sleep. He would stay up himself. When she objected, he told her in no uncertain terms that he was perfectly capable of monitoring Adam's condition and would wake her up if he took a turn for the worse.

If the worst came to the worst, Craig had said that he could rig something up so that a surgeon at Addenbrooke's could talk her through the operation. Katie had already had a preliminary chat with the surgeon and she had read everything she could find about it online. The anaesthetic was what she was most worried about. They'd covered it on the course, and she had talked it through with an anaesthetist in Cambridge, but still it was a daunting prospect.

When she'd mentioned that to Craig, he'd cleared his throat. "And – well, my mum's a vet. I used to work at the surgery during the holidays and I used to help when she was operating, so..."

She had trained him up so that he could monitor the

patient. She'd also need someone to hand her the instruments. Ernesto had told her that he wasn't worried by the sight of blood and had offered to help. So she had gone over the instruments with him, had let him handle them before re-sterilizing them, so that he was familiar with them. And of course he'd had enhanced first aid training and so had Craig, so they were the best assistants available.

Now and then her thoughts had strayed to what Graeme had told her about Kevin and the accident that might not have been an accident. But she didn't let herself dwell on it. She was inclined to think that after all he had probably slipped and was now misremembering. It seemed so unlikely that one of the guys on base, who were almost like family now, would have committed an assault that could so easily have had a far more serious outcome.

Outside it was minus seventy degrees. She yearned for heat and light. Her thoughts went back to last summer when she had visited Rachel and Dan and Chloe while work was still continuing on the boat. They had picnicked on the bank. She saw herself wearing a summer dress and sandals. They had drunk spritzers and eaten baked salmon and potato salad. The warmth had soaked into her bones. She closed her eyes and saw the light on the water, fronds of weeping willow trailing on the surface, swans with a string of cygnets drifting along behind them.

A noise at the door brought her to herself. It sounded as if someone was kicking it. A voice said, "It's me, Justin" and all was explained.

She opened the door. He was carrying a small tray wedged on one arm. "I come bearing gifts," he said, "or at least hot chocolate. I made it myself and Ernesto added a splash of brandy."

"Here let me take that. Come on in."

She took the tray from him and set it down on the table. "Are you OK?" he said.

"Not really," she admitted. "I'm not sleeping well." She took a sip of the hot chocolate. There was more than a splash of brandy in it.

"That always happens around this time. People start getting out of synch."

"I know, that's part of what I'm investigating. But it's not only that. This wasn't a situation I ever expected to find myself in." All of a sudden the strain of putting on a good face, maintaining an outward display of confidence, was too much. "What if I have to operate on Adam? What if I can't pull it off?"

"You'll be fine, I promise you. What you need is a break from all this. If we weren't stuck in this God-forsaken place, I'd, well, I'd ask you if you fancied going out somewhere..."

She gave him a sideways glance. "You mean – like on a date?"

"I don't always look like this." He made a gesture that encompassed his shaggy hair, untrimmed beard, and unironed T-shirt.

"I'm sure you scrub up very nicely. A date... well, now..." she mused. "I'd almost forgotten about those. Remind me, what is it that people do?"

"Oh, they go to see a movie ... or maybe have a drink in a pub or dinner in a nice restaurant."

"Sounds wonderful. Though to be honest, I'd settle for a walk in the park right now."

The light-hearted joshing cheered her, reminded her that there was a world elsewhere where people did go to the cinema or restaurants and that one day she'd be back there.

Justin sat down next to her on the bed. "You'll feel better if you can get a good night's sleep."

"You sound just like my mum," she said ruefully.

He put out an arm and it seemed natural to lean against him. "It'll be OK," he said. He pulled her in close and she put her head on his shoulder. Only now she realized how much she had needed the comfort of physical contact. Held in his firm grip, she felt some of the tension leave her. After a while he turned and lowered himself onto the pillows. She went with him and they lay together.

The next thing she knew she was waking up to find herself lying next to Justin with her head on his chest. He was asleep with his arm around her. Through the window she could see the glittering stars wheeling slowly across the sky. They seemed almost to move as she watched them. She felt a sense of vertigo as though she and Justin were whirling through space, clinging together. A half-thought formed: we *are* whirling through space on this crazy little planet. Then she fell asleep again. Later, without really waking up, she was aware of Justin disengaging himself and of the duvet being tucked in around her.

When she did at last wake up, she was alone. She stretched luxuriously. It was the best night's sleep she'd had for ages. It was a few moments before she realized that the room was darker and then she saw why. The moon and the stars had gone. The sky was overcast.

She got up, showered, and dressed. On her way to see Adam she passed Justin alone in the dining room. He was eating scrambled eggs and drinking coffee. She stopped.

"Thanks for looking after me last night," she said.

"No problem. I thought I'd better slip away before, well, before the others were up and about," he said. "I didn't want the other guys thinking... you know..."

"That we'd spent the night together?"

"Wouldn't be good, would it?"

"Them thinking that, or actually spending the night together?"

She couldn't resist teasing him. Though he was right. This wasn't the time or the place to be starting a relationship.

He laughed and was about to say something when Graeme appeared in the door. Katie saw at once that something was wrong.

"Oh, Katie, good, you're up. I was coming to look for you. I don't like the look of Adam. I think he's getting worse."

They headed for the surgery, Justin following behind.

At the sight of Adam, Katie's heart sank. He looked sweaty and uncomfortable. She took his temperature. It had gone above forty degrees. His heart rate had also shot up.

"It's hurting," he said, "hurting bad." He gripped her hand. She saw the fear in his eyes. "Am I going to be alright?"

"Yes, you are," she said firmly and his hand relaxed in hers.

"There's something I need to tell you, Katie. It was me." She could tell from the way he spoke that he was feverish.

"What was you, Adam?"

"It was me," he insisted.

Surely he wasn't confessing to attacking Kevin?

"What are you talking about?" she asked gently.

"It was just a bit of fun," he pleaded. "I didn't mean any harm."

"I know you didn't." She stroked his hand, soothing him. "What was a bit of fun?"

"The jokes. The milk carton that mooed and the other things."

"Oh, nobody minded that. Don't worry about it."

"And the little penguin. I'm proper sorry about the penguin."

So that *had* been him! But she didn't have the heart to be annoyed.

"All except the scalpel," he went on. "I didn't take the scalpel, really I didn't. You do believe me, don't you?"

"Of course I do."

He was reassured. He nodded and closed his eyes.

Graeme was on the other side of the bed. Her eyes met his and she indicated that they needed to talk.

Justin saw the movement too and said, "I'll stay with Adam."

She and Graeme went out into the corridor and once they were out of earshot, Graeme said, "It's not good, is it?"

"Nope. We can't risk his appendix rupturing. He needs to be operated on – and the sooner that can happen, the better his chances'll be. We can't wait for the Twin Otters to arrive at Rothera."

CHAPTER 26

"I wish I could help," Justin said.

"You *have* helped. You make a stellar hot chocolate."

"Good to know I have my uses. Tell you what, when this is all over, why don't we have that date? Let me spend some of that money I've accumulated while I've been on the ice. Where would you like to go? Somewhere really glamorous. The sky's the limit."

She remembered what Justin had said: that in another life he might have been mixing cocktails for a living. "OK. Well if you really mean it: how about the Ritz?"

He laughed. "Champagne cocktails for two? No problem. It's a deal. It'll be something to look forward to."

And now she couldn't delay any longer. "It's time," she said. "The guys are waiting for me."

Justin looked around. There was no one else in the corridor. He slipped an arm around her waist and pulled her into a hug.

The surgery had been converted into a makeshift operating theatre. Ernesto was waiting in the blue hospital scrubs that they were all wearing. Adam was lying on the examination trolley, now an operating table, with Craig by his side.

Best though not to think of him now as Adam. He was her patient and all her skill and attention must be focused on doing her professional job. She thought of that old cliché: "Is there a doctor in the house?" Yes, there was, it was her, and her alone.

She inserted a cannula to give the anaesthetic and prepared the drugs in syringes. She set up the basic monitoring equipment: a blood pressure cuff on his arm, a pulse oximeter clipped onto his finger to measure oxygen saturations, and an

ECG monitor. Adam's heart rate – still too high – was registered in a series of regular beeps.

The important thing now was to get him to sleep as fast as possible. She put a mask over his face and gave him a hundred per cent oxygen. Next were the drugs that would induce unconsciousness and then paralysis.

As soon as they took effect Adam would stop breathing. She would have to intubate the patient in order to get him breathing on the ventilator.

"You can do this," she told herself. "You've prepared for this."

She was glad to see that her hands were completely steady as she carried out the procedure with the laryngoscope. Moments later the tube was in the right place and the monitors were registering Adam's condition in a series of regular bleeps. She let out her breath in a sigh of satisfaction.

She turned on the anaesthetic gas that would keep Adam asleep.

"OK," she said, "over to you, Craig."

He nodded.

She went to scrub up and put on her hat, gown, mask, and surgical gloves. She swabbed Adam's abdomen with antiseptic and covered him in drapes, leaving only the area around his appendix visible.

She nodded to Ernesto to indicate that she was about to start. She put in her earpiece. Craig had fixed up the communications earlier and she knew that Rose, the surgeon at Addenbrooke's, was waiting on the other end of the line.

"I'm here," Katie said.

"OK," Rose said. "You're going to be fine. No hurry. Just take a moment. Relax. Focus. Let me know when you're ready."

She let her breathing settle. She said a little prayer. She saw everything with an extraordinary clarity: Adam, the regular bleeping of the monitors, Ernesto with his eyes fixed on her face.

"I'm ready," she told Rose.

"OK. Take the marker and draw a line between the umbilicus and anterior iliac crest. McBurney's Point is about two-thirds down that line and, as I said earlier, that's where you make the incision. Done that? OK? The incision needs to be about seven centimetres. You know all this, but I'll talk you through it."

Katie nodded to Ernesto and he handed her the scalpel.

Now that the moment had come, all her anxiety had dropped away. Her own feelings were unimportant. She was just a tool. Her whole being was narrowed down to this place, this moment. A great sense of calm descended.

Rose's voice continued in her ear. "OK?"

"OK. I've made the incision."

"Now you dissect through the subcutaneous fat..."

"There's a bit of bleeding."

"No problem. Just cauterize that and continue."

The calm voice in her ear was a lifeline. The ritual of the operation continued.

She was almost at the point of taking the appendix out when Rose's voice disappeared in a burst of static.

"Craig! She's gone!"

He was at her side in a moment. A quick adjustment and Rose's voice was back, loud and strong.

She sighed with relief. This was the trickiest part and she didn't want to be doing it alone.

She was just about to lift the appendix out when something happened. She paused with the scalpel in mid-air, alerted to a problem without knowing what it was. Then she did know.

The bleeping of the monitor had dropped a tone. And now it dropped another tone. She turned her head to look at the digital display. The oxygen saturations had dropped from ninety-eight per cent to ninety-four. What the hell was happening?

She forced herself to stay calm. OK, suspend the op, cover the wound with a swab, find out what had gone wrong.

Craig was looking at her with horror in his eyes. She motioned him back. Adam's oxygen level was continuing to drop. OK. Turn the oxygen right up to a hundred per cent. Check the ventilator. Was Adam's chest moving? No! He was not breathing! Stay calm, stay calm. Is the tube still in? No, somehow it had got dislodged.

All the time the warning bleeps were growing more and more insistent. Oxygen saturations were down to eighty-six per cent. Time was running out and if she didn't reintubate Adam, he would be dead or brain-damaged in a matter of minutes.

She reached for the laryngoscope. Stay calm, she told herself, stay calm. Stay calm. Stay calm. You can do it. You've done this before. Don't rush, gently, gently. It seemed to take forever and for a terrible moment she thought she hadn't got the tube in correctly – but she had. His chest began to move. She looked at the monitor and saw that his oxygen level was going back up. She was limp with relief.

Everything was back to normal.

Somehow her earpiece had stayed in. She told Rose what had happened and gave herself half a minute to let her heart rate settle.

Then she went on. She lifted the diseased organ out and put it in a kidney dish that Ernesto held ready. She would incinerate that later. She was on the home straight now. All that remained was to sew up the wound and that was the easy part.

"That's it, all done," she told Rose.

"Way to go, girl!" Rose said, and Katie could hear the smile in her voice.

Katie said, "First thing I'm going to do when I get home is come up to Cambridge and buy you a meal in the best restaurant in town."

"Looking forward to it. OK now, Katie? This is me signing out then."

Katie gave Adam morphine for the post-operative pain.

She turned the anaesthetic off and waited until he began waking up. She removed the tube. She knew what must have happened earlier. When Craig left his post to fix the line to Rose, he must have dislodged it without realizing. It had been concealed under the drapes. But no harm had been done. Adam was breathing nicely on his own now. She'd have to keep a close eye on him for the first few hours, but it was over, she had done it, and she had saved Adam's life.

She thought of what Shackleton had said. "We all have our own White South." Yes, there are some things that test you to the limit and change you forever. This was one of them.

CHAPTER 27

ELY

Daniel was so absorbed in what he was doing that he didn't hear Rachel come in with a cup of tea. He only realized that she was there when she said, "Dan?" It was Saturday afternoon and she'd been baking with Chloe. A warm and fragrant smell wafted in with her. He reached for the mouse but it was too late, she'd seen what was on the screen.

"What's that?" she said, looking at the pictures of smiling babies and happy parents. She leaned over his shoulder and read what was on the screen. "Surrogacy? You're looking at websites about surrogacy?"

There was nothing for it. He'd have to tell her what was on his mind – and it was time he did that anyway.

He swung his chair round to face her and said, "I've been thinking... about another child... one that might be a match for Chloe."

She pulled up a chair and sat down. "I've been thinking about that, too. About what's best for her – and what's best for us as a family and I've decided –" She hesitated.

He waited with bated breath. Was it really going to be this easy? Had they all along been thinking along the same lines? He hardly dared to hope.

At last she came out with it. "I'm ready to try for another baby, Dan."

He let out a sigh and leaned back in his chair. He might have known it was too good to be true. Assuming a patience that he didn't feel, he said, "We've been over this, Rachel. After what happened last time, it's out of the question. We agreed –"

"That was when it was all fresh in our minds. Maybe it's time to think again. OK, I'm not very likely to get pregnant, but the doctors have never said that I shouldn't try…"

"But Rachel, surrogacy is so much more common now. I know there's a lot that's dodgy – women in India or the Ukraine who are exploited because they are so poor – I wouldn't want to do that either. But there are women right here in the UK, who undertake surrogacy for altruistic reasons. And with surrogacy we could arrange things –"

She broke in. "It seems all wrong to expect a woman to take a risk that I'm not prepared to take myself."

His exasperation was mounting. "But there isn't a risk – not really – for a woman who's given birth without any problems in the past."

"There's always *some* risk."

"But not like with you!"

"OK," she admitted. "Yes, there is a bigger risk, but they know that, so it can be managed."

"And that's not all." He hesitated, knowing that he was on shaky ground.

A cloud crossed Rachel's face. He saw that she knew what was coming.

"We could select an embryo that would be a match for Chloe. It's her best hope. Rachel, can't you see that this is the answer?" he pleaded.

"We've been through this before," she said. "And we agreed it was a road that we wouldn't go down."

"That was your decision. I was never really on board, you know that, Rachel. But while we were agreed that you weren't going to have another baby, it wasn't worth arguing the toss."

Rachel's mouth was set in a stubborn line. "Embryo selection means that one is chosen and others are rejected – that embryos have to be destroyed. Even if I could accept that, what about those children who are born to be saviour siblings – does anyone know the long-term effect? How they'll feel knowing

157

that they owe their life to being a match, that they were born to provide stem cells for another child. And what about informed consent? How can a baby consent to anything?"

"It's not just for that," he protested. "We want another child anyway."

"But will he or she know that? And can we even really know that it's the truth? We didn't talk of having another child before we had Chloe."

He felt his temper rising. "OK, it's not perfect. Life's not perfect. We just have to do the best we can in the circumstances."

"And that is really the best we can do?" she demanded.

"Those embryos, they're not children, they're not even foetuses. They're just a..." – he sought for the words – "they're just a bundle of cells. Rachel, you're not being rational."

"*I'm* not being rational!" Rachel got to her feet, her eyes wide. "*You're* the one who won't accept the medical evidence – won't believe that it's safe for me to have another baby."

Now he too was on his feet. He was so angry that he scarcely trusted himself to speak. "You know what, Rachel. I can't talk about this now."

He left the room, slamming the door behind him. Chloe must have heard their raised voices. She was standing open-mouthed at the top of the stairs. He snatched his car keys from the table by the door and grabbed his coat from the peg.

Then he was outside, taking in long breaths of the fresh, cool air and feeling a speckling of rain on his face.

* * *

Without thinking about where he was going he took the road west out of Ely. He drove aimlessly, not caring where he went; he just needed to drive until his anger and frustration subsided. Why couldn't Rachel understand that he meant everything for the best? Why was she so obstinate?

He found himself heading towards Ramsey along a road that ran parallel with one of the dykes, straight as a ruler, that cut across the Fens. Curtains of rain were advancing across the vast, open fields and then the heavy rain arrived, beating against the windscreen. It occurred to him that he was driving too fast, but as his foot touched the brake, the car hit a patch of mud made slick by the rain. He felt the car float free from his control and his stomach lurched. He tried to steer into the skid. The car swung first one way and then the other. Then the tyres gripped again and he slid to a halt on the verge at the side of the road.

He sat with his hands pressed to his face and took in deep breaths. It had all happened so quickly and it was frightening to think how differently it might have ended if something had been coming the other way.

The rain was easing off, only flecks now on the windscreen. He got out of the car, leaving the door ajar. The gentle rain was welcome on his face. He stood looking out across the Fens at houses made tiny – like Monopoly houses – by the distance and the lines of bare trees were flattened by the misty drizzle.

Something moved on the periphery of his vision. He hadn't noticed that the verge sloped gently towards the dyke. The car was inching forward. Very, very slowly, so slowly that it was hardly moving – yet seeming possessed of malign purpose, it was lumbering away from him.

The driver's door swung open. Without thinking he launched himself head first into the car, intent on wrenching the steering wheel around. But he was too late. The car was picking up speed and was already moving too fast. He found himself on his knees, with his body half in and half out of the car. He tried to pull himself clear. He almost succeeded, but as the car plunged down the bank, the momentum swung the driver's door shut again and it closed on his left hand. Pain shot up his arm and he tried to pull loose, but his hand was trapped. His feet scrabbled for purchase on the slippery grass, but he was dragged along faster and faster down the slope into the dyke. The car hit the water with a fearsome splash. It came to a jarring halt and the brackish water rushed up over his head and filled his mouth and nose.

Still tethered to the car by his trapped hand, he swung around in the water. His free hand closed on the wing mirror. He pulled himself as high up the side of the car as he could and got his chin above the surface of the water. He coughed and spluttered, and water streamed out of his nose.

The water was swinging back and forth in the dyke like a solid block. Slowly it settled. There was no sound except for the patter of rain on the roof of the car. He was aware now of the pain in his hand, was aware of almost nothing else. His own ragged breathing was loud in his ears.

The car shifted. It was settling deeper into the dyke and taking Daniel with it. With his free hand he fumbled with the door, but the handle seemed somehow to have got jammed and he couldn't get it open. Was he going to drown? He thought of Rachel and Chloe. There were voices. Someone was shouting and, twisting his head around, he saw a figure against the sky. Then someone – a man – was scrambling down the bank. He plunged into the water and seized Daniel's arm. Daniel wanted to explain that his hand was trapped and he couldn't open the door, but the words wouldn't come. There was someone else there now, a young woman, two anxious faces trying to make out what he was saying. Then the man disappeared and the woman was stroking his face and saying, "It's alright, it's alright. Mike will get the door open." The car creaked and sank a little more. Then the car door opened from the inside and his hand came free.

Then they were both there with a shoulder under each arm and they were half supporting him, half dragging him out of the water and up the bank. They lowered him onto the verge.

"Thank you, thank you," he gasped.

There was someone else standing there, an older woman.

"The ambulance is on its way," she said.

He wanted to protest. "I don't need – I think it's just my hand..." He cradled it, held it close to his chest.

The younger woman said, "You're in shock. And they'll need to X-ray that hand."

"Thank you, thank you," he said again. "You've been... you've been..." His voice trailed off. He couldn't think what he wanted to say. He was shivering.

Mike said, "Nah, you're alright, mate. Good job we saw the car go off the road."

The older woman had gone back to her car. She brought back a blanket and put it around Dan's shoulders.

There was the sound of sirens. The ambulance arrived and the police, too.

Dan was helped into the ambulance. The younger woman said, "Let us know how you get on" and he had the presence of mind to ask for their names and email addresses, those of the older woman, too. The younger woman wrote them down and put the piece of paper in his jacket pocket. As the ambulance was about to move away, the older woman came hurrying over. "You'll probably be ages in A & E. Have these." She handed him a small bottle of mineral water, an apple, and a Penguin biscuit.

The ambulance drove off. When he arrived at Addenbrooke's hospital, he found he was still clutching the apple in his good hand as if it were a talisman.

* * *

"You've fractured your fibula."

Mr Wright, the orthopaedic surgeon, gestured to the X-rays pinned up on the screen. He looked as if he had stepped out of some US hospital soap opera. He was tall, broad-shouldered, and blonde chest hair curled at the V-neck of his green hospital scrubs.

"But it was my hand that was trapped – it's just a cut on my leg."

"'Fraid not. The hand looks worse than it is, nothing's actually broken. As for the fibula – look, you can see it here." He ran a finger along a chalky line on the X-ray. "Luckily it's quite straightforward – it isn't out of alignment – and it doesn't require surgery. It should be enough if we put it in plaster, but you'll have to rest it."

"How long am I going to be out of action?"

"Well, you'll have to be in plaster for a couple of weeks. You should be pretty mobile after that. The fracture will heal just fine. The soft tissue damage will take longer. It could be months before the wound on your leg heals."

"Months! But how did it happen without my realizing?"

Mr Wright examined Daniel's leg with gentle hands. "Well, judging by the pattern of bruising, my guess is that the back wheel of the car went over your leg. There's quite a bit of soft tissue damage there."

The painkillers had kicked in now and Daniel was having trouble focusing – or maybe he was still in shock. He couldn't make sense of this. "It went over my leg?" he asked. "But why didn't it hurt?"

"I imagine the pain in your hand was overwhelming and that distracted you from the leg. It must all have happened pretty fast. Now let's get this cast seen to."

A nurse came with a wheelchair. Outside in the waiting room he found Rachel. He hadn't had his mobile with him, but he had managed to ring her from the hospital.

Her face registered shock when she saw him in the wheelchair, dressed in a hospital gown.

"Daniel!" She leaned down and put her arms around him. He inhaled a mixture of workshop smells – wood shavings – and the soap she used. His head swam and he clung to her. She returned his embrace.

He pulled back. "Where's Chloe?" he asked.

"I left her at Stella's. She's playing with Phoebe. She's fine. But Dan, what happened?"

He gave a shaky laugh. "Looks like I ran over myself in my own car."

And that was the least of it. He'd been lucky, so lucky. Even now, they could have been hauling his drowned body out of the dyke. He saw a policeman arriving at his house, the door opening, and the expression on Rachel's face as she realized, and behind her Chloe's eager, innocent face, looking to see who it was, in the moments before her life changed forever.

How could he have been so stupid?

To his surprise and shame he began to cry.

CHAPTER 28

ANTARCTICA

Adam was sound asleep. Katie stood for a while looking down at him. He was a healthy colour, his heart rate was normal, and there was no fever. She was keeping him in the surgery overnight, but she wasn't worried. He would have to be careful for the time it would take the wound to heal – no heavy lifting for six weeks – but he was making a normal recovery, thank goodness. The operation had been a success.

She stopped off in the kitchen to collect a mug and the flask of coffee that Ernesto had left for her, then made her way to the quiet room, her footsteps sounding loud in the silent corridor. She'd volunteered for the night watch – might as well since she was up keeping an eye on Adam anyway. Usually she liked it. There were so few chances to be alone that it was good to have the base to herself. But tonight it was hard to settle. She picked up her Dante, and remembered she had been reading it when Adam had told her that Sara was missing. This was her first stint on night duty since that had happened. She wasn't always in the mood for Dante and that was the case tonight. It was a demanding read. She left Dante and Virgil in the icy wastes of the ninth circle of hell and went to the library to find an Agatha Christie. She took a dog-eared copy of *And Then There Were None* off the shelf and then had second thoughts. Ah, *The Man in the Brown Suit*. That was more like it.

She got a few pages in, but she couldn't focus. She found herself fidgeting and listening out for something – but what? She was restless and uneasy. It was the strangest feeling, a sense almost of foreboding. It was almost as

164

though she was waiting for something to happen – and it wasn't something good.

She got up and looked out of the window, though why, she didn't know. There was nothing to see except the reflection of her own face staring back at her. She went back to her book, but soon she started to yawn. She poured herself a cup of coffee and read on. She stopped in the middle of a sentence, suddenly on the alert. What had she heard? Footsteps – some way off. The hairs went up on the back of her neck. They were coming this way. She held her breath. She had left the quiet room door open and suddenly she was afraid of what she might see. Any moment now – and when the figure did appear in the doorway, she nearly jumped out of her skin.

"Justin!"

"I'm sorry. Did I startle you? I couldn't sleep. Thought I'd come and keep you company for a bit?"

"It's silly, it's just that –" she stopped, unwilling to go on.

"Just what?"

"I keep thinking there's someone there and then there isn't."

He pulled out a chair and sat down next to her. She put her book down.

"Can you say a bit more about that?" he said.

"It's just exactly what I said. I'll be in the kitchen making tea – or in the surgery – concentrating on the job in hand, not really thinking about anything in particular, and I'll be aware that someone's come in. I'll even be conscious of someone on the edge of my vision. But when I look round, there's no one there."

"It's not scary, though, is it?"

"No – not at all, it's more, well, friendly, that's what's so strange –" She broke off. "But – do you mean –"

"Yes, it's happened to me a couple of times. In here once, actually. Someone came in and sat down – behind me and off to the side, so I didn't see them clearly and anyway I was engrossed in what I was reading. I was so sure that I wasn't alone that after a while I actually turned to speak to them and that was when I realized that there was no one there."

They were silent for a few moments.

Katie said, "Justin?"

"Mmm?"

"It wouldn't be possible for someone to hide on base, would it?"

He considered this. "Possible, yes, maybe. But very difficult and not for days on end. We've looked everywhere over and over again. Sara's not here, Katie."

"No. I know that, really."

"Just our minds playing tricks on us."

"That must be it. Quite interesting really, from a medical point of view." She remembered something. "I'll need to go and check on Adam again soon."

"You did a great job. How does it feel, being famous? You're going to go down in Antarctic history!"

She groaned. "Don't tell me. Craig takes a sadistic pleasure in searching the internet for cringe-making headlines."

"*Unqualified doc pulls off emergency op! Med student saves life at South Pole!*"

"Oh stop it. I'm not a student. Just haven't done the final stage of my training."

"Why let the truth get in the way of a good story? But seriously, it was pretty amazing."

And then it happened. She felt a vibration coming up through her feet as if a train or a big lorry were passing by. The door to the corridor swung silently open as if pushed by an invisible hand. A wave of dizziness swept over her. Her head swam and she wondered if she was going to faint.

"What the hell –" Justin exclaimed.

She looked at him and saw from the expression on his face that he was experiencing it too.

The whole room was swaying with a gentle side-to-side movement. It was exactly as though they were on a boat at sea.

Her book slid off the table beside her and landed with a thud on the floor. A glass of water – the liquid sloshing from one side to the other – was about to follow it. She grabbed it with one hand and with the other – absurdly – she grabbed Justin's arm as if she could steady herself that way even though he was moving too.

As suddenly as it had begun, it was over. For a few moments neither of them spoke, then:

"Was that an *earthquake?*" she said incredulously.

"An icequake, more likely."

Katie had heard of those. The ripple effect of distant earthquakes could sometimes be felt in Antarctica, creating seismic shocks that could cause icebergs to calve and crevasses to open and close. She hadn't expected ever to experience one.

Gingerly she got to her feet, and was relieved to feel the floor solid beneath her.

She and Justin made their way out into the corridor. Pit-room doors were opening and tousled heads were emerging. Graeme appeared dressed in a T-shirt and boxer shorts.

"Everyone OK?" he asked.

"I'd better go and check on Adam," Katie said, "and I'll check the rest of the base for anything untoward." That was part of her job anyway while she was on night duty: to check that the generator was working, that the fridges and freezers were on, and, above all, to be alert for the risk of fire.

"I'll come with you," Justin said.

Craig came out of his pit-room, dressed only in a towel knotted around his waist. Presumably he slept naked and had grabbed what was closest to hand. Katie averted her eyes from his well-developed pecs and curly, dark chest hair.

Graeme said, "Craig, see if there are any reports of unusual seismic activity from any of the other stations, would you?"

"Will do. In any case I was wanting to check that everything is still working OK. I'll get dressed."

The surgery was at the other end of the building. As

Katie and Justin made their way there they saw evidence of what had happened. Photographs crooked on the walls, one actually on the floor with the glass in the frame cracked. In the dining room there was a broken salt cellar and salt all over the floor.

Katie opened the door to the ward expecting to see an agitated Adam who would need to be soothed and reassured. All she heard was a gentle snoring. The clipboard on the end of the bed had fallen off. The carafe of water on the bedside table had slid off onto the bed and drenched the sheets. But nothing had disturbed Adam. He was sleeping like a baby.

* * *

It took Katie and Justin an hour or so to go through the base and check that all was well, to pick stuff up off the floor, and return objects to their shelves.

They reported to Graeme and were in the kitchen making hot chocolate when the timer on Katie's watch went off. It was time for one of the regular night-time duties. "I've got to check the weather for the meteorological log," she said.

"I'll come with you," Justin said.

Katie wasn't sorry to have his company as they walked through the sleeping base to the kit room and put on their outdoor clothes. The earthquake – or icequake – whatever it was – had unnerved her.

As Justin stepped out ahead of her she heard him take a sharp intake of breath. She soon saw why. A crescent moon was rising in the sky. Its light shone softly on the sea of frozen waves, sculpted by strong winds, that stretched off to the horizon. And above, filling the sky, vast scarfs of lime green light folded and unfolded: the aurora australis, the Southern lights. There was a rhythm to their movement as if they were flowing to some music inaudible to human ears.

The music of the spheres, Katie thought as she stood

mesmerized, lost in the spectacle, Justin beside her. Justin put his arm around her and she leaned into him.

She saw something out of the corner of her eye and turned to see that light was spilling out of windows farther along the platform.

"What's going on?" she said.

"We'd better find out."

They went inside. Nick was coming down the corridor to the kit room, blinking and rubbing his eyes. Something must have gone wrong at the telescope. Graeme was close behind him.

"The alarm's gone off at the telescope," Nick said. "The computer's turned itself off."

"Probably the effect of the tremor. We haven't got off so lightly after all," Graeme said.

"It might just be a fan again," Nick grumbled, "but I have to get out there."

"I'll go with you," Graeme said, stifling a yawn. They headed for the kit room to dress for the journey.

* * *

In this temperature the Skidoos didn't work. Graeme and Nick set off to walk the kilometre and a half to the Dark Sector. The moon was high now and it was bright enough to read a newspaper. The flag-line was clearly visible, winding away to the telescope, a dark shape that blocked out the stars. Graeme put his head down and concentrated on trudging on, the snow crunching under his feet. *Nick does this twice a day*, he reminded himself. *But I'm not as young as I was, that's for sure.*

They reached the telescope. Nick was right about the fan. The atmosphere was so dry that lubrication evaporated out here. That was a relief. If it had been something outside, well, trying to do some delicate task when your hands in thin mittens begin to freeze in seconds was no joke. When a part failed on the telescope at forty degrees below it could take two people over an hour to fix what one person could do in a few minutes back home.

He made tea, reflecting as he did that he never drank as much tea in normal life as he did here in the Antarctic. There was nothing for him to do for the time being except wait for Nick, a rare moment to reflect and let his mind wander. The success of Adam's op had boosted the morale of everyone on base and he was feeling more optimistic than he had for a while. Of course it was a logistical nightmare trying to cover all the work on base when they were three men down. But it looked as if Adam was going to make a full recovery and Justin's hand would soon be better, too. Ah yes, Justin. He hoped it wasn't going to complicate things too much, Justin falling for Katie. Graeme had seen the way he gazed at her when he thought no one was looking. She liked him, too, Graeme could tell, but he felt that he could trust her to behave professionally. It was different on the bigger bases, but here with eight men and her the only woman now *and* the only doctor... He hoped they'd save it until they got home. They'd make a good-looking couple. Ah, what a sentimental old so-and-so he was becoming...

Nick broke into his thoughts. "I've done it now and we'd better be getting back. I think the weather's on the turn."

Somehow it never felt as far, going back, especially when you could see the comforting lights of the platform in the distance. But when they went outside the lights were not as clear as they had been before; Nick was right about the weather. The moon and stars and the Southern lights had vanished and the sky was overcast. A wind was getting up. Already they could hear it thrumming in the guy lines of the anemometer, as they placed their right hands on the flag-line and set off.

It was as if the frozen land were coming to life. There was something eerie about the little scrapings and rustlings all around them, as if little animals had begun to stir. Graeme turned to shout to Nick. "Get hold of the flag-line." But the instruction wasn't necessary. Nick was already gripping it. He too knew what was coming.

The glassy surface began to stream with ice crystals. It was like walking into the sea. The ice crystals foamed over Graeme's ankles, surged to waist-level and then were over his head. Graeme could see nothing. The ice stung the exposed parts of his face and the wind buffeted him. When Graeme turned to check that Nick was still with him, he could scarcely make out his outline through the whirling and dancing ice crystals. All that stood between them and total disorientation was the flag-line. Graeme leaned into the blizzard and forged on. Progress was one hard-earned footstep at a time. It was not quite as cold – that was one welcome effect.

The wind began to drop a little and Graeme glimpsed the outline of the summer station. They would soon be back on base. Everything looked different. The blizzard had resculpted the landscape, piling up banks of ice in new places, in others eroding the humps and hillocks that they had grown accustomed to.

And now the base loomed up ahead. Visibility was rapidly improving. Graeme stopped so abruptly that Nick cannoned into him.

"Hey, what's up?" he said

Graeme wasn't sure what he had seen. Over by the vehicle depot – that snowdrift. A mass of white had backed there. There was something – but what? He pointed...

"Oh my – oh," Nick said, and then they were both stumbling forward on the ice.

A hand, hardly visible against the surrounding white, was sticking out of the mound. Graeme dropped to his knees. Nick joined him and together they set about digging out the ice crystals, plunging their hands in and scooping it out, and then working more carefully as they gradually uncovered what lay below.

Sara's frozen face stared up at them.

171

CHAPTER 29

Katie was in Sara's pit-room. Restless and disorientated, she had found herself wandering around the base. She somehow felt that she wanted to be close to Sara and sat down on her bed.

There had been some debate about whether they should bring Sara's body inside.

"We've got to bring her in! Of course we have," Katie had said. They had gathered in the dining room as they waited while Graeme phoned headquarters.

Alex had demurred. "But, Katie, we won't be able to fly the body out for months. Let's face facts. We'll have to keep it frozen anyway."

"We can't just leave her out there in a snowdrift. Think of her family."

"Have we got a coffin?" Rhys said.

Alex snorted. "Of course we haven't got a coffin."

"But we have got body bags," Katie said.

"When Admiral Byrd led his 1928 Antarctic expedition his supplies are said to have included two coffins and a dozen straitjackets," Rhys said.

"We might yet need the straitjackets," Justin muttered, through gritted teeth.

"It's all academic anyway," Nick pointed out. "It's not up to us. HQ will tell us what to do."

Craig was looking thoughtful. "We could always *make* a coffin."

Katie had been close to tears. Graeme had come in at that moment. "We're to bring her in," he said.

They had reorganized the frozen food stores, and had cleared the smaller walk-in freezer near the surgery. Graeme

172

and Alex had brought the body in and that was where it was now, laid on a shelf.

Everyone on the base had been there, standing awkwardly in the corridor, but no one had hung around. Graeme and Alex had needed to get warm and the others had drifted off to the dining room where Ernesto had coffee and tea waiting.

It seemed to Katie now that they should have had some kind of ritual or ceremony. Sitting on Sara's bed, her eye was caught by a small book bound in red leather on a ledge by the bed. She reached for it: a New Testament. When she opened it there was an inscription on the flyleaf: "For our darling Sara on her Confirmation with love from Mum and Dad." She thought of the cross on a chain that Sara always wore around her neck. Perhaps she would have liked to have her New Testament with her.

She took the book and went down to the walk-in freezer.

She opened the door and shivered in the blast of icy air. The body, still fully dressed, was in a body bag. She unzipped the bag and folded it back. Her heart skipped a beat. Katie had seen plenty of dead bodies during her medical training, but it's very different when it is someone you know, especially when it's someone around your own age. And she had never seen a body that was frozen solid. Sara didn't look real, more like a wax model. She wondered how long it would take for the body to thaw out when it was finally thawed out: days, no doubt.

She decided to put the New Testament close to Sara's heart. She unzipped the parka and was surprised by what she saw. That was strange, very strange. Sara wasn't wearing a fleece underneath, just a white cotton T-shirt. Whatever had possessed her to go out without one? That would certainly have hastened her death. Did this cast doubt on her state of mind?

She placed the New Testament on Sara's chest and was about to pull the sides of the parka back together, when she noticed something on the T-shirt. Some kind of stain. She examined it closely: a small rusty patch around a slit in the fabric. It couldn't be, no... surely...

A wave of dizziness swept over her and she groped for support. She leaned against the shelf, trying to compose herself, hoping that she was somehow mistaken. But she knew that she wasn't. Sara had been stabbed. She had been murdered – and it had to be someone on the base. It seemed impossible that it could be one of these men, someone she'd laughed and chatted with, that she sat next to at meals, no, more, someone who had actually cooked dinner on Ernesto's day off. But it had to be. Who could she be sure of? Could she be sure of *anyone*? She hadn't known a single one of them until two months ago.

A flutter of panic stirred in her belly. She took a deep breath. She couldn't let fear and claustrophobia get a grip on her.

The door opened behind her and she spun around. Justin was standing in the doorway, holding a bunch of roses.

She stared at him.

"Katie? Are you alright? You look – well –"

"As if I've seen a ghost?" she suggested.

Justin's eyes strayed to Sara's body lying partly exposed. He quickly looked away. "What's going on?"

"Wait a minute." She went over and glanced up and down the corridor. There was no one else around.

She closed the door behind her. "Come across to the surgery."

"Why? What's the matter?"

"Just come!"

He stepped over the threshold and she shut the door behind him. They stood looking at each other. Justin laid the bunch of flowers on the desk. Roses? But where – then she saw that they were made of pink tissue paper, so beautifully constructed that at first sight they had seemed real.

Justin said, "I got Rhys to make these. It didn't seem right, just leaving her there with nothing..."

"I know. They're beautiful. Sit down," she said. They both took seats at the desk.

"Katie! What *is* it? Why are you looking like that?"

"Just wait. I have to think." There was a bottle of brandy in one of the cupboards. She got it out along with a glass and poured herself a healthy measure. She sat down and took a swig. The warmth spread through her and steadied her.

Justin was staring at her. She would have to phone headquarters and she would have to tell Graeme. But what was she going to say here and now to Justin? Should she tell him?

He reached over and got a second glass out of the cupboard. Awkwardly, he scooped up the brandy bottle in the crook of his right elbow and held it to his chest. He took the top off with his left hand, leaned forward, and put it on the table. Still using just his left hand, he now tipped the bottle and slopped some brandy into the glass.

And watching him struggle, she realized that he was the one person on the base who couldn't have killed Sara. And not only did that fact clear him, but it was something she could use.

"We've got a problem," she told him. "I need to have a better look, but –" She hesitated, but there was no way to wrap this up. She went on. "Sara's been stabbed."

Justin's jaw dropped. He stared at her, speechless.

"I want you to be a witness," she said.

"Witness? Witness to what? And why me?"

"If I'm right about what's happened, you couldn't have done it. You're right-handed," she explained, "and your right hand is out of action."

At that point, his gaze shifted and she saw that his rational mind was taking over. "Couldn't I have done it left-handed?" he asked.

"Not unless you're ambidextrous and I've seen you struggling over the past few weeks and I know you're not. I want you to come back in there with me. I'm going to have to cut her T-shirt away and have a better look."

She got up to look for a pair of scissors. Justin was looking down at his clasped hands and she couldn't quite make out what he said next.

"What was that?" she asked.

"I said, I've never actually seen a dead body before."

"Oh. I see." She'd taken it for granted that he'd be able to cope. He was a scientist, after all, but as an astronomer, he was more used to dealing with heavenly bodies than dead bodies. The awful pun came into her head from nowhere and she recognized it as a symptom of approaching hysteria. Any minute now she'd either be crying or laughing her head off – or both.

"You'd better knock back that brandy. It'll help."

They sat sipping in silence.

Justin put the glass on the table with a decisive gesture. "OK. Let's get it over with."

Katie pulled on a pair of surgical gloves. They went back to the freezer. Very carefully, Katie slipped the blade of the scissors into the neck of Sara's T-shirt and slit it open. She peeled it back from the body. Just under Sara's left breast, aligned with the slit in the T-shirt, there was a small wound. Justin, standing beside and a little behind Katie, made an inarticulate sound.

Katie said, "She's been stabbed through the heart."

"Is that – I mean, is that enough? It looks so small."

"Yes, the damage'll be mostly inside."

Already Katie's fingers had gone numb, but there was something else she had to check before they went back to the surgery.

* * *

Without asking Justin went over to the desk and poured out two more glasses of brandy. He sat down heavily. Katie sat down beside him. He reached over and took her hand and squeezed it.

Katie said, "Her parka's not damaged or bloodstained. I'm quite sure she wasn't wearing it when she was stabbed. Even if you could have –" She hesitated, not wanting to put it into words. "I mean to say, even if you could have done... it, and I know you didn't... you certainly couldn't have dressed her in her parka and carried her outside one-handed."

"She was killed here on the platform then? That's what you're thinking?"

"She wasn't wearing anything over her T-shirt, so she must have been indoors when it happened."

"It's crazy. The whole thing's crazy. Katie – sorry, but are you really sure? Why wasn't there more blood?"

"When a major blood vessel or organ is damaged, internal bleeding can lead to loss of consciousness fairly rapidly. There doesn't have to be very much to show on the outside. She'd have died very quickly."

They contemplated that awful thought.

The wind had got up again. Katie went over to the window. Justin joined her and together they looked out at the flying drift and the darkness beyond. There was no need to say anything. Katie knew that Justin too was thinking of the hundreds of miles of frozen wasteland that stretched away in all directions, the seemingly endless night, the almost ceaseless winds that swept across the Antarctic plateau.

"How did they think they could ever get away with it?" Justin said. "What am I saying? How did *he* think he could get away with it? Because it has to be a man, doesn't it? I mean – it wasn't *you*, Katie."

"Wasn't it? I mean, yes, it wasn't. But can I prove that?"

"I don't want to be sexist – equal opportunities and all that, but Sara was a tall woman and I don't see you hoisting her over your shoulder and heading out into a blizzard."

Katie was glad to see that the colour was coming back into his face. She took a gulp of her brandy. "I can't believe we are having this conversation. I really can't."

"How could something like this have happened? Was it spur of the moment? A quarrel that got out of hand and then he had to cover up the best he could?"

"I don't know." But there was something about that wound, just in the right place, the economy of it, exactly what was needed and nothing more, that didn't seem like a blow struck in anger. She said, "I don't think he ever meant the body to be found and it could easily not have been. I think he was caught out by the blizzard and he hid the body near the vehicle depot, planning to get rid of it later on. Then the direction of the wind changed and shifted the drift, so that her hand came to the surface."

Justin thought about that. "If he had managed to get her away from the base, he could have tipped her down one of those deep crevasses and that would have been that."

"We'd have gone on thinking that she'd got confused and wandered off base. Someone must be cursing their bad luck right now."

They were silent. "I'm frightened," she admitted.

He didn't say that it would be alright, and that was good, because she wouldn't have believed him. But he did take her hand and squeeze it.

"Come on. Let's go and see the Boss."

A horrible thought occurred to her. "But what if it was him, who... I mean, I can't imagine for an instant that it was, but –"

"You're not thinking straight, Katie. The Boss was the one who spotted the body. He didn't have to do that – and he *wouldn't* have done that, if he had killed her. All he had to do was wait for a chance to go back out and cover her up again until he could move her off base."

Katie heaved a sigh of relief. "Of course. Yes, he's in the clear. It was unthinkable in any case."

"But is it any less unthinkable that it is one of the others? We've got to face it, Katie. It has to have been one of us, and we can't wait until the police arrive in six months' time. We have to find out who did this."

179

CHAPTER 30

"The line's gone dead," Graeme said, putting the phone down. "I'll have to try again later. They got as far as telling me to secure the crime scene."

Katie and Justin were in his office. If Katie had ever thought that calling Graeme "the Boss" was a bit of a joke, she wasn't thinking it now. He had taken in the news with a calmness that was impressive. He hadn't questioned it, hadn't asked her if she was sure, or expressed disbelief. There was nothing showy or dramatic about it, he had just quietly taken charge. He and Katie had gone together to look at the body and Katie had shown him the wound.

"What crime scene?" Justin asked. "We don't know where it happened."

"We know where it didn't happen. It didn't happen outside," Katie said. "She wasn't wearing her parka when she was stabbed, just her T-shirt."

"Could she have been out at the caboose?" Graeme asked.

"No. She would have been wearing more, not just her T-shirt and the parka, but her fleece as well. It was somewhere on the platform. I'm sure of it."

Justin shook his head. "How could it have happened without anyone seeing anything? How could you murder someone and get them off the platform? It's incredible."

"It *is* incredible. But it happened," Graeme said. "And there are a lot of places we could rule out – like the dining room where Nick and Craig were playing Scrabble most of the afternoon. The kitchen too where people must have been coming and going all the time."

Katie found herself thinking of Adam's beloved Cluedo: Miss

Scarlett with a dagger in the library. For a moment she thought she wouldn't be able to hold back hysterical laughter. *I've got to keep a grip on myself,* she thought. *Justin and Graeme are focused on the problem, seeing it as a puzzle to be worked out. I must see it that way too – at least for now. I'll try not to think of Sara actually being dead, of someone actually killing her. I'll try and think of it as if it is a game of Cluedo: a matter of elimination and logistics.*

"Moving the body would be the problem. Somehow they got it off the base that afternoon," Graeme said.

"Do we know that for sure?" Justin asked.

"Yes. I *know* it wasn't here at six o'clock. I searched the platform from end to end."

And then Katie knew. "The surgery. That's where it must have happened. It's well away from the rest of the communal rooms." It had been planned that way, so that confidentiality could be maintained.

"Makes sense," Justin said. "That's where he could have found her alone."

"Even so... How long would he have needed?" Graeme asked.

"You mean...?" Katie's voice trailed off.

"To kill Sara and get her body off the base."

Katie saw Sara sitting in the surgery. Someone coming in. Did they speak to her or did they just – do it? All it would have taken was one swift blow. "Not long," she concluded. "She'd have died almost instantly. But if the killer had to dress her, that's what would have taken the time." She couldn't believe she was having this conversation.

"Why did he waste time doing that?" Justin asked. "Why not just take her as she was? The important thing was to get her out of the building, surely?"

Katie said, "I think I know the answer to that. He was setting it up as an accident. He needed it to look as though she had gone out of her own accord. That's why the radio went too."

"He had some nerve," Justin said.

181

"I thought that at first," Katie said. "But actually, was it all that risky? No one comes to that end of the building unless they are going to the kit room or the surgery or the generator – or leaving the building, and no one was planning to do that on the afternoon of Sundown day. He only needed to be in the corridor for maybe, I don't know, thirty seconds. And the fire doors cut off the view from further down the corridor."

"We'll have to time it," Graeme said. He caught the expression on Katie's face. "I know it's a grisly idea, but before I start to question people I need to know how long it would take. And there's something we need to get out in the open first." He looked at them in turn, held their gaze for a moment. "Are we absolutely sure that the three of us are in the clear?"

There was silence, then: "I am satisfied that it couldn't have been Justin," Katie said. "The burn on his hand rules him out. No one could have got that coat on her with one hand out of action. I don't think he could have stabbed her either. He's right-handed and it's his right hand that's out of action."

"And it couldn't have been you, Katie," Graeme said. "Because you weigh – what – fifty kilos wringing wet? You might be wiry, but you are still only five foot five. I can't see you carrying a big woman like Sara down those steps in a blizzard. No, I am ruling you out."

"And it wasn't you, Graeme," Justin said. "You'd have kept quiet about seeing Sara's hand. Katie and I had already worked that out. Not that we'd have thought it was you in any case," he added hastily.

"Alright then," Graeme said.

Katie and Justin nodded.

They went down to the surgery. No one spoke a word on the way. They went inside.

"Yes, I think it must have been here," Katie said, looking around. "Anywhere else on the base and the chances of being seen would have been so much greater. If it's a crime scene perhaps we'd better not touch anything."

"Your fingerprints are going to be everywhere anyway," Justin pointed out. "And plenty of other people's too. Just about everyone was at Doc School, remember."

"How could he be sure of finding her here – that is, if it was premeditated?" Graeme asked.

A thought so horrible occurred to Katie that she went cold. For a moment she couldn't speak.

Justin put his hand on her arm. "Katie, what's the matter?"

"There is a way he could be sure of finding her here alone. She was a doctor. He could have made an appointment to see her. Consultations are confidential so she wouldn't have said anything to anyone."

"But he couldn't be sure that no one would see him coming here," Justin objected.

"No problem," Graeme said. "He'd just abort the plan. He'd have made up a reason for seeing her – and he'd have waited for the next opportunity. Would she have written the appointment down?" he asked Katie.

"Probably wouldn't have bothered. It's not as if she was seeing dozens of people. But she would have made notes about the consultation on the computer."

"The computer wasn't on when we came looking for her," Graeme said. "He could have closed it down."

"I doubt if there was time to make notes," Katie said. She hesitated and then sat down in Sara's office chair. "She's sitting here. There's a knock on the door. And she tells whoever it is to come in."

"So he does," Graeme said, walking over to the door. "And then ... does he sit down?"

"No," Justin said. "He won't waste time. He wants to get back to the rest of us as fast as possible."

"Wait," Graeme said. "We don't know it *was* premeditated. What if it wasn't? What if it was done on the spur of the moment? What if he – well, what if he wanted to have sex with her – what if he *did* have sex with her – against her will. What if he raped her?"

Katie said, "I didn't see any signs of that, no bruises or anything, but I didn't undress her completely and I'm not a pathologist. All that will have to wait until the body's flown out. But there's something about that wound – so precise, clinical even. It didn't look like something done in anger or in a panic."

"So he walks up to her..." Graeme said, positioning himself in front of Katie. "Like so."

"No." Justin shook his head. "He'd walk up behind her so she didn't see the knife."

"So like this then?" Graeme positioned himself behind Katie's chair.

"She'd wonder what he was doing," Katie said. "She'd start to turn round..."

"The chair swivels," Justin said. "He could've just put an arm round her and pinned her back and brought the knife round to stab her with an upward motion."

"Does that fit with what you saw of the wound?" Graeme asked Katie.

Katie saw it in her mind's eye. Sara puzzled, wondering what was going on, and then the arm across her chest, and the blow. It would all have been over so quickly.

"It could have been that way. It probably was that way. And once she'd been stabbed, she probably didn't live more than a minute or two."

"Maybe five minutes for the whole thing?" Graeme said.

Katie nodded. "If that. Less, I'd think."

"And then what?"

"And then he bolts the door in case someone else happens to come along," Justin said.

"No," said Katie. "First he goes and gets her coat and mukluks from the kit room. Then he comes back and dresses her."

They were all silent. Katie seemed almost to see a shadowy fourth figure there in the room with them. Whose was the face that belonged to that figure? Could there really be someone on the base who would do something like this?

"So how long?" Graeme asked.

"It wouldn't have been easy," she said. "Ten minutes? And don't forget he has to get all his outdoor gear on too. So I'd add another five minutes to that."

"It would take hardly any time at all to get from the surgery to the exit," Justin said.

They went out into the corridor. "We'll time it," Graeme said. "He's carrying her either in his arms or in a fireman's lift over his shoulders. That'll slow him down."

They walked to the exit.

"Thirty seconds," Graeme said. "He has to put her down to open the door. That'd be awkward. And then he has to pick her up again. Then he's out of the door and out of sight. No one's seen him and the dangerous bit is over."

"I'd say a couple of minutes, tops," said Justin.

"But it wasn't just a question of getting the body outside," Katie objected. "He had to hide it. That must have taken a while."

"Let's give him fifteen minutes to do that," Justin said. "Allow a few minutes for him to get to the surgery from the living quarters in the first place. Then after he'd disposed of the body he'd have to get his outdoor gear off and get back to the living quarters. I'd say we're looking at not less than forty or forty-five minutes for the whole thing."

Graeme said, "Let's not hang about here in the corridor. We'll go back to the surgery."

When they were back there and had pulled up chairs, Katie said, "We are looking for someone physically strong and highly organized."

"As for being physically strong, essentially, that's everyone on base," Graeme said. "There's no one here – except you, Katie – who isn't capable of slinging a body over their shoulder. Isn't that the case, Katie?"

She considered. It was true that they were all young, healthy, well-nourished males with good musculature: the weeks of shovelling meltwater had seen to that. Ernesto was the shortest, only an inch or two taller than Katie. But he had a well-developed upper body. Adam had been in pretty good shape before the appendicitis. Alex was both tall and well-built and with his Mountain Rescue experience heaving a body around would presumably be no problem. But Craig was perhaps the fittest of them all and spent a lot of his spare time in the gym. And then there was Nick who was used to going out to the observatory twice a day, which would have built up his stamina. What about Rhys? He was the most sedentary, preferring reading to working out in the gym, but that was only relative. And anyway, how strong did you have to be to employ a fireman's lift, especially if you were fuelled by adrenaline?

Katie reluctantly agreed. "No one can be ruled out on physical grounds. But why would anyone want to hurt Sara? It's just crazy."

"Maybe that's what it is. Crazy," Justin said.

Graeme said, "What do you think he used? I mean, what was the weapon?"

Justin shrugged. "Look around you. The surgery is full of sharp instruments."

"That scalpel," Graeme said. "The one that went missing!"

Katie felt queasy. "That would do it."

"You know what that means," Graeme said. "It must have been premeditated. The scalpel went missing long before Sara disappeared."

"Should we do a search?" Justin asked.

"Even if we did find it, it probably wouldn't do much good," Katie said. "If he had any sense, he'd have put it through the autoclave. That would destroy any traces of DNA. He'd have plenty of opportunity to do that. There's no lock on the surgery door. People can come and go as they please."

Graeme frowned. "That's something that's going to have to change. And we'll also have to put bolts on the pit-room doors."

Bolts on the pit-room doors... That really brought it home: the trust that was such an essential part of wintering over had gone.

Graeme went on, "Katie, I don't think you should see any patients alone. In fact, I don't think you should be alone at all, except when you're in your pit-room with the door bolted."

"But how's that going to work?" Katie protested.

"One of us will be with you all the time. Me or Justin."

"But we've got months to go..."

"I can't let this go on for months. I was sworn in as a magistrate, remember, when I was appointed base leader. I'm going to get to the bottom of this."

CHAPTER 31

ELY

"Whatever possessed me to choose red for my cast?" Daniel grumbled. "I must have been spaced out on painkillers. I'll never hear the last of it in the office."

"I like it, Daddy." Chloe was playing with her Lego on the floor of the sitting room. "You look like Father Christmas."

"My point exactly."

Daniel was sitting by the window, with his leg up on a stool, his laptop wedged awkwardly on his lap, as he typed one-handed. His left hand looked as if it had been pumped up, like an inflated rubber glove. It was strangely smooth, the knuckles submerged, a fat person's hand. There were puncture wounds where the car door had locked onto it. He still couldn't figure out how that could have happened: it was one of those freak accidents, something to do with the force with which the door swung shut and his hand being in exactly the right – or wrong – place. He'd been told that the bruising wouldn't come until the swelling went down.

His leg and hand ached, but nothing that ibuprofen and paracetamol couldn't deal with. He felt exhausted and was sleeping a lot. His thought processes had slowed down. He kept forgetting what he had been about to say and leaving things half done. They had warned him at the hospital that it would take a while for the effects of shock to wear off.

It was Saturday now and he planned to go back into the office on Monday.

He and Rachel hadn't talked about their argument, but they had been gentle with each other. They both knew that Daniel was lucky not to be more badly injured or dead, and other things paled into insignificance beside that. His thoughts kept returning to what had happened – he felt again the horror, the helplessness, as the car, like some monstrous predatory creature, dragged him along. So quickly life could change utterly, could "turn on a dime" as he'd heard Lyle once say. What scared him most was his own lack of judgment...

"Dan?" Rachel broke into his thoughts. "What shall I do with this suit? There are grass stains on the trousers, but there's not much wrong with the jacket."

"Throw the trousers away," Daniel said with a shudder.

"That seems a shame," said his practical wife, "considering what the suit cost. We'll have it dry-cleaned and then we'll see."

She started turning out the pockets.

"Why have you got some of Chloe's Lego here? Did you put this in Daddy's pocket, Chloe?"

Chloe got up and came over to look. "No. Oh look, it's a little man. Can I have him, Daddy?"

Daniel stared at the Lego figure, then remembered. Kieran had given it to him. "Of course you can, sweetie."

That reminded him. He still hadn't managed to track down Alistair Johnson-Marsh. It was strange that he didn't seem to have any presence on social media, no Twitter or Facebook account.

Chloe began to chortle. "Silly Daddy! This isn't Lego. Well, it is Lego," she amended. "But it isn't as well."

"What are you talking about?" Daniel asked.

She came over with the little man. She pulled him apart and held up a piece of red Lego. Daniel saw a sliding catch underneath. Chloe pushed it with her thumb and a piece of plastic shot out of the end.

"It's a memory stick. I know, because Nathan's daddy has one and Nathan got it mixed up with his real Lego." Chloe could hardly control her mirth. "Nathan's got loads and loads and loads of Lego, a ginormous lot of Lego, and it took them ages and ages to find it. Look, it's got this little curved thing on the end. That's how you know. Nathan got into trouble," she added more soberly.

"You're a clever girl," Daniel said. "Do you mind if I have this back? I'll buy you some more."

"Well..." Chloe narrowed her eyes as she assessed the situation, clearly gauging how much she could milk it for. Then she thought better of it. "You can have it for free, Daddy, because you've had an accident."

Rachel said, "Chloe's saving her pocket money for a 'Mighty Dinosaur' kit."

Chloe's face lit up. "Francesca's got one. You can make a D. Rex. It's cool. Scary!"

"I think you mean T. Rex," Daniel said. "Tell you what, I'll give you a fiver towards it, Chloe."

"Yah!" Chloe was delighted. She had enjoyed knowing something that Mummy and Daddy didn't know, but she wasn't interested in what might be on the memory stick: it would just be boring grown-up stuff. She went back to building her tower.

Daniel slipped the memory stick into his laptop. There was only one document on it. It was called "Virus-mediated apoptosis". Daniel clicked on it. "Artificial Virus-Induced Apoptosis: A Paradigm Shift in Cancer Treatment," he read, "by Kieran Langstaffe and Alistair Johnson-Marsh for submission to *The European Journal of Molecular Oncology*." It was followed by an abstract that began, "Apoptosis can be caused by mitochondrial stress..." It was the second sentence that made him sit up: "We have used a self-assembled virus capsid decorated with monoclonal antibodies against the SKBR-3 human breast cancer cell line, to deliver cytochrome c-enriched buffer into the tumour cells with a resultant 100% death rate." He read on. When he reached the end and saw the date, he leaned back in his seat and gave a long, low whistle.

He reached for his mobile phone and called Lyle. Lyle answered on the third ring.

"I've got something here that you need to see," Daniel told him.

* * *

"OK, so, let's get this out in the open," Lyle said. "You're thinking there's a possibility that Flora got hold of this research and passed it off as her own?"

Daniel had sent the contents of the Lego memory stick to Lyle and Lyle had been sufficiently concerned to drive up from London to talk it over. Rachel had made them some tea and then taken Chloe out to the playground.

Daniel said, "Well, one team was working on breast cancer cells, the other was using lung cancer cells, but the actual therapy is remarkably similar. I don't know what to make of it. It could just be coincidence. That does happen."

"Sure it does. But you're not easy in your mind, are you?"

"It's what Sara said. Apparently Flora just came in one morning and said why don't we try delivering excess cytochrome c directly into the cytoplasm and seeing if it triggers apoptosis. It wasn't the most obvious development of what they'd been doing up to then. I noticed that when I went through the lab books. In fact I'd say it was pretty left field. Sara said so, that it was a leap of the imagination on Flora's part, a flash of intuition."

"And don't we all know instances of that?"

Daniel knew that was true. Intuition and imagination played a far greater part in scientific research than non-scientists might imagine. You had to be able to envisage a solution before you could test it to see if it worked.

"There's no evidence that Flora pinched the work of these other guys," Lyle went on. "I'd go further: I don't see how she could have. Their work was never published and she didn't know them."

191

Of course Lyle wanted to believe that. A charge of plagiarism was the last thing he wanted muddying the waters while he was negotiating with potential investors.

Lyle went on. "You said, this guy, this Kieran, he's got a screw loose? Could he have seen Flora's paper when it was published and concocted this from what he'd read?"

Daniel thought of what he had seen at the house in south-west London: the pages and pages of crazy diagrams; the rambling Lego constructions.

"I can't see him doing that," he said. "This is all too logically constructed. I mean, it's even fully footnoted! And then the date at the end. It fits with the dates when Kieran and this other guy, this Alistair, were actually doing their research. It does seem that this pre-dates Flora's research."

"So what's our next move?"

"I could go to see Kieran again, but I don't know how much joy I'll get there."

"And this other guy, this Alistair Johnson-Marsh?"

"Vanished without trace, as far as I can see. I'll go on looking for him. And I'll do a detailed comparison of the lab books and this article."

Lyle was scrolling down the article on his iPad.

"You know, something puzzles me," he said. "If this is the real McCoy, why wasn't it published?"

Daniel stared at Lyle. Yes, why hadn't it been published? "You're onto something there. Perhaps they intended to submit it, but didn't actually do it."

"That's one possibility. But there's another."

"That they tried to publish it and it was turned down."

They looked at each other. Scientific publications operate a system of anonymous peer review. If this paper had been submitted to a journal an editor should have sent it out to two readers, specialists in the same field.

"You're thinking it might have been sent out to Flora?" Daniel asked.

"It had crossed my mind."

"She wasn't sufficiently senior at the time, surely?"

Lyle thought about that. "No, no, you're right. It'd be a different matter now, but back then... no. It wouldn't have been her."

Daniel said, "But we are seriously thinking that Flora somehow got her hands on this paper?"

"Well, if she did... it'd be a prime example of the Matthew effect."

"The Matthew effect?"

"Matthew 25:29 to be precise. 'For unto every one that hath shall be given, and he shall have abundance: but from him that hath not shall be taken away even that which he hath.' In other words the rich get richer and the poor get poorer." He noticed the look of surprise on Daniel's face. "Oh, yeah, I know my Bible. And it's a term used in sociology. It refers to issues of status and to cumulative advantage of economic capital. That's exactly what's happened to these two research teams. With her publication Flora went from strength to strength – more research grants, so more money and more status, leading to yet more money and status."

"I see. While the exact opposite happened to Kieran. When he didn't manage to get his research published, his career went into a nosedive, he lost what little he had. He ended up with nothing – less than nothing, actually."

Lyle said, "I think I'll have a word with the editor of *The European Journal of Molecular Oncology*. I know the guy as it happens. I'll see if I can find out if it was submitted and if it was, if I can get a clue as to who the readers were."

There was the ping of an incoming text on his phone. "Better get this," he said. "It's my assistant. What the... It just says, 'BBC Breaking News'."

Daniel called up the site on his laptop in time for them to hear: "...her family have been informed. Her body was discovered close to the main platform. It is thought that she got disorientated in poor visibility. Dr Sara McKee was the base doctor..."

Daniel and Lyle stared at each other.

Daniel said, "We knew that there wasn't really any hope, didn't we? There couldn't be."

"Yeah, not quite the same as knowing that her body's actually been found, is it? What's going on, Daniel? Everyone involved in this research – both sets of scientists – everyone is either dead, or missing, or out of their tree!"

CHAPTER 32

ANTARCTICA

Everyone had gathered in the dining room, Adam included, and was waiting for Graeme. Katie was sitting off to the side, along with Justin, a little apart from the others. No one was talking – it was as if they had guessed that more bad news was about to be announced. In the meantime she tried not to meet anyone's eye.

But she couldn't help stealing sideways glances. It had never occurred to her to be afraid of anyone on the base. Now, looking at Craig's broad shoulders and huge hands, she was struck all over again by the sheer size of him. He wouldn't have a problem overpowering a woman. But wasn't that true of all the men on the base? None of them, except for Justin, could be ruled out on grounds of physical incapacity. And actually there wouldn't have been a lot of strength needed to kill Sara, taken by surprise as she would have been. Katie could have done it, though lifting or dragging the body would have been beyond her.

So it was more a question of who would be psychologically capable. Because it must have taken a lot of nerve, not only the actual killing, but removing the body and concealing it. The killer had chosen their moment: a day when the normal routine was suspended and people were full of food and drink, not keeping track of each other. All the same it couldn't help but be risky. It was hard to believe that any of these men was capable of that. They had all been vetted and had psychological screening. But it must be one of them and she felt a chill. Whoever it was knew, too, that part of their plan had failed.

He would be afraid that Katie had examined Sara's body and could guess what Graeme was going to say.

She stole a glance at Adam. His freckles stood out against his pallor. Surely he could be ruled out? She just couldn't imagine him having the audacity and the presence of mind for such a cold-blooded murder, even before he'd been taken ill. And she wanted to believe what he'd claimed in his fever, that he'd not taken the scalpel. As for Craig, she still felt that she hardly knew him, but she remembered that moment of kindness in the communications room. Nick? Despite his louche appearance, she happened to know he rang his mother every Sunday. Alex, so sensible, practical, looking out for Adam as he had been? Rhys, with his rather endearing nerdiness? Ernesto? He was sitting off to one side, clearly fretting to get back in the kitchen. He did have a temper and he did have butchering skills and he had access to knives. But then so did everyone else. There had been no need for locked doors on the base... until now...

Graeme came in. Katie exchanged glances with Justin. There were butterflies in her stomach. She didn't know what she was expecting. A confession?

Graeme said, "I have some very bad news for you all."

Every eye was fixed on him. Adam's mouth had dropped open.

Graeme went on. "Katie has examined Sara's body and concluded that Sara did not die accidentally." The silence was absolute. He went on: "Sara was murdered."

Every face registered shock and disbelief. Katie, watching carefully, couldn't detect anyone for whom this didn't seem to be news.

"As you'll have realized," Graeme went on, "she must have been killed by someone on the base. And we believe it happened on the afternoon that she went missing." He paused, letting this sink in. No one spoke. "I've been in touch with headquarters. Obviously there's no question of the police investigating this crime at first-hand. With the power vested in me as magistrate, I shall be taking charge. I am going to begin by interviewing every member of the team to establish who was doing what and where on the afternoon that Sara died."

Alex raised a hand. "But – when you say she was killed – what was it...?"

Graeme said, "I'd rather not say for the moment. But I am afraid there can be no doubt about it."

There was a gasping sigh. It was Adam. His face was as white as chalk. Katie jumped to her feet. Craig, who was sitting next to Adam, turned and grasped his arm. She got to him just in time to help Craig lower him to the floor, as he fainted clean away.

* * *

The killer had been unlucky. No doubt about it. If it had gone as he had intended, it would have been the perfect crime. It would have been explained as another tragic accident. People would have shaken their heads and murmured: "It's a hostile environment..." However, he'd been very careful. And even if he hadn't been, by the time the police got to the base, forensics would be useless. Everyone's fingerprints were everywhere. As for the scalpel, he had hidden that. Then the first time he had been on night watch and had the base to himself he had sterilized it in the autoclave and replaced it in the drawer in the surgery. Job done.

He could hardly believe his ears when that fool Graeme said that he was going to investigate the murder. The guy didn't even have a degree! It had been hard work not to burst out laughing, but he had managed to keep a shocked and solemn expression on his face. Katie had been watching closely. He had more to fear from her than from anyone else. She was a smart cookie and if she did show signs of guessing, it would be harder to get her on her own now that Justin had a good excuse to stick close to her. It was pathetic really. He probably thought no one had noticed those sideways glances and puppy-dog eyes.

It was all a matter of keeping one's nerve. They would never be able to prove anything. He didn't think they'd even get close. And if they did… well, he wasn't out of ideas yet, not by a long chalk.

* * *

Adam was asleep. Katie smoothed back the hair from his damp forehead.

He had soon come round from his faint and they had taken him to his pit-room. He had lain on his bed with his eyes closed and Katie had seen tears seeping out. Katie had sent the others away.

"I want to go home," she'd heard him murmur.

"I know. So do I," Katie had said.

He started to sob.

Poor kid, she thought, *on top of the operation it's all been too much.* She'd been unable to soothe him and in the end she had given him a mild sedative.

Now she sat there beside the sleeping boy – she couldn't think of him as a man, though that's what he was, really. Justin had taken Graeme's instructions seriously and was sitting on a chair outside the door. She knew that Graeme was waiting for her and Justin in his office. The rest of the men were waiting in the dining room to be called for interview, but she needed a few quiet moments first before she went out and joined them.

She was more certain than ever that they could rule Adam out. The question was, were they going to be able to get him through the winter mentally intact? He was already fragile. Graeme was right. They couldn't spend six months not knowing who was the murderer in their midst. She thought of *The Thing* and the scene where the crew are trying to work out who is an alien and who isn't. The adventure of wintering over in Antarctica had turned into a kind of horror movie. There was something monstrous here, something alien, and you couldn't tell who was harbouring it just by looking.

It still seemed incredible. What possible reason could anyone have for killing kind and harmless Sara? Had it been something sexual? Perhaps she should have examined the body further. But surely Sara would have fought back if someone had tried to rape her and there would be evidence of a struggle, bruises on her arms, broken fingernails maybe. There was nothing, nothing except that one little wound, that one sure blow. It was the very opposite of what they called a "frenzied attack". It was more as if someone had wanted to kill her as quickly and cleanly as possible.

There was a gentle tap at the door and she gave a start.

The door opened and Justin put his head round. "When you're ready, Graeme wants us both. How's Adam bearing up?"

"Not good," Katie said, speaking in a low voice. "I'm worried about him. He's pretty fragile."

"We'll interview him last."

Katie got up and went into the corridor, shutting the door behind her. "I'm hoping we might not have to interview him at all."

Justin looked doubtful. "Graeme won't want to make exceptions, Katie."

"I know, but what if we find that between us all we can give him an alibi, that he doesn't have half an hour unaccounted for?"

"He told me he'd spent the afternoon watching the box set of *Game of Thrones* with Alex," Justin said. "And drinking beer and eating nachos. So maybe we will be able to rule him out."

"Let's hope so."

Justin was leaning against the wall, and was showing no sign of moving.

"We'd better get going," Katie prompted.

"Katie..."

"Yes?"

"I know something about someone, but I'm not supposed to know it and I'm not even sure it's true."

"You mean, about someone on the base?"

Justin nodded. "It could have just been idle gossip."

Katie considered. "You're talking about something that might have a bearing on what's happened here?"

Justin sighed. "I suppose there's a chance – an outside chance, mind – and I don't believe it for a moment – but – oh, hell, I'm going to have to tell Graeme, aren't I?"

CHAPTER 33

"I didn't want to say anything," Justin said, "because I can't be one hundred per cent sure it's true, and even if it is, the guy has every right not to have it bandied about."

Still he hesitated.

"Spit it out," Graeme said.

"A mutual friend mentioned it a year or two ago. He thought I already knew. Apparently Nick had a serious drug problem when he was an undergraduate. I mean really serious. Had to spend six months in rehab."

Graeme frowned. "Surely that would have been picked up when he was vetted to come out here."

"His parents kept it under the radar. They've got pots of money and they picked up the tab. Officially he just took a year off. Look, I hate mentioning it, but…"

"But what?"

"My friend said that he stole to feed his habit. His parents paid for that to go away and it did. But I'm sure he's clean now. I've known him for five or six years and never had a clue that he'd ever had a problem."

Justin and Katie waited as Graeme turned it over in his mind. At last he said, "Would you know if there were any drugs missing from the surgery, Katie?"

"There's nothing obviously missing. But I'd only really know if I did a proper inventory."

Justin said. "Oh, you can't think – surely I'd have noticed if he was getting high!"

"There'd be a motive, wouldn't there? And opportunity, too, maybe? Because if Sara suspected that Nick had pinched something, what would she likely do? Wouldn't she call Nick in for a confidential chat? He'd be alone with her in the surgery. We can't ignore the possibility."

"Oh hell! The guy's my friend!"

"What's your take on this, Katie?" Graeme asked.

Katie shook her head. "I haven't seen any sign of drug use, but then I wasn't looking for it."

Graeme gestured to where sheets of paper were laid out on his desk. "I've drawn up a grid, so that we can work out who's got an alibi. If we can eliminate Nick, there'll be no need to raise this with him. But if not, it can't be avoided. OK, Justin?"

Justin nodded. "Fair enough."

"OK then. We've decided that it couldn't have been done in under forty minutes, so I've divided the afternoon that Sara went missing into half-hour slots. I've started with when everyone wandered off after lunch and ended with when Adam told me that Sara was missing. That's two thirty to around six forty-five. We'll interview everyone and see if we can fill some of these slots. Hopefully we can start eliminating people."

"Can we narrow the time down even further if we start from the other side and think about when Sara was last seen alive?" Justin asked.

"That was Rhys. He said he had an appointment with her soon after lunch at around two forty-five. But was he telling the truth?"

Justin said, "We've already agreed that the killer could have made an appointment to see her. So could it have been Rhys who killed her?"

Katie frowned. "Well, he did actually have a genuine reason for seeing her. Sara wrote up her notes on the computer after she had seen him. And he had a follow-up appointment with me after Sara went missing."

"What was wrong with him?"

Katie was uncomfortable. "I'm not sure I should tell you. Patient confidentiality."

"Katie! Under the circumstances..." Graeme said.

"OK, OK. A minor but embarrassing ailment. I'm not saying more than that. But I can promise you that it's real enough."

"Did you examine him?"

"No, but Sara did – and he's suffered previous bouts. It's in his medical notes."

They thought about this.

"Doesn't rule him out, though, does it?" Justin said. "He could have killed her after he consulted her."

Katie was sceptical. "You mean he waits until she's handed over the medication and then he whips out a knife? I can't see it somehow."

"He could have come back."

Did Justin *want* it to be Rhys? Katie wasn't buying it. Rhys was certainly the most irritating person on the base, but that didn't make him a murderer.

Perhaps the same thing had occurred to Graeme. He said, "Enough! This isn't getting us anywhere."

"Sorry," Justin said. "But it is more than likely that it happened earlier rather than later, isn't it? If she'd been wandering around the base someone would have seen her and no one is saying that they did."

"Did she say anything about what she was planning to do, Katie?" Graeme asked.

"Well, I was half-expecting that she'd come along and suggest watching a DVD, but I didn't think anything of it when she didn't show. Thought she might have fallen asleep. We'd all had a fair bit to drink."

"We'd better start filling in the grid," Graeme said. "Makes sense to do that first among the three of us. I'm distinguishing between what can be confirmed by other people and what can't, and we'll see what comes of that. Katie? Want to go first?"

Katie had had time to think about that while she was sitting with Adam. "It's fairly straightforward. I didn't see Sara at all after lunch. I went back to my pit-room and wrote a couple of emails. So that would be until just after three. Ten past, maybe? Then for the rest of the afternoon I was in the library reading. Justin was already there when I arrived. I didn't see anyone else until Graeme and Adam put their heads round the door when they were looking for Sara."

Graeme was writing on the grid. "You sure about that? Didn't you even go to the loo or get a cup of tea?"

"I must have done, but –"

"You went and got coffee, don't you remember?" Justin said.

"Oh, of course – I went and got a cup of coffee – I got one for Justin, too – and I saw Nick and Craig. They were playing Scrabble in the dining room. And Ernesto was in the kitchen, just putting something in the oven."

"What time was that?"

"Hard to say. Maybe around half past four?"

"OK. What about you, Justin?"

"I spent twenty minutes or so on the running machine in the gym. Adam was there when I arrived and he was still there when I left. And then I made a cup of tea. There was no one in the kitchen. I saw Nick and Craig and Alex, but they were engrossed in their Scrabble and I don't think they saw me. I took my tea along to the library and settled down with my book."

"Which was?"

"Eh?"

"What were you reading?"

"Oh, I was reading *Alone* by Admiral Byrd. Rhys had gone on about him so much, I thought I'd see what the fuss was about. I couldn't put it down! Great stuff! After a bit Katie came in and then it was just the two of us. No one else came in or out. I went out to the loo at some point, but I'm a bit vague about the timing of it all."

"You fell asleep at one point," Katie pointed out.

Justin looked sheepish. "Just briefly."

"Just briefly! Twenty minutes, more like. I was getting sleepy too. That's why I went and made coffee."

"OK, that's you two sorted," Graeme said. "As for me, after lunch I went to my office to catch up with some paperwork. Adam dropped in. That would have been around three fifteen. I'd asked him to come and see me, I'd been a bit worried about him. I wanted to talk to him about the importance of not letting his body clock get out of synch. Told him he needed to stick to a strict sleep regime. He told me that he'd just come from the gym and he was trying not to sleep during the day. We left the office together. I was in there for around an hour, so that probably takes me to around three twenty-five or three thirty. But I wasn't watching the clock."

"That's going to be the difficulty," Justin said. "Everyone was off-duty. They weren't thinking in terms of half-hour slots."

"True enough. Though actually the next thing I did took exactly half an hour. I went to the gym and did my thirty-minute workout. So that takes me to around four and then I made myself a cup of tea – Ernesto was in the kitchen – and took it to my pit-room. I was still there when Adam came looking for me. In fact I was asleep," he admitted.

For over two hours? Katie would have thought Graeme had more sense than to disrupt his body clock like that.

"I wasn't asleep all that time," he added hastily.

But Katie noticed that he didn't say what it was that he *had* been doing.

"We'd better start the interviews," Graeme said. "Katie, I want you to sit in with me. You can help me by taking notes."

Katie nodded.

"What about me?" Justin said.

"I'd like you to go and get people – and you might as well sit in on the interviews too. Any one of us might notice something that the others miss."

"Who shall we start with?" Katie asked.

"We'll start with Rhys. As far as we know he was the last person to see Sara alive."

* * *

Katie and Graeme could hear Rhys from halfway down the corridor. When Justin showed him in, he was still in full flow. "First time an investigation's been carried out like this, you must admit it's very interesting – quite a challenge," he concluded, looking around, bright-eyed and expectant.

Surely he's not enjoying *this*, Katie thought.

He plonked himself down in the chair that Graeme indicated.

"So," Rhys said briskly, "you want me to prove that I didn't kill Sara. I wouldn't be such a fool as to murder the best-qualified doctor on base – no offence, Katie, you did a splendid job on Adam. But still you can't take my word for it. But I think – *I think* you'll find that I can satisfactorily account for my movements. I see you've got a grid there – very sensible –"

"Rhys," Graeme said.

"Yes?"

"Shut up."

"Oh. Alright."

"Let's start at the beginning. When lunch was over, you went for your appointment with Sara?"

"I helped with the clearing up, then yes, my appointment was for two forty-five and I was there on the dot."

Katie couldn't help being amused. Of course he was!

"And when did you leave?"

"Three. Also on the dot."

"Quite sure about that?" Justin asked. "I had an idea it was three minutes past."

Graeme shot him a reproving look.

"No," Rhys assured them, "definitely three. And she was absolutely fine. Writing up her notes when I left her. Piles, by the way."

"Sorry?"

"Haemorrhoids. That's what I consulted her about."

"Ah." Graeme avoided meeting Katie's eye. "And then what did you do?"

"Went back to the kitchen and made myself a cup of coffee."

"Was there anyone else there?"

"Not when I first went in, but as I was making coffee, Ernesto came in. Then as I was going back to my pit-room, taking my coffee with me, I saw Nick, Craig, and Alex playing Scrabble in the dining room. Then, until six, I was in my pit-room, planning my next moves for my online chess games. So on the face of it, I would not seem to have an alibi for those two and a half hours. However," he beamed at them, "my computer history will prove otherwise. Analysis would show that I was absent only once, when at four fifteen I went back to the kitchen for another coffee. By that time Nick and Craig had gone, but this time Ernesto was there, planning his menus for the restaurant he hopes will one day be awarded a Michelin star. At six, I went to work out in the gym and that was where you found me."

"That all seems satisfactory," Graeme said.

"Excellent." Rhys got to his feet. "Shall I send someone in?" he asked.

"Not yet. Just one thing more." Graeme was looking down at his grid. "When you saw Nick and Craig and Alex playing Scrabble, did they see you?"

For the first time Rhys hesitated. "Yes, and I believe we exchanged a few words."

"Thank you." Graeme made a mark on the grid.

Rhys bounced out of the room.

When the door had closed behind him and his footsteps had faded away, Graeme said, "It does look as if he's in the clear. Unless he somehow rigged his computer. Not very likely, but we will have to check."

Justin shook his head. "He seems to think this is all a game."

"It's just his way," Graeme said. "Let me tell you something. When Sara went missing, Rhys was the very first to come to see me and he volunteered for every search party. No, he's alright is Rhys." He sat back. "I've updated the timetable. That gives us information about Ernesto, Alex, Nick, and Craig."

"One thing," Katie remarked. "If Rhys says it was three on the dot, it *was* three on the dot."

"We can't expect the others to be so precise," Justin sighed.

"Who's up next?" Katie asked.

"I think it'd better be Ernesto," Graeme said. "People would have been in and out of the kitchen fixing themselves drinks and snacks all afternoon. If we can establish who and when, we can fill in some of these spaces on the grid."

* * *

Ernesto spread his hands. "Yes, I am in my kitchen all afternoon – where else would I be? – but I don't remember now who comes and goes. My kitchen is a nice place to be. People in and out all the time."

Graeme and Katie exchanged glances.

"You were in the kitchen all afternoon?" Graeme asked.

Ernesto considered. "Yes, all afternoon. That is, after my rest. I always have a rest after lunch. Just half an hour. I lie down with Raymond Blanc and a double espresso."

Graeme's eyebrows shot up.

"Raymond Blanc's a chef," Justin explained.

"*Le Manoir aux Quat'Saisons*. It is my favourite book," Ernesto said. "And then I go back to the kitchen and get on with planning my menus. It gives me inspiration for a new recipe for chicken cacciatore. Traditional but with a modern twist."

"But you haven't cooked that for us, have you?" Katie asked.

"No, no, not for the base, for menu for my restaurant. And I am thinking again about the layout of the kitchen. But yes, I remember, around half past three I am thinking about what to bake for tea. Alex comes in to get some beer. He asks me, will I make scones and will I put sultanas in the scones for Adam. That is what Adam's mum does. At first I am doubtful." Ernesto pursed his lips and shook his head. "Sultanas in scones? It is not my way, but then I think why not? It is my job to provide good homestyle cooking, and I know the poor boy is homesick, so sultanas go in."

"No point in being precious about it," Justin agreed.

Katie had to resist the urge to kick him under the table.

"Nick and Craig and Alex, I see early in the afternoon, playing Scrabble and then for a while, they are not there. Then Nick comes in to make tea when I am getting the scones out of the oven. They have to wait for the scones to cool down to have with their tea. Then Nick and Craig are playing Scrabble again and are still playing Scrabble when you come looking for Sara."

* * *

"So Rhys said we exchanged a few words, did he?" Nick said. "Actually we told him to – well, to clear off. At least that was the gist of it. You know what he's like, he was hovering over us, commenting on our moves, and when he told Alex that he'd just missed an excellent word using a triple score, it was too much."

Katie scrutinized him, looking for indications that he'd been taking drugs. He was wearing a T-shirt so that his bare arms were exposed. She couldn't spot any needle marks – though the tattoo made it hard to be sure – and of course he'd be careful not to shoot up where they would show. He was pale, but weren't they all after the lack of sunlight?

"And did he?" Graeme asked.

"Did he what?" Nick said.

"Did Rhys clear off?"

"Yes, to be fair, he did. You do have to spell it out with Rhys, but once he gets the message…"

"So you and Alex and Craig were playing Scrabble from after lunch until when exactly...?"

"Well, Alex only played one game. And then he said he was going to go and have a shower. Craig and I had another game."

"And then what?"

"Well, I don't know about Craig, but I went to my pit-room. That would be about a quarter to four. I had a nap. I was there about an hour, I should think. And then I went back to the dining room. Craig was there, so I made us both some tea. Craig and I sat and chatted and drank tea. Then we played Scrabble again."

"What time was it when Alex left you?"

"Maybe a quarter past three? Something like that."

"Did anyone come in later while you were having tea and playing Scrabble again?"

"Yes. Someone did. At least once. Maybe more."

"So who was it?"

"I didn't really notice. I was absorbed in the game."

Graeme consulted his grid. "Was Ernesto there when you made the tea?"

"Ernesto? Yes, he was, now that I come to think of it. He was just getting some scones out of the oven. Craig and I had a laugh about it. He offered to make us espressos – strong enough..."

"...to blow your head off." They finished the sentence in a chorus.

Nick went on, "He had papers spread out all over the table. Menu-planning, he said."

"What time was that?"

"Must have been around quarter to five."

After he'd gone, Graeme said, "Well, Katie?"

"If he is taking drugs, he's doing a good job of covering it up. But then, he's a smart guy. I wouldn't like to say for sure."

Graeme sighed. "OK. We'd better have Craig in."

* * *

Craig was as taciturn as ever, but he did confirm Nick's story. They were together, playing Scrabble all afternoon except for an hour or so, when they went their separate ways. Alex had joined them for the first game – a fairly short one, he seemed to recall. Yes, of course he remembered sending Rhys away with a flea in his ear. He had been intermittently aware of Ernesto in the kitchen. Alex had probably left them around three fifteen. Then he and Nick had had a second game. He had no idea what Nick had done after that, but Craig had gone to his pit-room and watched an episode of *Breaking Bad* on his laptop. He had already watched the whole series at home. It was a modern masterpiece. He had brought the box set with him and was working his way through it again, one episode at a time.

Like Nick, during the second bout of Scrabble he had been vaguely aware of some comings and goings, but he hadn't registered who the individuals were. He had an idea that Ernesto had been in the kitchen throughout, but he couldn't swear to it.

Was that all? Could he get back to work now?

* * *

Alex frowned. "It's hard to remember precisely, but I'll do my best. Let me see... After lunch I stayed in the dining room and had a game of Scrabble with Nick and Craig."

"We didn't think to ask the others," Justin said, "but who won?"

"Oh, Nick did. He almost always does. One game was enough for me. After that, I decided to have a shower. After that –"

"Wait," Graeme said. "What time did you go for your shower?"

"My best guess would be three ten, three fifteen? Then I came back to the kitchen and collected some beer and nachos. I'd agreed to meet young Adam in the TV room to watch *Game of Thrones* and that's what I did. Not my favourite programme, but I like it well enough and I got the impression that he wanted the company so I was happy to go along with it. I knew he was finding the dark days hard going. And that's more or less it. Back-to-back box set viewing for the rest of the afternoon. We cracked open a few beers and I think he enjoyed it. But by around six I'd had enough. I was getting a bit antsy, wanted some exercise before supper, so I left him to it and went off to the gym. I'd just got there when Rhys arrived and that's where you found us when you came looking for Sara."

Graeme said, "So between around half past three and six o'clock you and Adam were together?"

Alex nodded. "That's right. Oh, I'm not saying that we didn't need to relieve ourselves of some of that beer once or twice, but neither of us were gone more than a few minutes."

* * *

"It does seem like Alex is in the clear," Justin said.

"As long as Adam confirms his story for the second part of the afternoon," Graeme agreed.

"And what about Adam? Is he in the clear, too?" Katie asked.

Graeme ran his finger down the grid. "He was in the gym with Justin until three. Then he was with me at three fifteen for around ten minutes. After that he went to the TV room and hunkered down for that marathon DVD session."

"The last half-hour or so isn't accounted for," Justin pointed out.

"We didn't think that was long enough. And anyway if he'd killed Sara, would he really have raised such a hue and cry at six forty-five?" Katie asked.

"If he was clever, that's exactly what he would have done," Justin said.

"Oh, please! Adam? Can you really see it?"

Graeme said, "I agree with you, Katie. I don't believe for a moment that Adam had anything to do with Sara's death. But we'll have to speak to him if only to confirm Alex's alibi. You must see that. And it wouldn't be right to make an exception in his case. We must be seen to be fair."

Katie thought this over. "OK, but he *is* my patient. If he starts to get distressed, I'm calling a halt."

* * *

Graeme said, "We're sure you didn't have anything to do with Sara's death, Adam, but you might be able to help with alibis for some of the others."

Graeme's voice was gentle, fatherly. Adam was still very pale, but he seemed calm enough. He nodded his understanding.

"Well, first of all, I went to the gym and then I saw you. And then I spent the rest of the afternoon watching *Game of Thrones*."

"On your own?"

"Oh no, with Alex. He brought along some beers and nachos, said we'd have a lads' afternoon."

"And you were together all afternoon?"

"Yes. Well, nearly. Alex said he was going to stop and go to the gym at six o'clock and that's what he did. I watched a bit more on my own and then it was nearly half past six and it was time for my table tennis with Sara and that was when –" He gulped and his lower lip began to tremble.

Katie gave Graeme a warning look.

He nodded. "That's fine. All done now. You can go back to your pit-room."

Adam left the room and they waited for his footsteps to die away.

"Well," Justin said, "where does that leave us?"

Graeme ran his finger along the grid. "At first glance it's not looking good for Craig or Nick. Both of them have an hour when there's no one to vouch for them."

There was a knock on the door and Ernesto poked his head round. "Dinner has been ready a long time," he said reproachfully. "The others have all eaten."

213

Katie looked at her watch and was surprised to see that it was nine o'clock. She had lost all track of time.

"OK, we'll come now," Graeme said.

When Ernesto had gone, he said, "There's nothing to be gained by slipping out of our routine – or neglecting the work of the base. Tempting as it is to just push on, I'm going to call a halt for today." He squared away his papers. "It's not as if anyone's going anywhere," he added with grim humour. "Also I need to have a good look at the grid and plan the next move. We'll meet back here tomorrow morning. The bolts should be on the pit-rooms by now and either me or Justin will escort you to yours, Katie, when we've had dinner."

CHAPTER 34

ELY

Rachel dropped Daniel off at his office. She watched as he made his way in, managing his crutches with difficulty. He was wearing one of his older suits with one of the trouser legs slit to accommodate his cast.

They'd already dropped Chloe at school, so now she drove home and parked. She walked slowly along the quayside, enjoying the sheen of green on the weeping willows, pausing to watch the Canada geese pecking the grass. In the marina someone was taking advantage of the fine weather to paint their cruiser. She told herself that she was making the most of a fine spring morning, but she knew really that she was putting something off. She reached home, unlocked the door and went in, leaned with her back against the closed door, and gave a sigh.

For the first time in days she had the house to herself. She wanted to be alone for what she had to do.

When she had gone out to get a prescription for Daniel a couple of days ago, she had bought something else for herself, something that she had been careful to conceal in a drawer. Five minutes later she was sitting on the toilet lid in the bathroom, looking at the two blue bars that had appeared in the little window of the white plastic wand. She looked again at the diagram in the leaflet, read the leaflet again, then realized that she hadn't taken in a word. But in any case she didn't need to read it. She was pregnant. She had known it from the moment that she had realized she was a week late. She was normally as regular as clockwork. How had it happened? She reminded herself that no method is a hundred per cent reliable. We may think that we are in complete control of our bodies, but we're not. Not really.

She thought Daniel trusted her enough to know that she hadn't done it on purpose. Though now she wondered if it had been completely accidental. What did Freud call it? The psychopathology of everyday life? Those things that happen accidentally on purpose! Perhaps part of her wanted this so much that she had somehow willed it to happen. Because she knew now how very much she wanted another child – and not just for Chloe's sake.

It didn't matter really how it had happened. A warmth was spreading through her, a warmth that seemed at one with the sunshine and the freshness of the spring day. Already she was beginning to love this baby.

But how was she going to break the news to Daniel?

* * *

"I got something from the editor of *The European Journal of Molecular Oncology* last night," Lyle said.

He had rung mid-morning on Daniel's first day back in the office.

He went on. "We had a drink together and I brought the conversation round to the article that Kieran Langstaffe and Alistair Johnson-Marsh submitted. He said he couldn't be expected to remember every article that was submitted and turned down, especially when it was several years ago. I pressed a bit more – mentioned that they'd later published something on similar lines – and I could see that he'd remembered something. Then *he* started quizzing *me* about it, wanting to know why I was interested. Then he admitted that he did remember it now, but he couldn't recall offhand who the referees had been. I said he was bound to have a record of it.

And he agreed, but then he said that it was confidential and he wouldn't be able to tell me."

"So that's that?"

"Not quite. More and more was coming back to him. He said it had been a rather unusual case. One reader was perfectly happy with it, enthusiastic even, and the other had slated it. In the end he'd felt that he couldn't ignore the negative report. I got the impression that the referee was a pretty big gun. I think I'd got him rattled, that he'd made some kind of connection that worried him. So when we said goodbye in the pub, I pretended to go to the bathroom. As soon as he thought I was out of sight, he got out his cell phone and made a call. Dollars to doughnuts he was ringing one of the referees."

"Well maybe, but it doesn't get us much further, does it?"

"Ah, that's not all. I thought long and hard about who those referees might be and I got an idea about that. It's a fairly small field. And I thought I knew someone who might be able to help. I've just spoken to her on the phone."

Daniel shook his head, marvelling. How was it that Lyle always knew someone or, at the very least, someone who knew someone else? This was the secret of his success, no doubt, especially as he usually got what he wanted from them.

Lyle said, "I thought bare minimum she'd be able to give me an idea of who the readers might be. But it was better than that. She was one of them! And she was pretty teed off when the paper was turned down. Her theory was – and I quote – that: 'one of the big beasts in her field had put the kibosh on it'. She gave me a shortlist of possible names and – what do you know – Cameron was on it!"

"Did she tell anyone about this?"

"I pressed her on that, and eventually she admitted that she had let something slip. She got drunk at a party and found herself talking to Langstaffe's research partner, Johnson-Marsh. She commended him for good work and told him that

217

she couldn't understand why the paper had been turned down. She says he could have worked out for himself that someone more important than her must have given it a bad report – and that he was probably capable of working out who that person might be."

"And then worked out that Cameron had passed on his and Kieran's research to Flora. Perhaps he went to confront her and ended up killing her."

"It's a possibility. But we still don't know where the hell he is, do we? I'm going to the police with this."

* * *

Daniel decided to take an early lunch. He needed to get out of the office and think about what Lyle had told him. He told his secretary that he'd be back in an hour, groped for his crutch, and made his way out into the cathedral close.

Clouds scudded across the April sky. For a moment he had the sensation that it was not they, but the cathedral that was moving, as though it were some vast ship swaying at anchor. He knew that Rachel often went in to sit in the cathedral and say a prayer. He tended to cross the threshold only for special events like midnight mass, but today he felt drawn to it. Perhaps that is where most of us do turn, when it comes to matters of life and death, he thought.

He made his way slowly across the green. He was more used now to his crutch and the swelling was going down on his hand, too. But still he hated being in plaster. It was like being hobbled – or having a ball and chain, frightening almost to have his freedom of movement curtailed. He felt an affinity with all those who were halt and lame and was humbled. He vowed never again to take his health for granted.

Inside the cathedral the sound of his crutch echoed on the flagstones. He struggled to find his resident's pass in his wallet, showed it at the ticket desk, and walked down the aisle. He wanted somewhere quiet to sit and saw that there was no one in Bishop Alcock's chapel. He went in. It was a small, dark chamber, crammed with carved and bristly canopies. He read a notice that told him that they had come from some other chapel, so that was, no doubt, why the scale was all wrong. In the dim light he seemed almost to make out skulls in the busy details of the carvings.

He sat down. He yawned and ran his hand over his face. They'd had another bad night with Chloe. He found himself thinking not of work, but of the accident that could so easily have taken his life. We think we are in control, but we aren't. It had been a mistake to live in fear of what might happen if Rachel got pregnant. Nothing is ever a hundred per cent safe. He knew that now.

The already dim light in the chapel was fading and pools of darkness were forming. Rain had been forecast.

When he got home this evening, he was going to tell Rachel what he had learned. *Life is short and unpredictable and we have to seize the moment. Let's try for a baby – and not just for Chloe either, but for its own sake and for what it will bring to our lives.*

From somewhere in the cathedral came a distant sound of children laughing and calling. It was hard to tell where noises were coming from in the vast echoing space of the cathedral.

That was why Daniel didn't realize that he was no longer alone until someone sat down beside him. His heart skipped a beat. It was Professor Cameron.

Cameron said, "I was on the way to your office and I saw you go into the cathedral."

Daniel eyed him warily. "What do you want, Professor Cameron?"

"Lyle's been asking questions about the Langstaffe and Johnson-Marsh paper. Larry rang me after Lyle had spoken to him. It mustn't come out."

So Lyle was right. Cameron had been one of the readers of the Langstaffe and Johnson-Marsh paper.

"You were the one who turned the paper down," Daniel said.

Cameron nodded. "That's right. Good idea, but it was seriously flawed, problems with the methodology."

"That's not true. You didn't turn it down because you thought it was no good. Quite the reverse. You turned it down because you'd seen its potential."

"No."

"I've read it, Cameron. I know what you did. You handed their discovery to Flora. You stole it. You took it and you made sure that Kieran's paper wasn't published."

Cameron was a dark shape in the gloom, sitting with slumped shoulders. They sat in silence and then at last he said, "It was very early days with me and Flora. No one knew about us. We were very discreet. Of course I knew all about her work, that was what had brought us together in the first place. She asked my advice, and I was flattered. It went on from there. We were in bed when I told her about the paper. It hadn't occurred to me until then that I might suppress it. But when Flora talked about getting a head start, I realized what she was thinking. It was something I could do for her. It's not as if she wasn't talented, she was a first-rate scientist. I knew what she'd be able to do with it. And then – I've never felt like that about anyone, I'd have done *anything* for her."

Daniel thought of Kieran, sitting in that room in south-west London, surrounded by towering Lego constructions, the brilliant mind occluded, the faithful mother mourning the loss of the man he had been.

"How could you do that?" Dan asked. "Someone of your stature, your eminence. You're a *scientist*, for God's sake. What's this going to do to your reputation when this gets out?"

"It mustn't come out. Flora's dead." Daniel heard the pain in Cameron's voice. "I don't want her name traduced. She didn't just take Langstaffe's idea. She understood the potential in a way that he hadn't, she took it further. It was a true breakthrough, a genuine scientific achievement. I want her to be remembered for that."

Daniel could find it in his heart to feel sorry for him. He had lost the woman he loved, and perhaps that was punishment enough. But still justice must be done. "Langstaffe should have his due, too," he pointed out.

"Is it really going to make any difference to him now? Would he even be able to take it in? Yes," Cameron said, catching the expression on Daniel's face, "I know about his illness."

"If you know that, you know that you blighted someone's career. No, worse than that. You blighted someone's *life*."

"Someone who wasn't normal, someone who was already... fragile. If it hadn't been that, it would have been something else."

Daniel was shocked. "You really think that this can be brushed under the carpet?"

Cameron put his hand on Daniel's arm. He spoke fast. "Well, can't it? It's not in Lyle's interest – or Theseus's either – to have doubt thrown on the validity of the patent. I'm sure the editor of *The European Journal of Molecular Oncology* would be quite happy for this to go away. He'd prefer not to have a scandal centring around his publication." His hand closed on Daniel's arm. "There's no real evidence either," Cameron continued. "Who's to say that Flora didn't stumble across the idea of stimulating apoptosis in cancer cells all on her own?"

Organ music came drifting into the chapel, a tantalizingly familiar tune, just on the edge of Daniel's memory.

He said, "You misjudge Lyle. He wouldn't be involved in a cover-up. And even if he would, I certainly wouldn't."

Cameron tightened the grip of his fingers. Daniel winced. He was conscious of the solid bulk of the man and of his own vulnerability, tethered as he was by his cast. Still he couldn't stop himself. "You're supposed to care about the truth. That is what science is all about. You cheated and you lied. And so did Flora. You still don't understand, do you? When you were indulging in the pillow talk with Flora, you –"

Daniel's phone rang, strident and shocking. He'd forgotten

221

to switch it off when he entered the cathedral. He pulled it out of his pocket and saw that the call was from Lyle.

He answered it.

Lyle said, "I've just heard from a contact – it's not public knowledge yet – they've found a stab wound on Sara's body –"

"A stab wound! You mean she was *murdered*?"

"Looks that way."

"I've got Cameron here. He's admitted the fraud."

"Keep him there. We need to talk. I've got a lead on Johnson-Marsh as well. I think he's going by another name. I'm going to speak to the police and then I'm on my way up." Lyle hung up.

"What's happened?" Cameron asked.

"Sara McKee was murdered. I don't think it's just coincidence that both she and Flora are dead, do you?"

"But that can't be – not Langstaffe…"

"No, it wasn't Langstaffe. But who else could have found out about you and Flora? Who could have guessed that you'd given her Langstaffe's research and made sure that his paper wouldn't be published? There was another name on that unpublished research paper."

Cameron let go of Daniel's arm and buried his head in his hands. "No, no, it can't be." His voice was muffled. Daniel understood that he was desperately trying to defend himself from this bitter knowledge. But sooner or later he would not be able to deny the truth and when that happened, it would destroy him.

CHAPTER 35

ANTARCTICA

Breakfast was a silent affair. Katie, Graeme, and Justin sat separately from the others, who had in any case arrived in dribs and drabs. Katie hadn't slept well. Lying awake, a horrible thought had occurred to her. Awful as it would be to discover which of them was a murderer, it would be even worse if they didn't find out. If they had to spend the entire winter not knowing, they might go off their heads and when outsiders at last arrived at the base they might be discovered barricaded in their pit-rooms, surviving on individual caches of tinned food.

And another thought occurred to her: something she and Sara had joked about. But perhaps it wasn't a joke. She voiced her suspicions when she and Graeme and Justin had convened in Graeme's office.

"Do you think there's something a bit odd about Craig?" she asked.

"How do you mean?" Graeme asked.

"Well, he never really says anything about his life before he came here. Had you noticed?"

"Actually he never says much of anything," Justin pointed out. "But now you come to mention it..."

"There can't be anything sinister about it, can there?" Katie asked. "I mean he couldn't be escaping from the law?"

"Not a chance," Graeme said. "He'd never have got the job here. Everyone's vetted. So we can be certain that he hasn't got a criminal record and he's not wanted by the police. More likely to be an unhappy marriage or something like that."

"But what if there was *something* shady?" Katie persisted. "I don't know – maybe he's not who he claims to be. And Sara found out."

They pondered this. "You might have a point," Graeme said slowly. "Because I've looked very carefully at the grid, and there's no getting away from it. Craig and Nick are the only ones with any length of time unaccounted for. Both of them claim to have spent an hour in their pit-room, but no one can corroborate that. We'll have to have them both in again. And I'm afraid this time, I will have to raise the question of Nick's history of drug-taking. I'm sorry, Justin."

Justin said, "Before you do that, I've had an idea. There's something I want to try. Let's call Craig in again."

"What's the idea?" Katie asked.

"I'd rather not say just yet. I might be quite wrong, but there's something I want to ask both Craig and Nick and I don't want them to have a chance to confer..."

Justin went to get Craig and brought him back.

Craig sat down and looked at Graeme, waiting for a lead. Graeme said, "Justin has something he wants to ask you."

Justin said, "It's just this. After Alex left, you and Nick went on playing Scrabble, didn't you?"

Craig nodded. Katie thought he looked wary.

Justin said, "Who won?"

"Who won?" Craig repeated.

"Yes, who won? It's quite a simple question, surely."

"I'm... not sure."

"Really? Competitive as you both are, you're not sure?"

"I think... Nick won... yes, that's right. Nick won that time and I won later in the afternoon. It was a draw. One all."

"OK. Would you mind waiting next door in the communications room?"

Katie thought Craig was about to protest, but he just bit his lip and nodded.

* * *

"Who does Craig say won?" Nick asked.

"Never mind about that." Graeme had taken over the questioning. "We are asking *you.*"

Nick considered. "Craig won the first game and I won the second."

There was silence. He looked at their faces, "Or it might have been the other way round..."

Justin said, "You know what I think? You didn't finish that first game, did you? That's why neither of you know who won. No one won."

Nick laughed. "It's a fair cop. I told Craig that we ought to come clean. He said, only if it's essential. Well, clearly it *is* essential and we've got nothing to be ashamed of. We've, well, we've fallen in love. I liked him right from the beginning, but he's not one to wear his heart on his sleeve and I wasn't sure how he felt about me. And then that afternoon I got the idea from reading *Anna Karenina*. There's a bit where Levin proposes to Kitty. They're playing a game with cards with letters on them. He spells out the initials of what he wants to say. I laid out a message on the Scrabble board. And Craig replied." He was blushing. "We went to my pit-room to talk things over and be alone together."

Graeme said, "So are you saying that you and Craig spent the whole afternoon together?"

"We weren't apart at any time for longer than it takes to go and have a slash."

Justin said, "And now we know why neither you nor Craig could tell us who came in or out during that second bout of Scrabble. You only had eyes for each other!"

Nick smiled. "It's true. I was in a bit of a daze."

"OK," Graeme said. "You can go."

Nick got up to leave and Graeme said, "Just one more thing. Do you know why Craig never talks about his life before he came here?"

Nick began to laugh. "Yes, I do, but I don't think it's for me to tell you. You'd better ask him yourself. One thing I will say though. It has absolutely nothing to do with anything that's happened on base."

When he'd gone, Graeme asked, "Do we believe him?"

"Yes, we do," Justin said. "I already knew that Nick was gay. I didn't see him and Craig kissing or holding hands or anything as obvious as that, but I had a feeling..."

"It's romantic, really," Katie said. "You know, I can see that they might be rather well suited."

"We'd better get Craig back," Graeme said.

* * *

"Oh alright then. Yes, if you must know, yes, we were together all afternoon," Craig said. "Nick wanted to tell you earlier. I couldn't see that it was anyone's business but ours. We knew that neither of us had anything to do with what happened to Sara."

"And now that we know it too, we're that much further forward," Graeme pointed out.

Craig had the grace to look embarrassed. "Sorry. I've never liked having my private life on display. And it's been that much worse –" He broke off.

Katie was willing Graeme to probe a bit more. He caught her eye and she made a face that said, "Go on!"

He took pity on her. "Is there something else we ought to know, Craig?"

Craig pondered. "Well, I suppose it can't do any harm. Maybe best under the circumstances to have everything out in the open. Yes, I had a special reason for coming here. I had to get away. You see, it's like this. For the past couple of years, my life's been hell. Ever since I won the lottery."

There was a stunned silence, then Katie said, "You won the lottery? How much did you win?"

"A million and a half. I wasn't one of those mega-winners.

Unless you followed the lottery closely, you wouldn't know. I thought I'd be safe enough here with other scientists – they tend to be a bit snooty about the lottery. The only person who thought he'd heard my name somewhere before was Adam, but he couldn't remember where."

"The odds are hugely against any one individual winning," Justin said. "I expect Rhys could give you the statistics."

Craig said, "At first it was great. I bought myself a house, looked after the family – bought a little flat for Mum – and gave some to charity. But everybody else wanted something from me. The begging letters, you wouldn't believe! And then one evening I was having a quiet drink on my own in a bar, and someone said to me, 'Aren't you that guy who won the lottery? Why aren't you buying drinks all round?' The next day I applied to BAS."

* * *

"They could be in it together," Graeme said when Craig had gone, but his heart clearly wasn't in it.

Katie said, "It's hard enough to believe that there's one person among us responsible for Sara's death, but two... what possible motivation could they have?"

Graeme updated his grid and then sat back. He drummed his fingers on the table.

"What's the matter, Graeme?" Katie asked.

"If we do rule out Craig and Nick on the grounds of their joint testimony, then I have a problem. According to the grid, I ought to be arresting myself. I'm the only one who had enough time to do it. At the critical time I was alone in my pit-room with no one to vouch for me."

"We must have got something wrong," Justin said.

"I can't see where. Everyone else is accounted for. See for yourself." He turned the grid around and Katie and Justin looked at it.

It was just as Graeme had said.

Katie said. "Someone's made a mistake about the time – or else two of them were in it together – unlikely as it seems."

"And not necessarily Craig and Nick," Graeme said. "Adam and Alex were also alone together for a long stretch of time with no one else to vouch for them."

"Frankly that seems even more unlikely than Craig and Nick."

Justin was still bending thoughtfully over the grid. He looked up and said, "There's another possibility. We've been thinking that it couldn't be done in under about forty minutes – that it would take that long to kill Sara and get her body off the platform. Maybe that's where we made our mistake."

"We timed it," Katie pointed out. "It must have taken at least that."

"I'm not sure. Perhaps it would have been possible to shave that down to half an hour. But let's go on saying half an hour. My question is this: did it have to be a continuous half-hour? I mean, did it have to happen all at once?"

"How do you mean?" Graeme asked.

"Well, what if the killer went along to the surgery and killed Sara and hid the body and then went back to establish his alibi? He could have gone back later to take the body outside."

Katie said, "But that would be even riskier than if he did it all at once. I mean what if someone had come looking for Sara? We might easily have realized that she was missing earlier than we did. If we'd started a search earlier, we would have found the body, if it was still on the base."

"Was it likely though, that anyone would go looking?" Justin asked. "If you had gone to look for her in the surgery, what would you have thought if you hadn't found her?"

Katie thought it over. "I'd have probably thought she was having a nap in her pit-room," she admitted. "I wouldn't have wanted to disturb her."

"Exactly. That's what anyone would have thought. It's

natural for someone to want a bit of privacy now and again and the rest of us respect that. It was only because she'd arranged to meet Adam at six that we discovered then that she was missing. Otherwise we wouldn't have realized until she didn't show up at supper time."

Graeme said, "So what are you saying? That he could have split it up into two tasks? – for want of a better word."

"Maybe even three. One: there's the actual murder. We're agreed that he probably went straight in and stabbed her. He'd have to hide the body. Maybe in the generator room? He could do that in ten minutes, maybe less. Two: he goes back to dress her in her outdoor clothes. Later he goes back a third time and takes the body outside and hides it. That's the most time-consuming bit. What if he'd prepared a hiding place earlier that day? But even if he hadn't, it could be done in less than half an hour."

Graeme said, "And between times he's establishing his presence, dropping into the kitchen for a chat with Ernesto or exchanging a bit of banter at the Scrabble table. He'd have to have nerves of steel, but I think you may be onto something, Justin. Let's have another look at this grid."

Katie felt cold. It was a nightmarish thought. It was bad enough to think of someone murdering Sara on the spur of the moment and hurrying to cover it up, but to imagine this level of cold-blooded planning and premeditation was chilling. She thought again of that perfectly placed wound...

Wound! How could she have forgotten! She looked at her watch. She should have dressed Adam's wound half an hour ago. The poor guy would be waiting in her surgery. She got up to go. Graeme and Justin looked up from where they were poring over the grid.

She said, "I'd forgotten about my appointment with Adam."

"Justin will go with you," Graeme said.

She was about to protest, but then thought better of it.

229

Justin said, "Can you take a look at my hand, while you're at it? It's been a while."

They walked down the corridor past the dining room. It was smoko time and Ernesto was doggedly sticking to the routine. Coffee and cake were set out on the table. But no one was gathering convivially any more. People came and took their coffee and cake away.

Adam was not after all waiting at the surgery. Katie took advantage of his not being there to examine Justin's hand. It had healed well. "You can keep these bandages off now," she said.

"Thank goodness for that."

Katie checked the time again. "I wonder what's happened to Adam."

Her eyes met Justin's and they exchanged uneasy glances.

"We'd better go and look for him," Justin said.

They walked back through the dining room and poked their heads into the kitchen where Ernesto was rolling dough for homemade ravioli. He said that he hadn't seen Adam since breakfast. They opened the doors to the TV room and the music room and gym – though he was hardly likely to be there. There was no one around except for Craig in the Communications room. Everyone else was no doubt at work in the labs on the floor above.

Adam had probably fallen asleep in his pit-room. But when they knocked on the door there was no answer. Justin pushed the door open and they looked in. There were dirty socks balled and scattered on the floor and Katie doubted if he'd changed the bed since he'd arrived in Antarctica. The man himself wasn't there.

By now Katie had butterflies in her stomach. Where could he be? They were still standing in the corridor outside his room, when Justin laid a hand on her arm and said, "What's that noise?" There was a kind of rhythmic rumbling coming from somewhere. They went on down the corridor to where the door to the library and quiet room stood ajar.

They went in. Adam was there, sprawled out on a sofa, a book about Sheffield Wednesday lying open on his chest. He was snoring loudly.

"Sounds like someone rolling potatoes down a corrugated iron roof," Justin said. He leaned over and shook Adam's shoulder.

Adam woke with a start. When he saw them gazing down at him, there was a flicker of panic in his eyes. "What? What's happened?"

"Nothing's happened," Katie said. "It's fine. Except that you were supposed to be in the surgery almost an hour ago to have your wound dressed."

He blinked and rubbed his eyes. "What time is it?"

She looked at her watch. "Half eleven."

"At night? Or in the morning?"

"In the morning!"

"Oh sorry – I'm always losing track –"

And he didn't have a watch, Katie had noticed. Even though he wasn't that much younger than her, it was a generational thing. He had always relied on his mobile phone to tell him the time, so he'd never bothered with a wristwatch.

"You really shouldn't be sleeping during the day," she chided him gently. "I know that Graeme's spoken to you about the dangers of disrupting your sleep pattern."

"I know." Gingerly, anxious not to pull on his stitches, he swung his legs off the sofa. Justin stuck a hand under his elbow and helped him to his feet.

* * *

All the time that Katie was examining Adam something was nagging away at her. The wound had healed beautifully. She couldn't help feeling proud of her handiwork. "You'll do," she said. "Normal activity will be fine now, but no heavy lifting for a couple of weeks more at least."

And yet still something was bothering her. It wasn't until Adam had left and she and Justin were walking back to Graeme's office that the penny dropped. She stood stock-still. Justin walked on without realizing that she had stopped. When he saw that she wasn't with him, he turned to look at her.

"Hey, what's up?" He looked at her more closely. "Katie, you've gone as white as a sheet."

She couldn't speak for a few moments. Could it really be? Had she discovered how the trick had been worked? She realized now that she hadn't completely accepted that someone on the base was a murderer. Some small part of her had clung to the thought that there must be some mistake and the interviews had allowed her to go on thinking that. If no one could have killed Sara, perhaps no one had.

She raised her eyes to Justin's. How tired he looked. The laughter lines around his eyes seemed to have deepened just in the last few days.

He came up and put his hand on her arm. "Katie? Katie, love! What is it?"

"I think I know how he did it," she said.

* * *

"Have I done something wrong?" Adam quavered. They had called him back into the office.

Katie was happy to leave the questioning to Graeme.

His voice was kind, reassuring.

"Just one or two details we need to go over." He glanced down at the grid. "You spent most of the afternoon with Alex watching *Game of Thrones*. How long are the episodes?"

Adam's face registered relief. He could answer that. "Around fifty-five or sixty minutes."

"How many episodes of *Game of Thrones* did you watch that afternoon, Adam?"

"Three."

"Whole episodes?"

"Well, no. I remember feeling a bit narked, like, because I hadn't finished the last one and it were time to go and meet Sara for our game of ping-pong."

"How much was there still to go?"

"Not sure exactly, but it weren't very near the end. If it had only been five or ten minutes, I'd have waited until it was finished. So it might have been twenty minutes or half an hour?"

Graeme was looking at the grid and frowning. "But it says here that you were in the TV room from three thirty to six thirty. If the episodes were an hour each, even allowing for loo breaks, why couldn't you manage to fit three in?"

Adam stared at Graeme, nonplussed. "I hadn't thought of that..." His face cleared as an explanation occurred to him. "We must've started later than I thought. Aye, that'll be it."

The lights flickered and went out. They sat in darkness, waiting for the outage to be over, but nothing happened. Katie could hear Graeme fumbling in his desk and cursing and then the beam of light from a torch split the darkness.

A moment later the lights came back on, only to flicker, and go off, and then come on again.

Adam said, "I'd best go and see what's up with the generator. Is that alright?"

Graeme nodded. "That's all I wanted to know. You can go now."

Adam left the room.

They listened to his footsteps retreating down the corridor.

"They didn't though, did they?" Justin said, as soon as he was out of earshot. "Start later, I mean."

Graeme's face was grim. "No, I don't think they did. Can you go and find Rhys and bring him here, Justin? And then Alex."

* * *

233

Katie was sitting against the wall, where she could watch the door. Her mouth was dry and looking around she saw her own tension mirrored in the faces of the others. Graeme was behind his desk. Justin was sitting close by, his chair angled protectively towards her. Craig was in a chair by the door, leaning forward with his hands clasped on his bare knees. He was under strict instructions not to speak.

When Alex came in, he scanned the room and Katie thought she saw something wary in his expression when he spotted Craig. If so it was gone immediately and he was back to his genial self.

"What's all this?" he asked, smiling.

"Please take a seat, Alex. I just want to verify something that Adam told us. You said earlier that you were with him solidly between three thirty and six."

"That's right."

"He wasn't absent for any length of time – a toilet break – or anything else that took more than a few minutes?"

"No, I told you. He went for a pee once, I remember that, but he was gone hardly any time at all. I'm sure he's in the clear."

"I think Adam *is* in the clear."

"So if that's all..." Alex pushed his chair back, preparing to leave.

"It's not all," Graeme said. "Sit down." There was something in his voice that Katie hadn't heard before, a steeliness and a command that had the effect of freezing Alex halfway to his feet.

No one spoke. Katie held her breath. The room had gone very still.

"Sit down," Graeme repeated.

Katie thought that Alex wasn't going to obey him. But then he shrugged and sank back in his chair. His face was impassive. She knew what was coming next and she wondered if Alex did too. A shiver ran up her spine.

Graeme said, "Adam is in the clear. But you are not. Alex

Marsh, with the power vested in me as a magistrate, I am arresting you on suspicion of murder. I am issuing a police caution. You do not have to say anything. But it may harm your defence if you do not mention when questioned something which you later rely on in court. Anything you do say may be given in evidence."

Alex's jaw dropped. "You can't be serious?"

Katie thought that his surprise was genuine. It hadn't occurred to him that he might be found out. He recovered himself and laughed. He looked around at the others as if to see whether this was a joke and they were all in on it. No one wanted to meet his eye.

He turned back to Graeme. "When exactly am I supposed to have done this? I was watching telly all afternoon."

"No, you weren't. You stole some of that time from Adam – I don't know how much. It might have been as long as half an hour, but it was certainly over twenty minutes. You waited until he had fallen asleep. You noted where you'd got to in the episode of *Game of Thrones* that you were watching. When you got back from disposing of the body, you rewound the DVD and woke Adam up, giving him the impression that he'd only dropped off for a few moments. You knew he wasn't wearing a watch and had been getting confused about time and would be unlikely to realize what had happened."

Alex gave a snort of laughter, but his eyes were cold. "A plan that relied on someone falling asleep in front of the TV? It's ridiculous. Absolutely bonkers."

"Is it?" Katie said. "You knew that Adam was struggling with his sleep patterns. And that he'd had a large meal with beer. And then you made sure that he had more beer. Along with nachos. So plenty of beer *and* carbs. The chances of him dropping off were excellent; in fact, it was pretty inevitable."

"And anyway," Justin said, "You were just being careful, covering all the bases. You didn't think you were going to need an alibi, because you thought Sara's death would be regarded as an accident. If Adam hadn't fallen asleep, or if he'd woken up and found that you weren't there, you'd have made some excuse or other and Adam wouldn't have thought anything of it. You didn't need to be away long. Typical of you, really: belt and braces. Clever – but a bit too clever as it turned out."

Alex shook his head in apparent disbelief. "I killed Sara and took her body out into a blizzard and hid it? In under half an hour?"

Graeme spoke with calm authority. "No. You killed her and hid her body, probably in the generator room, earlier in the afternoon – after you had played Scrabble and before you joined Adam in the TV room. During the time that you claimed to be having a shower."

Alex said, "You can't prove that. You really don't have any evidence for these allegations."

Justin said, "How did you know the body was taken out in a blizzard? That didn't start until around four o'clock."

Katie saw a flicker of something in Alex's eyes. Doubt? Fear?

She said, "And are you absolutely certain that when the police finally get here, they won't find forensic evidence that ties you to the murder? You do know that DNA is preserved by freezing?"

No one spoke for what seemed an eternity. Then the silence was broken by a sound that couldn't have been more ordinary, and yet was shocking in its incongruity. The telephone rang.

* * *

It could only be HQ.

They sat and listened to Graeme's side of the conversation.

Graeme nodded. "I see, yes…" His eyes rested on Alex. "Yes, I have him here. I'm not surprised to hear that. We'd reached pretty much the same conclusion."

He listened some more and his eyes widened in surprise.

"Will do." He put down the phone.

"We'll be keeping you in some form of custody, Alex, until the winter is over. We're not the only ones who have been putting two and two together. The police also want to question you about the death of Sara's research colleague, a woman called Flora Mitchell. They say that they have evidence against you and that you're their main suspect."

Alex sat back and folded his arms. He stared at Graeme defiantly. Was he going to go on denying it all, Katie wondered? And what would they do if he did? And come to that, how on earth were they going to find somewhere to lock him up for six months or more?

The silence stretched out.

When Alex did speak, it wasn't what Katie was expecting.

"I'm not sorry. They deserved what they got, both of them."

Katie could hardly believe her ears. "They deserved it?" she said. "Sara deserved to be stabbed to death? She was a good woman! How could you think that? You must be mad."

Alex's expression didn't change. "I don't *think* it. I *know*. You didn't know Kieran, you haven't seen Kieran as he is now. Some things are worse than death. He was..." Alex groped for words, "...he was this brilliant towering intellect, always coming up with ideas for new ways of doing things. I was the down-to-earth one, the organizer, the plodder who could keep their head down and work out the details. We were a team. He had this idea for using cytochrome c to trigger apoptosis in cancer cells and between us we managed to get it to work. Kieran wrote a paper and put it forward for publication. It would have made our names. Kieran should have had his own lab by now and in the end, maybe, a Nobel Prize, why not? He really was that good. Nothing was impossible, and he'd have taken me along with him. Instead the paper was turned down and that was the end of everything. We were dead in the water. We couldn't get research money. Kieran couldn't get another job. It was after that that he started to get ill. And then we saw the paper that Flora Mitchell had published in *Oncogene*.

Using our research! We couldn't understand it – how had she got hold of the results of our experiments? She *had* to have had them. But we couldn't *prove* that she'd even seen our research, let alone stolen it. And then it all happened so fast. Almost before we knew it, Kieran had been sectioned. I'd been a mature student when I went to university in my mid-twenties to do medicine and later research. When I couldn't get another research post, I went back to my old trade as a mechanic. But Kieran..." He shook his head. "Well, your friend, the patent lawyer, has seen him. Kieran's mum told me that. So he knows..."

Katie went cold. To think that someone could become so obsessed with revenge that they could kill the people they thought had wronged them. But now that she knew, it seemed almost that it should have been clear all along that it was Alex. Who after all was better equipped to deal with the ferocious blizzard on the day that Sara disappeared? She understood why he had been so disconcerted when she had caught him out over the plaster cast. He *had* done it before as part of his medical training – the training he hadn't wanted anyone on base to know about, the training that had enabled him to wield that scalpel with such speed and precision.

Alex went on. "We didn't know who the readers of our paper had been. I thought for a long time about how I could find out what had happened – why it had been turned down – and in the end it was just luck. I was at a party and this woman had had a bit too much to drink and told me that she'd been one of the readers for our paper. She'd recommended publication and been overruled. She didn't know who the other reader had been, but mentioned one or two people who had the clout to do that. I looked them up online and one of them was Cameron. He and Flora Mitchell had just got married. So then I knew. It was obvious. He'd passed on our ideas to her and had made sure that our paper didn't get published. I tracked her down the day before I flew out here. I thought of killing Cameron as well, but this way is better. I want him to know what he's lost and I want him to be exposed for what he is. I want him to really suffer."

Everyone was staring at him now, struck dumb by his admission.

Katie was lifted up on a wave of incandescent fury. At the same time her eyes filled with tears. She wanted to hurt him, to hit him, to slap his face, to pull his hair, to knee him in the balls.

"But Alex, Sara! Why did you kill Sara? She didn't know! She didn't have anything to do with stealing your research. She was completely innocent."

Alex stared at her. "Of course she knew! How could she not? She was working with Flora. Her name was on the paper."

"Sara hadn't a clue. I'm sure of that. She thought it was all Flora's idea. Flora came in one day and suggested that they try something new. She told me that it was down to Flora's generosity that they both had their names on the paper. And she told me all about Kieran coming to their lab and accusing them of stealing his research. She wouldn't have talked about it the way she did if she'd thought for a moment that what Kieran said was true!"

The lights flickered. Katie realized it wasn't just that she felt cold. It *was* cold. The heating must have gone off.

They heard footsteps in the corridor. The door was flung open and Adam appeared in the doorway, flushed and breathless. "Graeme, can you come? Now, please? We've got a problem with the generators."

And then the lights went out.

CHAPTER 36

Graeme cursed and fumbled in his desk for a torch. His fingers closed around it just as the emergency lighting came on.

He sent Adam back to the monitoring room and told Justin and Craig to take Alex to the quiet room and keep him there until further notice. He caught up with Adam at the door of the monitoring room. They went in and Adam explained that the generator in the office block had apparently overheated and switched itself off half an hour ago. He'd thought that it might be a blocked pressure release valve or a faulty thermostat, but now that a second generator had gone, the one that served the living quarters...

Two generators failing at the same time! Graeme had never known that happen before. Four separate generators provided heating as well as all the rest of the base's electrical power needs.

A loud bleeping began. Adam went over and switched the alarm off. He turned to Graeme.

"Flaming Nora! Number three's gone! That's the one that feeds the workshops and the garage! That only leaves the one for the summer quarters."

This was crazy, totally unprecedented in Graeme's experience. What on earth could have happened?

"OK," Graeme began, "the first thing we need to do is –"

The bleeping began again. Adam swung round to look at the monitor and turned back to Graeme, his mouth a perfect O. For a few moments he seemed lost for words, then he darted across and switched off the alarm.

"That's number four gone! That's all of them! What are we

going to do?" There was panic in his voice. "With no heating – it's fifty below outside – what will we do? We'll freeze!"

Graeme assessed the situation. The emergency lighting would last for only a few hours and already the temperature was plummeting. With the generators gone, everything was gone – heating, lights, running water, sewage system. Communication, too, very likely. It was vital they isolate the fault and fix it as soon as possible – and for that he needed Adam.

He put his hand on the younger man's arm. "Listen to me, Adam." But Adam wasn't hearing him. He was breathing hard and his eyes were unfocused. "Adam? Adam! No one is going to die. OK? Even if we can't restore the power, we'll survive. There's enough fuel and food to last until the winter's over. Do you understand?"

Strictly speaking this was true. They had basic survival equipment of the kind that field parties used when they went on trips: tents, camping stoves, heavy-duty sleeping bags. They weren't going to meet the fate of Scott and his companions. But they were in for a difficult and dangerous time with the margin of safety reduced to a narrow edge – not to mention the psychological impact of having to survive for months in such conditions. And what the devil was he going to do about Alex? But one thing at a time. Focus on the present, on the immediate problem. And that was Adam. He was their plumbing and heating engineer and he was on the verge of losing it, poor kid. And no wonder! Appendicitis. A murder on base. Graeme felt like losing it himself.

He took a deep breath. He gripped Adam's arm and looked into his face. He spoke sharply. "Look at me, Adam. We're going to find out what's wrong. And we'll sort it. OK? We can do this. I need you to focus, Adam."

He held Adam's eyes with his own and saw rationality return.

Adam sighed. "Yeah. Sorry. Of course." Something occurred to him and he brightened up. "I wasn't really thinking. We've got the backup generator, haven't we?"

"That's right. So we have." He clapped Adam on the shoulder.

He hadn't the heart to point out that that might be as big a problem as trying to fix the main generators. Because the backup generator was a kilometre and a half away in the Dark Sector. To haul it back to the base they would need to somehow get the bulldozer out there over treacherous terrain in the pitch dark. It would take hours and hours – if it was even possible. And the man with the best chance of pulling it off, the man who had the most experience and requisite know-how, was the man he had just arrested on suspicion of murder.

But the first task was to find out whether the failure of the generators was due to an electrical fault in the monitoring system or if there really was a loss of coolant. Fortunately there was an easy way to check.

"Someone will have to inspect the expansion tank," he told Adam. It was housed in a separate building next to the garage. "I'll go. No point in both of us getting togged up."

"No. I'll come, too. It's my job."

"Sure you're up to it? Physically, I mean. What about those stitches?"

"I'm grand now. The doc said so. No heavy lifting, that's all."

Graeme considered this. On balance it was probably best that Adam came too, best to keep him busy and his mind occupied – and after all it was his job.

"Alright then," he said. "Let's go."

He and Adam got kitted up and they went out. The sky was clear. There was only a crescent moon but with the stars it was enough to light their way. Cold seemed an inadequate word for the medium in which they moved, as cumbersome in their layers of clothes as floating astronauts. Graeme heard a rustling sound that puzzled him until he realized that it was the vapour in his breath freezing as it left his mouth. Even dressed as they were, in the minutes that it took them to get to the building that housed the expansion tank, his hips and shoulders began to ache. *I'm getting too old for this lark*, he thought.

The expansion tank was a large pressured vessel that looked like the hot water tank for an outsized immersion heater. It was supposed to be half full of coolant with an air space to allow the coolant to expand when it got hot. No high-tech measuring equipment was needed to assess the situation. Graeme simply picked up a spanner, left conveniently to hand for just this purpose, and tapped it smartly on the side of the tank. The hollow ringing sound told him all he needed to know. His heart sank. The tank was empty – or virtually so. The coolant was no longer circulating around the generators. It wasn't a fault in the monitoring system. There really was a leak somewhere. All four generators were linked to the same cooling system. If they were lucky, the leak would be in one of the feeder pipes that split off from the main pipe to supply the individual generators. The problem would be local to one of them and they could isolate it and then get the other ones working.

They set about testing the pressure in the pipes of each generator and an hour later they knew the worst. The leak was not in one of the feeder pipes. There was only one possible explanation, now that all the others had been eliminated. The unthinkable had happened. The main coolant pipe must have cracked – and it was buried outside a metre down in the permafrost.

CHAPTER 37

Katie was helping Ernesto in the kitchen. It seemed the most useful thing she could do and besides it was the warmest place in the building. With admirable pragmatism Ernesto had set up camping stoves and was preparing as much hot food as possible while the emergency lighting held out.

"Good soup is always necessary," he explained, as he chopped one of their last remaining onions.

When Graeme and Adam came in, she knew at once from Graeme's face that the situation was serious. "I'm calling a meeting," he said. "You stay here, Adam. I'll go and get the others." He went off.

Adam's face was thin and drawn. He slumped into a chair without taking off any of his outdoor clothes – as the temperature was approaching zero, there wasn't much point. Katie could only hope that he had the emotional resources to survive another crisis.

"What's happened?" she asked.

"Large coolant leak from the main arterial pipe. It's a disaster. Dunno how we're going to fix it."

"Espresso, Adam?" Ernesto asked. "Or a mug of soup?"

"Ta. Yorkshire tea, please."

Ernesto shook his head and sighed as he got out a mug. It was beyond his comprehension that someone could prefer a teabag to a good cup of coffee. "I wonder, what Graeme will do about Alex?" he said.

Katie shrugged. "Hard to know what he *can* do."

Adam frowned. "What do you mean? Why should he do anything about Alex?"

Katie and Ernesto exchanged glances.

"Graeme didn't tell you?" she said.

"Tell me what?"

She made him sit down while she told him. At first he couldn't believe it. "But Alex was with *me*. He was with me the whole time. We were watching *Game of Thrones*." Then when she explained what had happened, how Alex had pulled the wool over his eyes, she saw comprehension dawn – and with it, she was glad to see, anger. Anger was good, anger was positive energy that could be harnessed. "How could he? How could he?" Adam kept saying.

Yes, how could he? Katie didn't believe that Alex had done it just for Kieran. He had done it for himself, too.

Adam and Katie lit lamps in readiness for when the emergency lighting went off. Craig came from the Comms room and told them that the only contact with the outside world was now by hand-held satellite phone.

Last of all came Justin and Rhys with Alex, sullen and silent, between them.

They pulled chairs into a circle and listened as Graeme outlined the situation. They would have to dig out the whole length of the embedded pipe to find the break. They would only be able to work for very short spells because of the extreme cold. Even with a digger it was going to be back-breaking work. They would have to do the last part by hand with pickaxes so that the digger wouldn't cause further damage to the pipe. Then when they had found the leak, they would have to repair it using the MIG welder.

Justin put up a hand. "How can we do that with no power from the generators?"

"That's the other thing. We'll have to retrieve the emergency generator from the Dark Sector. It's air-cooled, so it should work OK. Someone – more than one person – will have to take the bulldozer out there and haul it back."

At that moment the emergency lights went out.

The lamps that they had had the foresight to prepare were

dim after the florescent lighting. They sat blinking in the gloom as their eyes adjusted. Katie looked round the group. There they sat, surrounded by some of the most advanced technology in the world, their breath rising in clouds around them, dressed in their outdoor gear, prevented from freezing to death by the same means that human beings had employed for thousands of years. She and her companions were no more than tiny sparks of life, flickering in the vast, dark wastes of Antarctica, sparks that could so easily be snuffed out. And the temperature was continuing to drop.

Graeme went on. "We'll try to keep this room warm – above freezing at least – and use it as our base – sleep in here if necessary – but I don't think there'll be much time for that. We'll be working round the clock. We'll split up into two teams, one to work on the pipe and the other to go for the generator."

Alex said, "Let me go for the generator."

There was silence. He looked round at their faces. "Oh, come on, guys. What do you think's going to happen? You think I'm going to pick you all off one by one?"

"You've killed a woman. You killed *Sara*," Graeme said. "And the police want to interview you in connection with the death of another. I don't know what else you might be capable of."

Alex was silent. At last he said, "Aye, well, in ordinary circumstances maybe you'd be right, but these aren't ordinary circumstances. You need all the hands you can get. The backup generator is a kilometre away and I'm the one who can best manage the bulldozer. Not to mention that it's more than fifty degrees below out there and no one else has got my experience of these kind of conditions."

Graeme said, "Even if I agreed, it's not a one-man job."

"So let me take two of the guys with me."

Graeme looked round, inviting responses. "I can't force anyone to work with you. What do the rest of you think? Nick? Rhys?"

Nick cleared his throat. "I'm afraid he's right. None of us really have the expertise or as much experience."

Rhys said, "Looked at logically it's a no-brainer. I mean it is not as if he can escape, is it? Where would he go? Also he had a reason for killing Sara and that other woman." He raised a hand to forestall indignant comment. "OK, it was a terrible reason and it was based on a false premise. Just saying that he doesn't have a reason to murder any of the rest of us. He needs us and we need him if we're all to get through this."

Graeme said, "Valid points. Anyone else? Craig?"

Craig scowled. "Goes against the grain, but yeah. Rhys is right. He can't go anywhere. It's hundreds of miles to Vostok and even if he could get a Skidoo to go that distance in these temperatures – what would he do when he got there? They're just as isolated there as we are here."

Justin said, "I agree. We do what we have to do to survive, doesn't matter how we feel about it. Whoever goes out there for the spare generator has got a much better chance of surviving and getting back with Alex than without him. We'll be shooting ourselves in the foot if we don't use him. So, yes, I am in. Reluctantly."

Ernesto said, "I myself would lock him up and throw away the key. Sara was a good woman, a fine woman. So I don't like it, it is all wrong, but..." he shrugged, "yes, he cannot get away, so OK. We should make use of him."

Katie said, "There's also the practical stuff to consider. Even if we find a way to lock him up, we'd have to squander our resources heating another part of the base. So yes, we'd better use him."

Graeme said, "That just leaves you, Adam."

Adam didn't say anything, but sat, biting his lip, while they waited silently for his reply. After a few moments he nodded his head in reluctant agreement. *He can't trust himself to speak,* Katie thought.

"That's settled then," Graeme said.

Nick raised a hand. "I'll go with him."

"And I will," Rhys said.

Other hands shot up all round.

"I think it should be me and Nick," Justin said. "We're used to trekking out to the Dark Sector."

Graeme considered. "Not so much lately, Justin. It had better be Rhys. And anyway I need you here. You had plenty of experience with the digger last winter. So did Craig. Those of us left on base will take it in turns to work outdoors and get the pipe fixed. Between shifts I want Justin and Craig to work on backups for the IT systems to protect the scientific data. OK, let's get going."

CHAPTER 38

It wasn't easy, working the digger with hands in gloves so thick and heavy that they were like bear paws, but Graeme's stint was nearly over. Craig was up next and then Justin and then Ernesto. Graeme was allowing each man to work for only half an hour at a time. With the cloud cover the temperature had gone up a few degrees, but it was still nearly fifty degrees below. With no moon or stars and no lights from the platform it was pitch black. Lighting   had to be jury-rigged from the Skidoos.

He was aware of a figure on the edge of his vision and turned to see Craig signalling that he was ready to take over. He clambered down and Craig climbed up to take his place.

* * *

It was seven hours now since the loss of power. Katie had transferred most of her drugs to the kitchen – it wouldn't do them any good to be deep frozen and the temperature on the rest of the base had already dropped well below freezing. Then she had taken over for Ernesto, though in truth there wasn't much to do. Ernesto had made vast quantities of soup and several casseroles which he'd stored in thermos flasks. She poured herself a mug of lentil soup.

There was no running water and they were relying on emergency supplies of bottled water, all arranged close to the stoves so that they wouldn't freeze. She stood cradling her mug of soup and looking out at where she could see the patch of light in which the digger was working. As she watched, there was a flurry of ice crystals and she lost sight of it for a few moments. It was frustrating that she couldn't help, but she had had less experience of using the digger than anyone else on the base. She had after all only been out here a couple of months, even if it did seem a lifetime. The world she had left behind, the world of sunlight and living things and the friends she couldn't contact, seemed as if they might be only a dream. Only the cold and the dark were real. One day, she thought, unimaginably far in the future, as our sun cools, the whole planet will be like this, covered in permafrost. And what about us as a species, we human beings? Will we be long gone, wiped out by our profligacy, too clever for our own good, or will we have fled away and made our home on some distant planet?

She was overcome by a wave of fatigue. She sat down and closed her eyes and instantly she was walking in the woods near where her mother lived. A sea of bluebells shimmered in the sunlight that filtered through the trees, the bluest blue she'd ever seen. The colour and warmth and light of the May afternoon soaked into her. She wanted to wade into the bluebells and plunge into them as into the Mediterranean sea.

She woke with a jerk, her mouth dry.

She'd been disturbed by the door opening. Justin and Adam came in. Adam wasn't allowed to drive the digger and was helping Justin and Craig in their efforts to salvage data. Hardly anyone was doing the job that they'd come out to Antarctica to do.

She poured out soup for them and coffee for herself.

There was a clattering of boots down the corridor and they all looked around. They heard Graeme singing before they saw him. "When this lousy war is over..." But when he came in, he was smiling. He said, "We've dug deep enough to work on one section with pickaxes while someone else uses the digger on a different section."

Justin put down his mug. "I'll come."

"Can I take over on the digger?" Katie said. She knew that

there was no point in offering to wield a pickaxe. She simply didn't have the upper body strength of the men.

Graeme said, "I'll keep you in reserve, Katie. Ernesto's OK for a bit longer. But the guys hauling the generator are due back for a breather. Could you take soup and coffee down for them?"

"Sure, we'll keep the home fires burning, won't we, Adam?" She smiled at Adam and he smiled wanly back. She knew it was hard on him, but she wouldn't allow him to take a more active role. She couldn't risk that wound breaking open.

* * *

Alex was cold, so cold. He told himself to focus. Lives depended on his competence. His thoughts kept sliding away to – something he would rather not put into words. It was not that he regretted what he had done to Flora Mitchell. He felt justified. She had done a terrible thing. She had destroyed a brilliant mind. But Sara – how could he have known that she wasn't involved? It was the joint authorship of the paper that had foxed him, had convinced him that they had been in it together.

Everything had changed with the other guys. They obeyed his instructions, but that was all. Of course out in the field it wasn't possible to do more than that. They couldn't hear themselves speak above the roaring of the wind. In any case no one wanted to open their mouth and suck in searing air that could have you coughing up blood.

They returned to the garage to warm up the Skidoos – and themselves – every hour. Hot-air blowers, powered by a small diesel generator used to defrost machinery, had been rigged up.

There was none of the banter or gallows humour that there would have been in the past. Nick and Rhys didn't speak unless it was essential and they didn't meet his eye. They were scientists, surely they could understand what a terrible thing Flora had done? And Kieran had been his *friend*. Such a tepid word for a relationship that had been the most important

251

thing in his life. He saw now that his own relationship with Kieran was so close that he had simply assumed that Sara had been hand in hand with Flora, that they had each been as guilty as the other. And he still thought that was a reasonable assumption. Flora and Sara had worked together for years, after all, and where did Sara think the idea for cytochrome c had come from? Had she really thought that Flora had just plucked it out of the air? Hadn't that been remarkably unintelligent of her?

Every hour Katie brought out soup and coffee and she brought it out for him as well. She had asked him one question. "Was it you who tipped over the Monopoly board?" Well, of course it had been: he had been losing and losing was for – well, for losers. And Alex was no loser.

After that she didn't speak again and she wouldn't look at him either. Sara had been her friend – Sara, Sara – like the needle of a compass swinging to magnetic north, he couldn't stop his thoughts swinging back to Sara. He would wrench them away and then moments later...

He drained his mug and looked at Nick and Rhys to indicate that it was time to head back out. They nodded and when he turned to go, without a word, they followed him.

As he stepped out into the bitter Antarctica night, he understood that no amount of hot soup, no layers of thermals, or heavy-duty parkas could protect him from a chill that seemed to penetrate to his very core.

CHAPTER 39

It was ten hours since the loss of power and this was the third time that Katie had taken soup down for Nick and Rhys and Alex. She fought her way around the entrance to the platform, passing on the way the little island of light, where the guys were labouring to uncover the pipe, two at the bottom of the trench and one on the digger. It was impossible to know who was who. Their faces were covered by balaclavas and goggles, without which the ice on their eyelashes would freeze their eyes shut.

Inside in the kitchen Adam was asleep in a chair. Justin on his rest break was sitting at the table, resting his head on his folded arms. He looked up when she came in and she saw that he was almost too exhausted to speak. She made him tea with plenty of sugar in it and sat next to him while he drank it. There was ice in his beard and his eyes were red-rimmed. She took one of his cold hands and rubbed it in hers.

They were still sitting in companionable silence, when there was a commotion in the corridor and the next moment the room seemed full of great hulking figures, bringing with them a rush of cold air.

One of them pushed back his parka hood and pulled off his balaclava. It was Graeme.

"We've found it!" he said. "We've found the break. There's a thirty centimetre split down one side of the pipe."

"Can we fix it?" Katie asked.

"Yep. We can use the MIG welder. But not till the others get back with the backup generator."

Ernesto and Craig were emerging from their parka cocoons, but they didn't remove any of their other layers. The temperature in the kitchen was above freezing, but not by much.

Adam had woken up. He began bustling about, dishing out soup.

"How could that have happened, how could the pipe split when it's protected by all that insulation?" he wondered. "That's what I can't figure out."

Graeme said, "The insulation's split too."

"That unusual seismic activity last week," Justin said. "It might have done more damage than we realized."

"Time for post-mortems later," Graeme said. "Coffee for me, please, with a dollop of brandy. When are the others due back for their next break?"

In all the excitement Katie had failed to keep track of the time.

She looked at her watch. "Well, around now actually."

Adam said, "You're alright, Katie. Stay where you are. I'll keep a lookout."

He went to the windows to watch for the lights of the Skidoos. Their appearance was the signal to go down to the garage with the flasks of soup and tea. No one wanted to be outdoors a minute longer than they had to.

Time passed. Katie began to feel uneasy and she could see that the others were too. The conversation grew sporadic and faded away. Alex was punctilious about sticking to time. Why were they late?

"Ay up! They're coming," Adam exclaimed and then a moment later: "But there's only two of them!"

Already Graeme was on his feet, pulling on his parka.

* * *

Katie went with him. When they reached the garage the Skidoos had already arrived. One of the figures had dismounted and was supporting the other who had slumped to one side on his vehicle. Katie and Graeme rushed to help.

The one helping spoke. It was Nick and his voice was hoarse.

"Rhys came off his Skidoo – he's hurt –"

"OK," Katie said. "I need to know if he hit his head. Did he lose consciousness?"

Nick said, "He hit a hump at an awkward angle and the Skidoo flipped over. I was just behind him when it happened. I don't think he hit his head and he certainly didn't lose consciousness. I got to him right away and he was already cursing."

"No – no, it's just my side," Rhys said and gasped. "I think I might have cracked a rib. I can walk – I think."

Katie thought quickly. Impossible to examine him here. "We'd better get you inside."

They got him back to the dining room. The others got a mattress and helped him to lie down. Kneeling beside him, she was able to examine him. Rhys was badly bruised and it was likely that he had fractured a rib – maybe more than one. She would need to get the X-ray machine up and running before she could be sure about that, but she was fairly confident that he hadn't punctured a lung or sustained any serious internal damage. For now all she could do was give him a painkilling injection. As she did so, she was aware that the wind had grown worse and was making a sound at the windows like someone knocking to get in. She looked around for Graeme to tell him her verdict, but couldn't see his face among the faces clustered around.

"Where's Graeme?" she asked.

Nick told her. "He and Justin have gone to look for Alex. We'd got to the telescope and we'd attached the generator to the bulldozer. Alex sent us back for our break. He was about to start back to base on the bulldozer. He should be back soon. Though it *is* getting a bit breezy," he added.

When Katie went to the window she saw that as a masterly understatement, that could hardly be improved on. Just in the time it had taken them to get Rhys inside and get him examined, the world outside had become a whirling mass of snow. The lights rigged up over the trench had all but disappeared.

* * *

The swirling snow, visible only in the lights of the bulldozer, combined with the continual slow judder of the engine had a hypnotic effect. And though Alex wasn't much of a one for poetry, a piece of verse that he couldn't quite grasp was running in his head to the same tempo. Something about a man on a horse and woods filling up with snow. "The woods are lovely, dark and deep." Yes, that was it, they had learned it at school. Now that he had grasped one thread, the rest was coming. "But I have promises to keep, and tum te tum te tum te tum." What *was* that last bit? Yes! "And miles to go before I sleep." He wanted sleep, he craved sleep. If only he could escape those tormenting thoughts about Sara. A couple of times he had felt himself slipping away, had almost fallen asleep at the wheel, but the jolting had jerked him awake. He had to keep going. He had miles to go before he could sleep. And promises to keep, yes, and woods were filling up with snow and they were lovely, dark and deep.

He was aware that it was hard to marshal his thoughts and wondered in a detached way if he were suffering from hypothermia, but it didn't matter. All that mattered was keeping his promise and getting back to the base. He would be there soon. He had only to follow the flag-line and... where was the flag-line?

Cautiously he pulled back on the throttle and peered ahead. He could see nothing but whirling snow. He turned – with difficulty, he was so bulky in his outdoor gear – but there was nothing to be seen behind him. Somehow he had managed to veer away from the flag-line. Was he still more or less on course for the base or was he heading out across the vast ice shelf? There was no way of knowing. If he had lost his way, the bulldozer, towing the generator, would simply trundle on until it ran out of fuel. He would be dead, frozen behind the wheel, long before that happened.

* * *

Graeme and Justin were ready. Every possible layer had been donned including neoprene face guards and they had their VHF radios strapped on. Once outside they would be deafened by the roar and shriek of the wind, so Graeme gave Justin his final instructions. There was only one instruction that really mattered. Don't let go of the flag-line.

And yet still Graeme hesitated.

Again he ran over the possibilities in his mind. How likely was it that Alex had realized how perilous the weather was becoming and had decided to stay at the telescope – or had retreated there, if he'd already begun the journey? He was their most experienced outdoors man and he had climbed Everest. If anyone could be trusted to survive out there it had to be him.

Even in the time it had taken them to get kitted up, the weather had worsened. The wind was ferocious, gusting, Graeme guessed, at maybe a hundred miles an hour and visibility was virtually nil. Justin, he knew, would not hang back. He was raring to go, fired up by a sense of adventure. When the guys called Graeme the Boss, he was secretly pleased and even a little bit proud. Because of all the Antarctic explorers, Shackleton was the one he most admired and wanted to emulate. Shackleton had never lost a single man under his command. He had stopped within a hundred miles of being the first to the South Pole and had called a halt to the expedition because he knew there was not enough food to get his men back alive. "Better a living donkey than a dead lion," he had said.

Most likely Alex was safe and sound at the telescope. In which case Graeme was not justified in going out in a blizzard like this and even less in taking Justin with him.

He decided to wait until the storm blew itself out.

* * *

Alex tried to reason it out. The flag-line had been on his left, therefore he must have veered right. The question was how far right? If he swung round to the left, he ought to get back to the flag-line. The danger was that he would swing round too far and end up moving away from the base – or even going round in a circle. It was hard to think clearly. The roaring of the wind filled his ears. It was as if the blizzard had got inside his head and was muffling his thoughts.

Yes, he must go left. He turned the steering wheel.

In all the years he had climbed mountains in many different types of weather he had never known anything like this. He was in a world of white and it was in constant motion. He could no longer see even the headlights of the bulldozer.

It was then that he realized that he wasn't alone. The sense of a presence was so strong that he was sure he would see someone when he turned his head. Had Nick come back on a Skidoo? But there was no one there. He had heard of this phenomenon. It wasn't uncommon among mountain climbers and others in circumstances of extreme danger. It must be a hallucination brought on by fatigue and stress. Yet the sense of having a companion was overwhelming. He couldn't shake off the feeling that someone was beside him. More: that they were giving him instructions, telling him to correct his steering, to go right. He couldn't ignore the voice. It seemed to know what to do. It told him to look up. He did and what he saw astonished him.

At ground level he was in the grip of the storm and could see no further than the end of his arm, but a few feet overhead the layer of drift had thinned. He brushed the snow from his goggles and gazed up at a swathe of starlit sky. In the centre was the Southern Cross. By that he could orientate himself.

The voice had been right. Somehow he had got on the other side of the flag-line. He was on the right-hand side instead of the left and had been heading out onto the ice shelf. Knowing this he was able to compensate and hold the steering steady. It seemed too that the wind was dropping a little.

Fifteen minutes later he glimpsed the lights of the garage and knew that he had made it.

People were waiting there. They were helping him off the bulldozer and uncoupling the generator. Katie was helping him to take off his gloves so that he could drink his soup. She was Sara's friend and he was touched that she would do that, after what had happened...

The woods are lovely, dark and deep. I have kept my promise, he thought. *Now I can sleep.*

* * *

Katie waited with the others in the dining room. They sat in silence, too drained to talk.

It hadn't taken long to weld the pipe and repair the insulation. After that they used the digger to fill in the trench. The coolant in the expansion tank had been replenished and now it was time for the moment of truth: Adam and Graeme had gone to restart the generator.

Rhys was lying in a nest of sleeping bags on a mattress on the floor. He was fast asleep, doped up to the eyeballs with painkillers. For everyone else Ernesto provided espressos all round.

Even that was hardly enough to keep Katie awake. Her eyes felt sore and gritty. Her watch said three o'clock, but she couldn't remember whether it was supposed to be day or night. Her body clock had gone haywire.

The room was dim. They were conserving energy and only one lamp was lit. *It must have been like this in our prehistoric days in the cave*, Katie thought, looking at the shadowy bearded figures huddled around a single source of light. *We'd be wearing animal skins instead of heavy-duty parkas and thermal underwear.* Justin was sitting next to her and the pressure of his leg against hers was comforting.

When the lights flickered and came on, she was dazzled.

Graeme and Adam appeared in the doorway and there was a ragged cheer.

When Katie's eyes had adjusted, she saw how exhausted the guys looked and how filthy they were. They were like those men in the early black-and-white photographs of Antarctic explorers, men who had barely survived the rigours of the Antarctic winter. No doubt she looked much the same – minus the beard. It was a long time since she'd had a shower and she wouldn't be having one for a while yet. Power would be limited, and they would have to survive without running water or working toilets, perhaps for weeks, until everything was up and running.

But none of that mattered. They had come through, they had survived.

Ernesto was twisting the wire on a bottle of champagne.

"No problem keeping this chilled!" he joked.

Justin was setting out glasses on a table and there was a lively buzz of conversation. Everyone was getting their second wind – or more like their third or fourth wind.

There was a pop and Ernesto filled the glasses. With a flourish and a little bow he handed one to Graeme. Graeme took the glass, but absently, looking around as though something was puzzling him.

Justin handed glasses out to the others. He took one himself and raised it. "To the Boss!"

"To the Boss!" everyone said, raising their glasses.

He had earned that title, Katie thought. She was in awe at the way Graeme had dealt with the situation – and at his stamina. He put the younger men in the shade.

Graeme was still scanning the faces around him and frowning.

"Where's Alex?" he said.

CHAPTER 40

MIDWINTER

Email from KATIE to RACHEL:

I haven't felt I could write about this before, other than just the bald fact that Alex was missing. We searched the platforms from end to end, though all along we knew it was no good. He had gone. Graeme organized a search party, but after a few hours he called it off. Some of the others would have gone on for longer, but Graeme said he wasn't going to risk their lives, when it was clear what had happened. Alex deliberately went out, knowing that he wouldn't be coming back.

I don't think he could live with knowing that he had killed an innocent person when he killed Sara. I keep wondering what it was like for him, setting off into the dark and bitter cold. How long could he have lasted out there? Not very long – and they say death from hypothermia is a painless way to go. Perhaps his body will be found when the summer comes – perhaps not. There are plenty of deep crevasses out there. Either way he will become part of the mythology of Antarctica and future winterers will tell stories about him and pretend that his ghost haunts the place. And perhaps it will at that.

Justin says it's maybe for the best, but I don't agree. I think justice should have been seen to be done. That would have been best for Flora's and Sara's families. On the other hand, as Graeme says, it would have been hell having to stay out here with him for the remaining six or seven months. How could we have kept him under lock and key?

As for the rest of us, we've got back into a routine. Now

that we are down to eight, it's harder work than it was with ten, but we manage. Rhys was sore for a while, but no serious damage was done. Adam has almost recovered physically and is in much better shape psychologically than I would have expected. In any case we don't talk about what happened. It's better not to when we still have so long left here. Overcoming the generator breaking down has somehow been cathartic. It's pulled us all together. We came so close to complete disaster that I think we're all just glad to be alive. Ernesto goes on cooking up a storm and we play board games in the evening. There's a lot of laughter, even Craig's more communicative these days. We've come through and that's all that matters. But of course there's sadness, too. We're grieving for Sara and I often think of that other woman, Flora. Such a waste.

As for what I'll do when I get back home, I don't know yet, and it doesn't seem to matter like it did. I'll think of something.

Today we're at the halfway mark of our stay. So we've reached the summit and it'll be all downhill from now on. And then one day it'll happen: the rim of the sun will burst through the line of the horizon. Adam as the youngest will raise the British flag. It feels sometimes as if we're existing out of time, here in our own little bubble, where one day is very much like the next and outside it is always night. But today's special, it's midwinter, a holiday, and of course I am thinking of the last time we had a celebration when Sara was with us. I miss her every day. Still we'll do our best to celebrate in a quiet way. As I write, Ernesto is roasting a chicken and some of the boys are decorating the dining room. And later on I've promised to thrash Adam at table tennis.

I keep thinking about you and the baby. Such lovely news. Only hope I'm back in time for the birth. The thought warms me through the coldest day. New life...

Give Chloe a big hug from me.

All my love,

Katie

THE END

Acknowledgments

I like to visit the places that I write about, but in the case of Antarctica, that wasn't possible. So I am hugely grateful to Dr Rose Drew, one of the few medics who have wintered over in Antarctica, for sharing her experiences, giving me advice about the medical aspects of the novel, and reading a draft of the novel. Her help was invaluable and it has been a pleasure getting to know her.

I have also drawn on accounts written by others who have recently wintered over in Antarctica, notably Gavin Francis in *Empire Antarctica: Ice, Silence & Emperor Penguins* (London: Chatto and Windus, 2012) and Alex Gough's *Solid Sea and Southern Skies: Two Years in Antarctica* (Kindle Edition: Alex Gough, 2010). I'd also like to mention an earlier classic of this tiny subgenre: *Alone* by Richard E. Bird (London: Neville Spearman, 1958).

I have tried to read as much as I could about Antarctica. Gabrielle Walker's *Antarctica: An Intimate Portrait of the World's Most Mysterious Continent* (London: Bloomsbury, 2010) was the book I most often turned to while writing.

Heartfelt thanks are also due to the following.

Dr John Olsen, who was my scientific advisor, developed a (sadly fictitious) cure for cancer, and commented on a draft of the novel.

Dr David Poulson, who helped me to bring about a technical breakdown on an Antarctic research station.

Gary Moss, who once again shared his knowledge of patent law with me.

Dr Paula Bolton-Maggs, haematologist, sister-in-law, and friend, who gave me medical advice and put me in touch with Dr Kate Ryan.

Dr Kate Ryan, who kindly told me about treatments for Diamond Blackfan Anaemia.

Dr Helen Crimlist, who gave me advice on some of the medical aspects of the novel and kindly read a draft.

Dr Beverley Howson, who discussed post-partum haemorrhage with me.

Prue Chiles and John Moreland who shared with me their memories of a medical emergency. Thanks also to Jo Burn, who read and commented on a draft of the novel, and to Lisanne Radice for a very helpful discussion.

Thank you to all at Lion Fiction, and especially my splendid editor, Jessica Tinker, and my assiduous copy editor, Drew Stanley.

As for Sue Hepworth, who comments on everything that I write, what can I say? Thank you seems hardly adequate for all the years of friendship and patient reading – and even rereading – of many drafts.

And finally I dedicate this book to the memory of my husband, who gave me the time and space to write this book and the others that came before it.

MIDWINTER IN ANTARCTICA.

SIX MONTHS OF DARKNESS ARE ABOUT TO BEGIN.

Scientist Katie Flanagan has an undeserved reputation as a trouble-maker and her career has foundered. When an accident creates an opening on a remote Antarctic research base she seizes it, flying in on the last plane before the subzero temperatures make it impossible to leave.

Meanwhile patent lawyer Daniel Marchmont has been asked to undertake due diligence on a breakthrough cancer cure. But the key scientist is strangely elusive and Daniel uncovers a dark secret that leads to Antarctica.

Out on the ice a storm is gathering. As the crew lock down the station they discover a body and realize that they are trapped with a killer...

UK £7.99
US $14.99

ISBN 978-1-78264-216-9

9 781782 642169

www.lionhudson.com